SISTER
GOLDEN
HAIR

D0003936

SISTER GOLDEN HAIR

a novel

DARCEY STEINKE

Tin House Books
Portland, Oregon & Brooklyn, New York

Airdrie Public Library
304 Main Street S
Airdrie, Alberta T4B 3C3

Copyright © 2014 Darcey Steinke

All rights reserved. No part of this book may be used or repro-
duced in any manner whatsoever without written permission
from the publisher except in the case of brief quotations em-
bodied in critical articles or reviews. For information, contact
Tin House Books, 2617 NW Thurman St., Portland, OR 97210.

Published by Tin House Books, Portland, Oregon, and
Brooklyn, New York
Distributed to the trade by Publishers Group West, 1700
Fourth St., Berkeley, CA 94710, www.pgw.com

Library of Congress Cataloging-in-Publication Data

Steinke, Darcey.
  Sister golden hair / by Darcey Steinke.
    pages cm
   ISBN 978-1-935639-94-7 (paperback)
 1. Teenage girls--Fiction. 2. Dysfunctional families--Fiction.
3. Roanoke (Va.)--Fiction. 4. Virginia--Social life and customs-
-20th century--Fiction. 5. Domestic fiction. I. Title.
  PS3569.T37924S74 2014
  813'.54--dc23
                              2014011909

"Hospital" by Jonathan Richman © 1971 Wixen Music
Publishing / Modern Love Songs. Used by permission.
All rights reserved.

Printed in the USA
Interior design by Diane Chonette
www.tinhouse.com

For Abbie

*I'll seek out the things that must have been
magic to your little girl mind.*

—THE MODERN LOVERS

✦

CHAPTER ONE

SANDY

The Vagabond Motor Lodge sat across the street from the Fiji Island restaurant, wedged between Johnny's Auto Parts and a gas station with a flying horse on its neon sign. Our first few days staying there felt like a vacation. In the morning, after Dad left for his new job, we swam in the motel pool, doing cannonballs off the diving board as my mother lay out under a blue canvas umbrella with white fringe, watching cars go by on the highway. In 1972, I'd just turned twelve, and my family had moved for the third time in so many years. The August heat was ruthless on the bright cement, relenting only in bluish spots of shade. There was glamour in the way the heat slowed my body down and penetrated every moment with languor. In the late afternoon, when it was time for my little brother, Philip, to nap, we walked in our wet bathing suits across the parking lot, heat rising around us in visible waves. Our mother let us stop at the gumball machine outside the front office. Inside, the motel owner, a bald man who wore a Texas string tie, sat with his little dog, Mr. Buddy, on his lap, watching television.

We were moving again and the reason was, as my father frankly told us, that there were not many jobs for defrocked ministers. The members of First Methodist hadn't liked when my dad let his hair grow so long it brushed his coat collar, or that he traded his clerical collar for bell-bottoms and blue shirts with wide ties. They didn't like it when he encouraged the youth choir to sing "I'd Like to Teach the World to Sing" accompanied by guitars rather than the organ, and they really didn't like it when he started a Gestalt workshop in the church basement and began preaching against Vietnam. When he held a commitment ceremony for Barry and Don, a parishioner complained. This led to a clergy trial, with a jury of nine Methodist ministers who decided that his actions were not compatible with Christian teaching. They read from the Book of Discipline, stripped him of his credentials, and—from what I heard—my dad, who refused to defend himself anyway, walked down the center aisle and into secular life.

After getting fired, Dad stayed in bed and read from a pile of old *New York Review of Books* that we dragged from the rectory to each new rented house.

He read books about history, science, and psychology. Once he was over the shock, he started to get enthusiastic: church doctrine was draconian; we'd figure out our own relationship to God. He gathered us together and explained that we were going to make a fresh start in Virginia.

It would have been nice if my mother was the strong, long-suffering type, but this was not the case; with every move she got a bit more unhinged. When we were supposed to be asleep, she cried to my father about how unhappy she was. Explained the she felt like a zero, a nothing. Listening to her, I tried to judge her freak-out level. She was at a 5 pretty much all the time. Brow furrowed, vaguely unhappy. Often, say, around the dinner table, she got to a 4 or even a 3 if my dad was sullen or my little brother complained about the food. She'd been at a 2 the whole drive down, but now she was at a 3, a good 3, not a bad 3.

When we got back to our room the owner's wife had made up our beds, vacuumed, given us new towels. She was skinny as a skeleton as she pushed her cart, loaded with tiny bars of soap, glasses in white paper, and clean towels. Every day while she worked inside the rooms, jerking her bones around as she pushed the vacuum, I gazed at the cart until I got up enough courage to ask for more motel writing paper. She turned off the vacuum, gave me a sour look, and told me the stationery wasn't kiddie stuff, but she guessed I could have a page or two. She didn't know I was writing a long letter to Francie from *A Tree Grows in Brooklyn*, telling her about myself and also how sorry I was her father drank.

By midweek we still hadn't moved into our duplex in Bent Tree. We no longer walked down the highway, parking lot to parking lot, to Sambo's for dinner, but instead ate American cheese sandwiches and chips from a big foil bag we bought at the convenience store.

After dinner we took baths and got into our pajamas, and our mother let us out in front of our room to play in the parking lot. Across the street the Fiji Island was lit up so we could see the huge carved Easter Island statues on either side of the bamboo doors. The sign out front, bookended by plastic palm trees, read PINA COLADAS—TWO FOR THREE DOLLARS. For some reason nobody could explain, an old railroad car sat to one side of the parking lot. My mom knocked on the window from inside our room, pointed to the highway and shook her head vigorously. Then she leaned against the orange headboard and read a magazine, occasionally glancing to the television screen where Nixon's head was huge and wiggly like the bobblehead dogs older people liked to put in the back windows of their cars.

In the half-light we ran around the motel to the Dumpster. Across a mangy field was a farmhouse that had wandered out of an earlier time period, gotten lost, and was now unable to find its way back. Fireflies floated over the field and above the farmhouse. Tiered up the side of the mountain were brick ranch houses, lit in two colors: incandescent gold if the families inside were having dinner, or indigo blue if they were watching television.

I wanted to crouch down in the field and pretend the Viet Cong were after us. But I could tell this game frightened Phillip. Whenever he was scared he pretended to look very carefully at some object on the ground, in this case chunks of parking lot gravel.

As it got darker the fireflies rose up and we went back around to the front of the motel to spy on the owner. Mr. Buddy sat delicately on the bald man's lap as if he were the dog of a French diplomat. The owner and his wife lived behind the office and we could see them through the doorway at the back; the wife rattled around the kitchen.

The parking lot was packed with cars, license plates from Alabama, Mississippi, even Florida and Texas. The backseats were jammed with coolers, stacks of magazines, and clothes hung from hooks above the back doors. A fat man who held his pants together with an expanse of rope had dragged a chair from his room and was sitting out smoking.

The fireflies multiplied; there were so many it was easy to reach out and catch one and hold it in the palm of your hand. Phillip got his Wiffle bat and swung at the bugs until he had a patch of glowing tails stuck to the plastic. He smeared the tails over his forehead so his skin glowed.

After we caught as many as we could in the ice bucket, I opened the motel-room door and told my mother we had a surprise for her. "Now what?" she said, letting the magazine she'd been reading fall to the bedspread. She and my dad had yelled at each other earlier and now he was in the motel bar reading his book and drinking a beer.

I turned off the overhead light, then lifted the top of the ice bucket so the fireflies rose into the room and began to blink over the bed and around the night table. One flickered so close to my mother's face that I could see the white of her eyes.

"How will we get them out of here?" she said.

Though her voice sounded worried I could tell by the way her eyes followed the little lights around the room that she liked the fireflies. After a while she helped us trap the bugs again and let them go outside.

I had trouble sleeping. To try to calm myself I thought about our life before we left the church. Dad used to say prayers before every meal; he sat on my bed and prayed with me at night. There were Sunday services, Sunday school, funerals, baptisms. When I slipped into the church in the late afternoons, the altar was dark and beautiful. The crimson carpet, the blues and greens from the stained glass like a doomed kingdom under the sea. We visited the lonely, we collected cans of food for hungry people, coats for people who were cold. We prayed for sick babies. We were at the center of what I thought of as THE HOLY, and our every move had weight and meaning. But out in the world away from church, we floated free. What if my dad did not come back? What if he met a lady in the bar he liked better than my mom, one who wasn't always complaining about money? One who didn't tell stories about giant worms in New Guinea that lived in your intestines or housewives who laid their bodies down over railroad tracks? He might go off when the bar closed and we'd never see him again. I sometimes imagined my father had another family. Rather than upsetting me, this gave me a certain respect for him. This second family would explain why he was always so preoccupied.

Our room was not far from the motel lounge with its orange hanging lights with wrought-iron filigree. Cars came and went; as it got later people laughed loudly in the parking lot and used the cigarette machine just outside our door. I watched the few remaining fireflies bob in the air, blinking on and off. I tried to stay awake to see my father, but I must have fallen asleep. When I woke again he was lying beside my mother and there was just one bug left flying frantically by the doorway.

✦

The next day my mother forced my dad to go over to Bent Tree and give the manager an ultimatum: if we couldn't move in by Friday, we were going to ask for our deposit back and look for another place to live. Usually when my parents talked seriously my father sat beside my mom, but on his return he paced the floor and his eyes kept opening wide as he went up on his toes. He talked as if the details of our life were an exciting movie, not anything that actually affected us.

"Get this!" he said. "The woman who is in the unit we're supposed to move into has barricaded herself inside. She told us through the door that while she was moving out Sunday morning, her ex-husband threatened her with a knife."

"Lovely," my mom said.

Her mouth turned down around the edges and her chin started to quiver like it always did when she was about to cry. Seeing my mother in such misery jolted my sleepy bloodstream like a candy bar. My mind started to click down my well-worn list of ways I could help her: (1) Write an anonymous letter about what a great person she was. (2) Spend my allowance on lottery tickets. If I won, which I figured I was bound to do if I really concentrated hard, I could buy her the house she was always talking about. (3) Run away from home so she wouldn't have me to worry about anymore. I knew that last one would hurt her more than help her; a few items on my list were radical. Rather than make her feel better, they were meant to throw a glass of cold water in her face.

My father continued to talk about the evil ex-husband. I pictured him sitting in his pickup truck looking at the duplexes through binoculars and playing with his Swiss army knife. He wore a red bandana on his head and mirrored sunglasses. I pretended to shift in my sleep, so I could see my mother in the dark hotel room. Her eyes were large and wet as she watched Johnny Carson. A 3 moving toward a 2. To my mom, the intrigue with the woman was just another example of how our life was in decline, one more detail added to the long list of others, chief among them the fact that we couldn't afford to buy a house on my father's tiny salary.

+

Sometimes when my mother cried and said she wanted a house, Phillip, who was four, would rub her back and tell her not to worry, he was going to buy a big house when he grew up, and everybody could live there—not just us, but all our friends, grandmas and grandpas, birds, all the rabbits and mice. Even polar bears, if they promised to be nice and not eat anyone.

I'd had the same fantasy for a while, that I'd grow up, get rich, and buy her a house that looked like the Taj Mahal; to me the pink marble and deep purple reflecting pools looked like heaven. But I was getting tired of her endless longing. Wherever we lived wasn't good enough. We might call it a house, and think of it as "our house," but to Mom no place we'd lived in was nice enough to be a house. It was as if the walls had fallen down, and we were just camping out, completely exposed to the elements.

+

It rained all day Friday. We watched television as heavy drops pelted the big plate-glass window. We fought over whose turn it was to get ice from the machine at the end of the open corridor. The ice machine sat next to the candy machine, each bar of chocolate lit up like a tiny god.

In the evening the rain cleared and we drove over to Bent Tree, passing Long John Silver's, Hardee's, and a 24-hour do-it-yourself car wash. There was a drive-in movie theater playing a film called *Dallas Girls* and a string of brick ranch houses with Christmas lights up around the porches and a sign by the road that read MASSAGE.

Eventually the strip malls got farther apart, interspersed with black glass professional buildings and churches on both sides of the highway. Just before we turned off, there was a brick church with white columns, a steeple, and a sign that read SIN KNOCKS A HOLE IN YOUR BUCKET OF JOY. The parking lot was empty and glittering under the overhead light.

Off the highway I counted thirteen NIXON FOR PRESIDENT signs stuck in front yards. My father hated Nixon, but I felt sorry for the president because he always looked so dazed and miserable. Warm air came through the window, damp from the rain and tinged with the scent of dirt and grape juice.

I didn't understand why we couldn't rent a different duplex in one of the other developments—Lux Manor, Sans Souci, Evergreen Estates—spread like bread mold over the side of the mountains. My dad was acting like he did when he was a pastor, like everyone else's life was more important than our own. He drove slumped back in the seat, his hand dangling over the wheel, the motel envelope holding the rental listings from the local paper on the dashboard. He intended to slip the envelope under the woman's door and gently encourage her to think about moving out.

When he told us his plan, my mother had been folding clothes she'd just brought back from the Laundromat, a pair of my little brother's corduroys on her lap. She looked up at him.

"That's your plan?" she asked.

In the last few days she'd rolled her eyes whenever my father talked about how much he liked his brandnew job at the VA hospital, or said something about the beauty of the Blue Ridge Mountains. Most of the car ride she'd been silent, her head pressed dramatically against the window frame, but as the car climbed the mountain and my father said we were close, she started to talk. Her features became unfocused, and when she opened her mouth I knew she was going to say something about rich people.

"Did you know in Hyannis Port the Kennedys keep a pony for the children to ride?"

"I wish we had a pony," Phillip said.

Between places, while we were in transit, she always went back to the Kennedys. Once settled in a town she picked a nearby rich family. In Philadelphia it had been the Westerfields. She knew the girls went to Emma Willard for boarding school and that they summered in Lions Head, Maine. She knew that their house had six bedrooms and that each bathroom was fitted with delft tile.

I was sick of the Westerfields as well as the Kennedys. I had to hear about Caroline, how she had christened the USS *John F. Kennedy* with her mother, Jackie, how she once received a puppy from Khrushchev and was moving schools from Sacred Heart to Brearley. My mother went on reviewing. John-John had spent the summer on a dude ranch. The Onassis yacht had a hot tub and a steam room. Then, as my dad tapped the brakes and took a left turn onto a road lined with freshly planted pine trees, she turned to new information she'd gotten out of the *Roanoke World-News*. She'd learned that the Vanhoffs were Roanoke's first family. Mr. Vanhoff was president of Shenandoah Life Insurance Company. His great-grandfather had been governor. The paper said Mr. Vanhoff had hosted the fund-raising golf tournament at the Roanoke Country Club while Mrs. Vanhoff had taken her children to the family's vacation compound on a private lake in Michigan. There they raised rabbits and took French lessons. While my mother spoke, I bent my fingers up and back so slowly I was able to slow time down, so the syllables of what she said were so far apart the words were unrecognizable. I imagined that I was one of the astronauts on *Apollo 15* landing the *Falcon* on the Apennine mountain range, taking the lunar rover for a spin on the silent surface of the moon. After trying to catch our eyes in the rearview mirror she realized neither Phillip nor I were going to respond.

"Here we are!" my dad said as we passed the Bent Tree sign and pulled onto a street lined on either side by two-story duplexes. Twenty-five units climbed up the side of the mountain, each a boxy red-brick building with six front windows, two doors, and tin chimneys like mushrooms springing up from the roof. My dad had made the place sound like a fancy mountaintop resort, the sort of hotel in which the young heroines in the books I read spent their summers. But the duplexes in Bent Tree looked more like army barracks.

The manager, a short man with a comb-over and a huge set of keys dangling from his belt, was waiting for us. He looked like an even smaller version of Sonny Bono, bereft without his Cher.

Dad followed the manager into the duplex and we sat in the car waiting. Insects throbbed and a bird shrieked back in the woods. My little brother crawled over the seat and got in Mom's lap. The top half of each duplex was covered in beige aluminum siding; strips had fallen off here and there, exposing patches of gray cement. Most of the windows were covered with blinds, but a few people had strung sheets over the glass. One showed a Confederate flag. A rusty grill lay on its side and a few motorcycles were parked along the street. In the yard next to our unit was a concrete birdbath.

✦

As we drove out of Bent Tree, my father told my mother how the woman inside our duplex wouldn't speak to him or the manager. The manager said Bent Tree's owner felt once you'd signed the contract, you'd committed yourself to spending at least a year in the development. Still, if an annulment was needed, if we really wanted our deposit back, he would issue us a check. My mother didn't answer; she just ran her hand through my brother's hair as he slept on her lap. I kept waiting for Dad to tell us about his plan B but he was quiet. I knew my father wouldn't get his first check for another week and we were down to our last forty dollars and that the motel room cost $19.95 a night. I knew, too, that we couldn't go back to Philadelphia; our house held a new family, a young couple with a baby. Once, when a job hadn't worked out, we'd gone to live with Dad's parents. Another time we'd stayed with my mother's sister for a few weeks, but my aunt had made it clear when we left that that would be the last time.

The sun had gone down and my dad turned on the car headlights. After a while he stopped on the side of the road and spoke to a hitchhiker waiting on the soft shoulder. The man wore a small backpack, a cheesecloth shirt, and jeans with a *V* cut in the bottom of

each leg and a triangle of paisley material sewn in
to make the bell swing wide. His curly brown hair
fell at his collarbone and he had a mass of freckles.
Most thrilling was the string of seeds—Love Beads—
around his neck. The young man got into our station
wagon. I was all the way in the back lying on my stomach, reading the funny pages of the newspaper with
a flashlight. I peered over the seat. My mother had
smeared white cream on a rash around my mouth and
I was terrified an actual hippie might see my greasy
face, or worse, the red dots all over my chin.

"Hi, everybody!" he said. "My name is Guy."

"Where you headed, Guy?" my father asked in the
nothing-to-lose voice he always used when talking to
hippies.

"Up to Floyd," Guy said. Floyd was farther up in the
mountains, the place local hippies hung out. I could
tell my father was disappointed with Guy's reply. I
knew my father felt if Guy was free enough to be a real
hippie, he would march in protests against Vietnam,
or head for the Deep South to register black voters. I
knew Dad had been sad to miss the fund-raiser that
spring for McGovern, the one where James Taylor
and Carole King sang.

"Do you live up there?"

"Oh no," Guy said. "I'm just checking it out."

Wow! I thought. *Guy doesn't have a home either.* But
unlike us, he didn't seem to care; he was living free and
easy. Sitting sideways in the backseat, looking out the

window, he told us he'd hitched up to Maine, which was crazy beautiful. He was thinking about checking out Japan. A guy he knew was teaching English. My mother pressed her body against the passenger-side door, as if Guy might have head lice. Just before we pulled off the highway we let Guy out. I turned to see him receding in the glow of our headlights. He walked backward carrying a cardboard sign that read: HELLO, FELLOW HUMAN! CAN YOU SPARE A RIDE?

✦

After Guy was gone, my father talked about life on the road, speculating on the potential for adventure. We could buy a camper and just take off, live in the moment. I knew he was saying this so he wouldn't have to talk about Bent Tree. Finally he asked my mother what she thought we should do. She didn't answer. She stared out the window, her lips pressed together.

Back in the motel room she went into the bathroom to change into her nightgown and take off her make-up. When she came out she flung herself on the bed. At first my dad continued to try to talk to her, saying if the woman—whose name was Miranda—wasn't out by Sunday, that was it, that was absolutely the cut-off date. Mom didn't say anything. She just lay on the bed staring at the dull ceiling, her eyes open and empty like a dead person's.

After a while Dad gave up trying to talk to her. He got us changed into our pajamas. I heard the television in the room next door and in the parking lot a car door slammed. My brother fell asleep immediately. I pretended to sleep, every now and then letting out a long dramatic breath to prove I was unconscious.

My mother stood up and walked over to the phone on the dresser beside the television. She had on her mint-green nightgown and she'd taken off her mascara so the skin around her eyes was smudged.

"I'm going to call my parents and see if I can take the children there."

"Don't do that," my father said from behind his newspaper.

She picked up the receiver and put her finger into the plastic dial.

"I'm sick of this," she said. "I'm calling right now."

"Don't!" My father lowered the paper.

My mother pulled the rotary to the end and let it ratchet back.

He stood up and tried to take the phone from her hand, but she held on so hard the skin over her bones turned white.

"Don't touch me," she said, holding the receiver over her head.

"You'll feel better when you're in the duplex," he said, taking the receiver from her hand and placing it back into its cradle. "You're just tired."

29

She let him lead her over to the bed, but when he tried to put his arm around her she shrugged him off and moved back to her earlier position on the far side of the mattress, her face to the wall.

In the night, when the train whistle woke me, rattling the window beside my bed, I saw through the dark that my mom was still lying on top of the covers, now in her quilted bathrobe, her back to me, her face toward the wall. I thought she was at a 2 moving toward a 1, but then I heard her long, even breaths and realized she'd fallen asleep. My dad was sitting in the vinyl chair by the television. At first I thought he was sleeping too, but then I saw the whites of his eyes gleam in the parking lot light slanting through the break in the curtains. Of course he was worried about my mom, where we'd live, if we had enough money, but I think his *grand plan* was also failing. He'd given up church stuff, the prayers, the creeds, the vows that he had told me were a waste of time. He didn't want to dig a channel, he wanted to find the spring and let it flow over us. We were, he had told me with great enthusiasm, in a period of devolution, unlearning what we knew. It seemed crazy to me that my dad was trying to get to a place without maps, or directions. He was tired, confused, despairing. And what if God actually was dead like a lot of people said? Then, rather than finding Him, my Dad was going to have to invent Him all by himself.

✦

Early in the morning, Dad came in with donuts. He told us he'd already been back up to Bent Tree. Miranda was gone and we could move in. We got dressed and threw everything into our suitcases: On the drive Dad played the radio, and he kept glancing over at my mom in her paisley head scarf and sunglasses.

"You look like a movie star going incognito," he told her.

She turned her head toward him and softened her mouth.

As we pulled up in front of our duplex, Mr. Ananais, the manager, stood by the curb waiting for us.

"She's still in there," he said. "I had her out earlier this morning but she got spooked and locked herself back in."

"Now what?" my mother said.

"Well," the manager said hesitantly, "I think if she heard the children's voices—"

"No way," my mother said. "I'm not having my kids exposed to some lunatic."

"Come on," my dad said. "It's worth a try."

"I'm not going," my mom said, looking straight out the window.

"I'll go," I said.

"Me too," said Phillip.

Inside the duplex a few boxes were stacked against walls. The floor was covered with mangy gold shag and the walls were white, holes here and there where pictures had hung. The rooms smelled like incense.

31

Mr. Ananais led us upstairs, down a short hallway to a closed bedroom door.

"Miranda," Mr. Ananais said, "the new tenants are here."

Beyond the door, mattress springs released and I heard soft footsteps moving closer. I could hear Miranda breathing against the wood.

"I'm in a very bad mood," she said.

"Do you want me to tell you more stories about my cat?" Mr. Ananais asked.

Dad looked at me with his eyes wide open. Mr. Ananais was more accommodating to the woman than either of us had expected.

"Yes," Miranda said, "that would be nice."

"Well my cat, Hector, likes to watch TV. *Bonanza* is his favorite show. He knows exactly when it comes on each afternoon. If it's not on, he gets mad and goes to the television and meows until I turn it on. I put a pillow down and he lies with his paws folded in front of him."

Mr. Ananais looked at my father, who was flushed and smiling. More than anything else in life, Dad grooved on surreal situations. If my mom had been here, she'd have been whispering that this was crazy.

"Why don't you say hello, kids?" Mr. Ananais suggested.

"Hi," I said. "I'm Jesse. I'm twelve . . ."

What else would she like to know about me? I could tell her how I loved to read or that lavender was my favorite color, but in the end I went with my favorite candy bar.

". . . and I love Almond Joy bars . . ."

"I like fire engines," Phillip said. "And pizza!"

There was silence but it had a different texture, more like macramé than leather.

"Come on, *koukla*," Mr. Ananais said. "Remember how we talked about having to call the police? I really don't want to do that."

"Are you threatening me?"

"No, no, no," Mr. Ananais said. "But really, what do you want us to do? This nice family wants to move in here, these children need a place to sleep, you can't just stay locked in there forever."

"What if he comes back?"

"I already told you," Mr. Ananais said. "His mother says he's gone to Texas."

There was quiet from behind the door.

"Are you still there?" Mr. Ananais asked.

"Where else would I be?"

"Are you coming out?" he asked.

"Could you sing me a song?" she asked. "I think that would settle my nerves."

The only song we all knew was "Jingle Bells," and before we got through the first verse, our car horn sounded.

"That's him!" Miranda screamed.

Mr. Ananais looked at my father. I knew he was worried that any gains would be lost if Miranda got frightened.

"We'll go," Dad said. "We'll come back in an hour or so."

In the car my mother's face was fixed in a smile that was not a smile at all. She'd moved over to the driver's side and before we had our doors shut she took off down the mountain, speeding past the ranch houses in the subdivision below.

"Getting us killed," my father said, placing a hand on the dashboard to steady himself, "isn't going to solve anything."

"Is she coming out?"

"I think so," my father said. "Though you may have ruined it by laying on the horn."

"Now it's my fault?"

"I didn't say that."

My mom swung around a corner, coming so close to a boxwood hedge that the branches scraped against the side of the car.

"Remember that guy who came to our door in Philadelphia saying he was a narcoleptic?" my mother said.

"He was very convincing," my father said. "He fell asleep several times right in front of me!"

She pulled onto the highway and sped out toward the interstate. We were going so fast that the buildings and trees melded into one long ribbon, unfurling behind the car.

"Remember the time you gave a hundred dollars to that slut?"

"She was a member of the congregation and she was pregnant," my father said.

"Remember how you used to go to the loony bin every single Saturday?"

"I was making pastoral visits."

"When you let that drug addict sleep in our guest room he drank all our cough syrup."

"For God's sake slow down," my dad said.

"You want me to stop?"

"Yes."

"Say please," she said.

"Please," my dad said.

She hit the brake and we all flew forward, then fell back hard against the seats as she rolled the car onto the shoulder. The tires crunched on the gravel and the fender pressed against a patch of weeds.

Throwing open the door, my mother stumbled out of the car and started to walk down the side of the highway, her dress whipping around her knees in the wind and the silky tails of her head scarf bobbing. Heat made the air muzzy and thick as if she were going through a time warp, moving away from us into another dimension.

My dad slipped into the driver's seat. I made funny faces at Phillip. We were screwing up our mouths and shaking our heads, but when Dad turned around we froze.

"Your mother's upset," he said.

"Understatement of the universe," I said.

"I want Mommy," Phillip whined.

My dad put on the hazards and drove up behind her.

He kept so close that I could see the muscles flexing in the backs of her legs. She was pretending to enjoy her little walk along the highway, looking at the weeds in the ditch, glancing up at the hazy sky.

"Just tell her you're sorry," I said. "That's all she wants to hear."

Dad leaned his head out the car window.

"I'm sorry," he said. "OK? Just please get back in the car."

She turned, took off her sunglasses, and looked at us through the windshield. Her face was pink and wet and her eyelids were so swollen she looked like a sea creature. Behind her was a string of fast food restaurants, a McDonald's followed by the Long John Silver's and the Hardee's. Every time a car sped by, her clothes sucked against her body. She stared at us for what seemed like a very long time—at least a million years.

This is it, I thought, *this is when she decides to leave us and start her new life.*

✦

Maybe because Phillip was so much younger, moving didn't seem to bother him in the least; he loved packing up his toys in his old suitcase, and once we got to Bent Tree he knew how to hang around out front in the mornings, running his remote-control tank up and down the sidewalk, until he attracted a kid his own age.

At Bent Tree, Eddie was the first kid to come around.
Though he was only four, the same age as my brother,
he looked like a tiny adult, his white hair cut in a mul-
let, short in the front and past his shoulders in back.
He had a white plastic knife tucked under his belt and
a bandolier made of toilet paper rolls attached with
electrical tape to his T-shirt.

My mother was pleased Eddie had come over because she wanted Phillip to stop running in and out of
the duplex. All week, while she tried to unpack, he'd
been sliding down the banister and jumping off the
couch. Mom agreed that Phillip and Eddie could play
together in the woods if I walked with them. On the
way, Eddie showed us the unit next to ours; it looked
OK from the outside, but inside wires hung from all
the ceilings. The wood frame next in line was over-
grown with weeds. On the lot beyond, the builders
had given up completely. There was only a large hole
and a few bags of cement ruined by the rain and dried
to hard chunks in the sun. Eddie told us that in the
spring, rainwater collected at the bottom of the pit
and he had caught tadpoles there in a Dixie cup.

The tree line was scattered with stuff people had
dumped: a television with a smashed screen, a plastic
bag of clothes, a broken-down playpen. Vines covered
everything. I'd always thought of nature like the happy woodlands in my childhood storybooks. But now I
was frightened by the large shiny leaves, the heart-
shaped ones veined purple, and the ones small as doll

hands covered with white hairs. The trees seemed angry; I felt if I turned my back, they might poke a sharp branch into my heart. I wanted the woods to be a place where I might make friends with a fawn or see a unicorn. I wanted to meet a squirrel wearing a little vest or a frog walking on his hind legs, leaning on a tiny carved cane.

Eddie felt none of my anxiety. Once we got a few yards into the forest he insisted that no girls were allowed in the hooch, that he and my brother would walk the rest of the way alone. I watched their thin legs moving over the packed dirt path. Where they made a sharp right, the trees thickened first to dark green and then to black.

✦

When I got back, our nearest neighbor, Mrs. Smith, was standing in her doorway wearing a housedress with metal snaps down the front. She wore her hair teased up in a beehive and smoked a cigarette with a long dangling ash.

"Would you mind getting me my newspaper, honey?" she said. "That boy threw it onto your side."

I pulled the paper out from under the ratty boxwood.

"You all moved in?"

"Still unpacking."

"Where you all from?"

"Philadelphia."

"Up there," she said. "My Lord!"

I nodded and smiled.

"I hear your daddy's a preacher."

"He was one. But he's not anymore."

Mrs. Smith frowned. She was the sort of character I'd imagined lived down South. Someone who made fried chicken and loved okra, someone who watched the Grand Ole Opry on television.

"Was it him I heard up in the middle of the night?"

"Either him or me," I said. "We both have trouble sleeping."

"Y'all and me both," she said. "I haven't gotten more than a couple hours' worth since my husband passed."

"When was that?"

"Twenty years ago," she said. "But it feels like twenty days."

Her cheeks sucked in as she pulled on her cigarette and let the smoke out of her small nose, the stream thick and gray.

✦

Eddie's mother, Sandy, lay out on a lawn chair beside her unit in a leopard-print bikini, spreading oil mixed with iodine over her legs. When she turned over on her stomach, she undid her top so her back was bare. To me she was exotic as a lizard soaking up the sun. Listening to Lynyrd Skynyrd on her transistor radio and drinking a can of beer. I stared for a while at her brown back and perfectly shaped butt from my bedroom window—until she glanced in my direction and I went back to unpacking my few possessions, hanging my dress and arranging my shoes in the closet. I had three pairs of shoes: red Keds, sandals with tire-tread soles, and a pair of Mary Janes that my mother had made me pack but that I swore I would never ever wear again even if someone held a gun to my head.

I opened the box that held the old encyclopedias I'd gotten at the Philadelphia library sale. Wedged in between the volumes was my baby doll, Vicky, her ratty sleeper scrunched up under her arms and her blue glass eyes clearly frustrated. I could tell she was mad I'd left her in the U-Haul for so long, and so I let her lie on my chest and I stroked her bald head as I sang "American Pie," the song that was now always on the radio.

After a while I got up and peeked out at Sandy. She had turned back around and was eating orange Cheez Doodles out of a big plastic bag. I went out to see if we had any mail and to get a look at her up close.

As soon as I came out our front door, she raised her sunglasses.

"Are you a teenager, honey?" she called to me. Her voice, like a little girl's, made no sense coming out of her brown body.

"Almost," I said, walking over to her chair.

"You babysit much?"

"Sure," I said. I didn't want to appear too anxious, but I was thrilled she might actually hire me. My heart fluttered. It was as if I were talking to a goddess from another galaxy.

"For who?"

"My brother mostly, but once I watched a new baby while its mother got her hair done."

"Sounds good," she said. I realized from the way she waved her hand that she was going to offer me the job no matter if I'd said I'd watched sea monkeys and babysat goldfish.

"Could you come over at seven? My boyfriend is taking me out to dinner."

When I arrived that evening, Sandy's boyfriend opened the door. Sonny was a tan, thin man with huge white teeth, his hair feathered back perfectly like birds' wings. I'd heard from Eddie that he was an oral surgeon and that he was rich. He poured himself a drink from a decanter with a gold top. Sandy's living room was filled with spider plants hanging in macramé holders. One wall was mirrored. There were ceramic lamps with large silk shades and a geometrical print suspended on the wall over the long, low, brown couch.

"I hear you're a Yankee," Sonny said, turning back toward the living room. He wore an Izod shirt with the collar turned up, khaki pants, and loafers without socks.

I nodded.

"We'll try not to hold that against you. Right, Eddie boy?"

Eddie, who sat on the couch holding a Tonka cement mixer, turned his head slowly, squinted his eyes at Sonny as if trying to remember who he was, shrugged, and went back to the television.

I sat down next to Eddie on the couch.

"What are you watching?" I said.

"Chitty Chitty Bang Bang."

It was early in the evening on a Saturday; the cartoons were long over and the sporting events too. Eddie slumped his body against mine. He was the kind of kid who would lean on anybody. Though I'd known him only a few days, he was already all over me, wanting to sit on my lap and hold my hand.

As Sonny lifted his glass to his mouth, I heard ice clink against his teeth. At first I thought he was watching the stairs, waiting for Sandy to come down, but then I realized he was staring at my profile.

"Let's see what else is on," I said, turning the channel. Though Eddie protested, I knew we were near the part where the Child Catcher appears with his greasy hair and *Chitty Chitty Bang Bang* changes from a kids' movie into a horror flick.

I kept waiting for Sonny to stop staring at me, but his gaze was insistent. I wondered if I didn't have a smear of sloppy joe on my cheek. I sunk down deeper into the couch. Finally Sonny reached over and put his cold hand on my chin.

"Open up, honey," he said.

I didn't want to, but with his fingers pressed against my jawbone what else could I really do? He turned my head toward the lamplight and looked carefully down my throat, tipping my head from side to side.

"Those wisdoms will have to come out," he said. "Tell your folks when it's time I'm their man."

Footsteps on the stairs. Sandy appeared in a powder-blue dress with ruched sleeves and a puka-bead choker. Her eyes were lined with black like a baby raccoon's.

"Whoa-wee," Sonny said, standing. "My own little Cleopatra!"

"No jumping on my water bed," she said to Eddie, sounding like a girl playing the part of a mother in a high school play. She wrote two numbers on a pad by the phone and picked up her leather patch bag. She leaned down and Eddie reached his pale arms up around her neck and squeezed. He held her head tightly, whispering something into her ear that made Sandy smile.

"Whoa there, little man," Sonny said, winking at me. "She's your mama, not your girlfriend."

As soon as the door closed behind them, Eddie ran upstairs and got his Hot Wheels case and a bunch of bright orange segments of track. I helped him set them up in the kitchen. He showed me, by bending the top of the track up between two soup cans on the counter, how the little green car with the racing flames had no trouble making the antigravitational loop-the-loop. He placed two ramps facing each other so when we released a car from each end the Hot

Wheels smashed into one another. After a while the collisions got boring.

"I'll tell my mom you're my favorite sitter if you give me some ice cream," Eddie said. "But if you don't I'll say you talked all night on the phone."

Eddie was clearly experienced with babysitters. I admired his negotiating skills.

Swinging open the freezer door I saw TV dinners, frozen pizzas, and two different flavors of ice cream: cherry and butter pecan. The lower fridge held gallons of soda and thick packages of cold cuts in white butcher paper, a delicacy in my own house. They had strawberries and Cool Whip. They had every kind of cereal: Cap'n Crunch, Froot Loops, Lucky Charms. I used the scoop to curl the ice cream into coffee cups and we ate it while we watched *The Sonny and Cher Comedy Hour*.

I knew everything about Cher, how her first memory was of being lost in the woods, that she'd had a dog named Blackie and two imaginary friends, Sam and Peter, who were lumberjacks. Ever since I'd first seen her a few years ago in her fur vest and elephant bells tied up with rawhide lacing, I knew she had a message for me. I let Eddie eat Cool Whip with his fingers right out of the container so he'd stay quiet as Cher came out in her red and purple gypsy dress and hoop earrings to sing "Gypsies, Tramps, and Thieves." She sang in her low, muddy voice with a certain remove, as if she were embarrassed by the song's rawness.

Eddie fell asleep while I was washing the cups. I watched him, the freckles over his face and his tiny rib cage moving up and down, before I picked him up, his body warm against my chest, and carried him up the stairs to his bed.

"My dad brought me a monkey home from Vietnam but the monkey stopped eating, all its hair fell right out and it died," he said sleepily. I pulled the covers up around him. The air conditioner was high and the room felt chilly. "I like you," he said. "You let me watch as much TV as I want."

I closed his door and stood in the hallway on the gold shag carpet. The walls were covered with sepia-colored mirrors. I looked at my reflection. If I stared long enough I could convince myself that I had nothing to do with the body before me; it was like I resided someplace else entirely and this body was just a puppet that I controlled by remote.

Sandy's room was beside Eddie's, one wall covered with the same smoky glass, the curtains and the bedspread printed with leopard spots. Everything in Sandy's house was oversized. Even her cat, Lulubell, had a fat furry stomach that dragged on the carpet. I looked through Sandy's colored eye pencils and Mary Quant lipsticks. The stuff was all of a good quality, much different from my mom's dime-store lipstick and clumpy mascara. My mom had given up on glamour. She had an all-or-nothing philosophy; if we didn't have money to buy clothes in real materials like linen and silk, she'd just go around in housedresses and white athletic socks.

I was different. I was drawn to the objects of womanhood. To me they were sacred items: the mascara wand, the cotton balls, the leopard-print panties with the pink bow I found in Sandy's dresser. My mother wore white bras and big cotton underwear and insisted I do the same. She said lingerie was for tramps.

I kept snooping. Sandy's closet was jammed. There were a dozen white uniforms—she worked at a nursing home—and lots of party dresses. Many had sequins and were nearly as flamboyant as the ones Cher wore on her show. Sandy was like a tiny Cher, small enough to fit into the parameters of life at Bent Tree. I wondered if I should risk trying one on. Sandy was so petite she was almost exactly my size. I pulled a slinky green dress with a beaded bodice from the hanger.

Once I had the dress on I looked at myself in the mirror. Over the past few months I'd grown so much I looked like a big freak and my hair was cut short just like my brother's. It wasn't unusual for people to think I was a boy. Just the day before, the pharmacist at the drugstore had said to my mom, *Two boys! How nice.* I knew everyone was waiting for me to turn into a young lady and so sometimes I practiced; I had a few moves I was working on. I tried to walk like a woman, to get the rhythm of my hips just right, so that the motion was smooth. I'd noticed that teenage girls always moved as

if people were watching them. It was important somehow to move like people were watching you, so that
people would eventually watch you. I moved on to the
next gesture I was working on: the hair toss. This move
was modeled after my fifth-grade teacher. She'd had
thick brown hair that lay lightly on her shoulders, and
every few moments she would lean back and give her
head a little shake. Since my hair was cropped short,
I wrapped a towel around my head, stood in front of
the mirror, and tipped my head back. But no matter
how many times I tried to move like my old teacher it
was always too jerky, like someone had told me I had a
spider on my neck.

I shook the towel off my head and lifted the dress over
my shoulders, then arranged it back on the hanger and
pulled my clothes back on. As I was hanging the dress
in the closet I heard a car door slam and tires peel out
roughly on the gravel driveway. I ran down the stairs
and threw myself over the back of the couch. Sandy
flew in the door, dropped her bag on the table, and got
a wine cooler out of the refrigerator. She plopped down
beside me on the couch, shook off her high heels, and
put her feet up on the coffee table. Her black mascara
was smeared. The skin below her eyes was pink and
puffy. I could tell she'd been drinking.

"That jackass is never going to marry me," she said.
"I don't know why I keep fucking him."

She swigged from her bottle and stared at the label.
"But if I break it off, where will I be?"

I was watching her small perfect feet, the toenails blood-red and shiny.

"You're so pretty," I said. "I can't believe you have any problems."

"Right!" Sandy laughed.

I could tell what I said had made her remember how young I was, and she jumped up and pulled a five-dollar bill from her wallet.

"I hope it went all right," she said. "He can be a handful."

I took the money but I didn't want to leave. I had heard adults swear only a few times; my dad said "shit" when he got really angry. But the way Sandy swore was different; it made what she said raw and affecting. I wanted her to keep on talking that way to me all night.

"Why do you keep fucking him?" I said.

"Oh honey," she said. "Don't talk like that. It's just not nice."

+

At home, my father was already in bed and my mother sat sideways on the couch, with her legs under her, eating from a plastic container of grocery store macaroni and listening to *Camelot* on the record player. In Philadelphia she'd met with a reducing group that made her wear a pig's mask if, during the weekly weigh-ins, she'd gained more than a pound. My mother had worked in a department store. On Saturdays, her day off, she sometimes sang along with the records of *Camelot* or *Fiddler on the Roof*. I knew to stay in my room. If I came out, she'd tell us how sad it was that Jackie Kennedy had lost two babies; Arabella was stillborn and Patrick Bouvier died just a few days after his birth. Or she'd yell at me for leaving dirty clothes around or opening up the refrigerator door so long all the cold got out.

As she opened her mouth, I prayed she wouldn't tell me again that James Vanhoff had won the State Junior Tennis Championship two years in a row and that he was now on the board of the Roanoke Historical Society or, worse, about the woman who claimed she was possessed by a devil or the toxic mold particles that were suspended in the air all around us. And I was in luck; she just asked me if it went OK, and all I had to do was nod.

✦

I'd set up my stuff in Miranda's old room. On the little wooden table beside my bed I'd placed my busts of Emily Dickinson and Shakespeare. I liked the way I'd painted Emily's necklace with tiny dots of gold, and I'd highlighted Shakespeare's gray hair with silver streaks so he looked like a superhero. My Venus flytrap had survived the journey. I had to remember to place a grain of raw hamburger into its clawed blossom once a week. My record player was in the corner beside my box of 45s, and I spread out my posters, one of a kitten and another I'd gotten from the Philadelphia Museum of Art, an Egyptian with eyes outlined in sparkly black. I loved how you could never tell the girl Egyptians from the boy Egyptians and how they were all so ridiculously glamorous.

From where I lay on my bed I could see my dad through his open bedroom door across the hall. He was under the covers reading his Ram Dass book. The relief he'd felt after we left the church was fading; at first when I asked how God would find us outside the rectory, he'd laughed and told me God was everywhere, you didn't need any particular prayers to find him. But now he seemed worried; he stayed up late every night reading and writing in his notebook. Though he wouldn't admit it, I think my dad was disappointed in Roanoke and the world outside the church; neither were the paradise he'd imagined.

Even though I had my things around me and my dad was nearby, being in Miranda's old room was still spooky. My room felt penetrable. I had taken precautions, moving my mirror directly across from the window, dumping salt in all the corners to ward off bad spirits, and keeping cloves of garlic on the windowsill to scare off vampires. I felt for the bottle of sage I'd taken from the kitchen spice rack—a safeguard against ghosts—and now kept under my pillow, and I knew my squirt gun, full of holy water, was in the top drawer of my dresser. True, I'd blessed the water myself, but I figured as a minister's daughter I had some powers, though they were probably diminished now that my dad had left the church. None of these things made me feel safe. I imagined the ex-husband crouched in my closet, his eyes rolled back to white, and I could almost feel the black hairs growing out of the pink skin of my underarms and down between my legs. I figured the sooner I became a woman, the sooner the ex-husband would be threatening me with a knife. It didn't seem fair that I had to change shape. I wished someone would have asked me; I might have said yes but I would have liked a choice.

At least I didn't have the curse yet. One of my friends had gotten the curse at nine; during gym a line of blood ran down her leg, staining the canvas edge of her tennis shoe. I knew I was "developing," as my mother so annoyingly called it. I knew too that it was natural, but I felt like a skinny monster.

What if the hairs filled not just my underarms and crotch but kept growing until I was covered with hair like a werewolf, thick strains growing over my forehead and around my eyes? I was getting puffy as well, and while I knew I was moving away from my old self into a new place, I didn't want to look like the Playboy Bunny I'd seen on television with the huge breasts and wide idiotic smile. I still prayed that I might swerve away from being that sort of creature and toward something else entirely. I felt my forehead. If my chest could puff out, why couldn't my forehead develop a horn? I got so excited by this idea that I got out my journal and tried to sketch a unicorn girl. But the horn looked like one on a rhino and I couldn't figure out how to draw the bone moving out of my forehead. I drew several variations of hooves, but it was tricky to make them delicate; I had heard that female unicorns were so sensitive, they never stepped on living plants.

None of my pictures satisfied me, so I wrote instead about how the unicorn girl ran away from her duplex up into the forest. There she lived among the deer and baby foxes, eating raspberries and soft leaves. She loved the taste of moss and she often had tea parties for the squirrels where she made cakes by mashing crab apples with butternuts. In the night she stared down at the duplex windows floating in the dark like little rafts of light.

✦

All the next week Sandy emerged from her duplex each day at noon looking sleepy and carrying a six-pack of beer; she lay out in her leopard-print bikini and sunglasses. Eddie watched television inside. Sandy's skin nearly purple, she seemed as drunk off the light as from the beers she popped one after another. I watched her pitch the cans toward the trash in time with whichever song was on her transistor radio.

I tried to force my thoughts away from her, thinking about Barnabas Collins, or trying to decide if I should go down to the fridge and see if we had any cheese. But Sandy had found a latch door into my head and stuffed her body inside.

I couldn't stand just watching her. I pulled on my bathing suit, grabbed a towel from the bathroom, and left the cool duplex for the blinding outdoor light. The only sunglasses I had were a pink pair from when I was little, but I figured they were better than nothing.

As I stood at the foot of her lounger, I saw how pale my skin was in comparison to hers. I asked if I could lie out beside her, and to my amazement she said yes. I hated my bathing suit with its pattern of strawberries and eyelet ruffles. Sandy said it was cute, but I knew it was babyish. She smelled like dirt and radiator heat and once I lay there I began to feel like a larva, pale and glassy beside her.

Sandy talked, pausing only occasionally to sip her beer. When she leaned up to spread oil over her legs, her bikini top gaped open and I saw her nipple and large areola. I listened to her voice with my eyes half closed, watching the skin around the crotch of her bikini; I saw a bevy of black nubs that made my eyes unfocus.

She told me Sonny was not really a good person; he sometimes told people they needed root canals when their teeth were fine. He called his teenage sons lazy and said they smelled bad. Sonny never listened, just waited for his turn to talk. She had thought she loved him, but now she realized she actually hated him.

"To be perfectly honest," she said, "I'm still stuck on Eddie's father. But I fucked that up by fooling around when he went off to Vietnam." He had a new girlfriend now and she was the one who got to fly over to Hawaii to meet him when he got R and R.

She spoke about herself with a certain distance, as if she were talking about a character on *General Hospital*.

"When I think about it," she said, "I can see what a terrible person I am."

"I don't think you're a terrible person," I said.

"But you would, Jesse, if you really knew me."

After that she was quiet and I could hear the hot wind in the leaves.

"Sonny took me to the grocery store and let me buy whatever I wanted."

She didn't know what she would do if he didn't help with the rent and the car payments. No way could she ask her family for money. Her parents had five teeth between them and the house she grew up in, if you could even call it a house, didn't have indoor plumbing.

"I'd rather gnaw my own arm off than go back there."

The sun beat down. Tree leaves singed around the edges, curled forward like burnt paper, and my skin was dry and stiff no matter how much baby oil I spread over myself. The weeds looked brown and miserable. Sandy's radio said we were in the dog days of summer, then a buzzer rang over the airwaves and the DJ told us it was time to turn or burn. The sun made a slow lava lamp under my closed eyelids, and I felt my head getting swimmy and realized how thirsty I was. I asked if I could go inside her duplex and get myself a drink.

Inside Sandy's unit it was dark and cool. All the furniture looked like it was underwater and covered with algae. It was true I was thirsty, and I drank down a jelly glass filled with water and then another, but I also wanted to be inside Sandy's house. I thought about going upstairs into her bedroom and lying across her water bed, and while I liked the idea of my bare skin against her fuzzy bedspread, I knew I would leave grease stains. What if I just quickly held one of her bras against my bathing suit top? She kept several hanging on a hook on the back of the bathroom door. Once I thought of this, the urge to do it was magnetic. It would be like holding Wonder Woman's bodice against my chest. Who knew what superpowers would spark from the material into me? I started toward the stairs, but then I saw Eddie and Phillip through the back window, making their way through the trees down the side of the mountain. All afternoon they'd been in the hooch, a tree fort made of particleboard with a skull drawn in Magic Marker on the door. The one time I'd been allowed inside, Eddie told a story about how his father had to unload a helicopter filled with body parts.

I walked out the back door and handed Sandy a beer; Phillip and Eddie ran down the raw edge of red dirt, toilet-paper rolls of ammunition taped to their T-shirts.

Their tennis shoes sent up a cloud of pink dust.

"Why are you running?" Sandy said.

"The gooks are after us!" Eddie yelled.

"You're not supposed to call them that!" Sandy said, but by the time she finished talking they had disappeared back up into the trees.

✦

That night, while we waited for my dad to get home from work, my mom browned hamburger in the Teflon skillet and I stood over the trash can and peeled potatoes. The wet strips curled off the blade and landed in the garbage in artistic configurations.

Mom was talking about rich people again, her voice growing lively and familiar. Mrs. Vanhoff was pencil thin and always wore her hair up, highlighting her long and elegant neck. The Vanhoffs had been in last night's newspaper eating lobster thermidor at the Hotel Roanoke.

"Carolyn Vanhoff is head of the mayor's art council, and I heard she takes tennis lessons with the pro at the club."

She sprinkled the Hamburger Helper flavor packet over the ground beef.

"Every January she goes off to a spa in North Carolina to lose the few pounds she gains over Christmas."

"You and Dad should go away," I said. "I could watch Phillip."

"Your father? Take me on a vacation? Like that's ever going to happen."

A peel flew off the blade and stuck to the wall. I wanted to defend my dad, but what could I really say? That he read a lot, that he had a great vocabulary, that he helped people. These would only get grunts and eye rolls from my mother. I decided to change the subject.

"Sandy is having trouble with her boyfriend," I said.

I thought my mom might like this information, but I could tell by how she pressed down the spatula so grease oozed out of the hamburger that she did not.

"I hope you're not looking up to that woman," she said.

I didn't say anything.

"You know Sonny is married."

"Separated," I said.

My mom swung around, holding the fry pan in front of her. It was rare; she'd gone from a solid 5 straight to a 2. The grainy hamburger and the greenish grease pooling in the tilted pan looked disgusting.

"Jesse, you have no idea what you're dealing with."

At least they're people I actually know, I wanted to say to her, *not strangers I read about in the newspaper.* My mom would rather pretend to have relationships with people than actually deal with our real-life neighbors. But I just grunted and ran out of the kitchen, up the stairs, and slammed the door to my room.

I held my View-Master to my eyes, pushed the lever down: Alice's head poking out of a thatched roof, then the wide, menacing smile of the Cheshire Cat. The colors reminded me of the stained-glass windows in my dad's old church, gemlike and glorious. But I couldn't move myself into the tiny 3-D colors like usual, so I tried to read the book I'd gotten from the library on worldwide burial rituals. I was on the part where mummies, after being swathed in linens, are first placed into one coffin and then a second. Through the wall I could hear Mrs. Smith playing hymns on her piano. She had a long list of things that were bad luck. Some of them were obvious, like breaking a mirror, but others I'd never heard before, like sweeping after dark and cutting your fingernails on Sundays.

I had always felt it was good luck that my mom was prettier than all the other moms, and that even though she didn't dress up anymore, she couldn't help but look stylish in her paisley head scarf and big dark sunglasses. But now her face was the color of a mushroom and she had velvet bags under her eyes like a zombie in a monster movie. Incrementally, she had transformed from the mom I used to love into a creature, weepy and miserable, a dark thing to be afraid of in the middle of the night.

✦

"You're getting good color on your front," Sandy said as I spread my towel beside her on the grass, "but you need more on your back."

It was late in the afternoon. Shadows fell over our toes, but the sun was still hot. We lay before the mountain like virgins about to be sacrificed. I pulled down the side of my bottom, to show her the line of lighter skin.

"Malibu Barbie!" she said, as she shook the baby oil and iodine and squirted a glossy puddle between her breasts.

"He still hasn't called," she said, motioning to the phone she'd pulled outside, which now sat on the welcome mat. Eddie sat beside it. He had on a pair of huge stereo headphones that had been accessorized with tinfoil sticking out at odd angles.

"He's in the Head Crusher," Sandy told me matter-of-factly.

"My eyes are going to squirt out of my head," Eddie yelled cheerfully, as he turned the page of his comic book. He wore his father's recon gloves, the tips of the fingers cut out, he'd told me earlier, so he could better grip his weapon.

"I'm sure there are good reasons he's not calling," she said, laying her head against her arm. "Emergency root canal, or that lazy son of his might have gotten busted."

I watched sparrows rub themselves with dirt in the ditch beside the driveway and listened to Mr. Ananais mowing down by the road. Lulubell lifted her furry head and looked at me.

My dad came out of the duplex in his bell-bottoms, a striped shirt, and a wide tie. He was going to his second job at the psych center, but before he got in the car, he walked over to where Sandy and I lay.

I sat up and pulled my knees into my chest; he held his hand over his eyes, blocking the glare, so he could better see us. I was terrified he'd say something stupid, tell Sandy about my rashes or that as a baby I was always constipated.

"Not much sun left," he said.

Sandy pulled off her sunglasses.

"There's enough for me, pastor," she said.

Before we left the rectory, everybody called him pastor—even people who didn't go to church called him that. Now, though, the title embarrassed him; he blushed and looked up into the trees blowing around on the side of the mountain.

"Help your mother with dinner," he said.

"Yes sir."

He walked back to our car, got in, and started up the engine.

"Your father," Sandy said, "is a good-looking man."

"What?"

"He's a looker."

"If you say so," I said, rolling over onto my stomach and pressing my cheek into the grass.

✦

When Sandy let me in she was dressed for her night out with the girls: white short shorts and a puffy-sleeved blouse tied high up to show off her belly, and her hair teased up and sprayed. She looked like one of the Dallas Cowboy cheerleaders. I had to admit she was disturbingly tan.

Eddie was already asleep, and when a horn honked, she jotted a number on a pad by the phone and said she'd be back no later than eleven. I got myself a jelly glass full of Pepsi and a handful of Fritos and watched a made-for-TV movie about a senator's daughter who ran away to join a bunch of hippies who lived in an old school bus. The head hippie—a long-haired guy in an embroidered vest and dirty jeans—took the senator's daughter to McDonald's, where he searched through the garbage for food. He tried to get her to eat the food he'd retrieved, but the senator's daughter couldn't make herself taste the limp, leftover fries. Then there were scenes of hippies handing out daisies and swimming in rivers. I got bored and turned down the sound.

I'd brought my favorite book, *Half Magic*, with me, and I opened the pages to where the oldest boy presses the magic coin firmly into his palm and all the children are suddenly transported to the court of King Arthur. The idea that certain objects had magic powers, a concept I'd clung to for so long, was starting to seem ridiculous. I'd also lost the ability, which I'd once reveled in, to pretend I was an animal. I used to spend whole afternoons thinking kitten thoughts or hiding in my closet like a shy baby deer. I'd imagine I was a mother badger living in a civilized badger hole, with a tiny stove and wooden breakfast table.

It was depressing, really, to be stuck always in my own skin. For a short while when I was small, between the time I realized I was myself and when I knew I had to stay a girl, I thought I could go back and forth between girl and boy. I used to imagine I could trade my body for a boy's. It wasn't until I said *I have a penis*, and watched my parents' faces break apart in laughter, that I realized I'd have to stay a girl forever. I turned the sound back up on the television. On the screen I could see the head hippie and the now-hippified senator's daughter. She was barefoot, in a patchwork dress with a braid of leather around her forehead. They had returned to the McDonald's, and they were foraging food left on the tables just out front. The head hippie fed the half-eaten hamburger to the hippie girl, the camera lingering on the girl's lips as she took the hamburger into her mouth. I could tell by the sad music that played over the closing credits that I was supposed to feel sorry for her. But why? Because she didn't have money for a fresh, clean hamburger? Or was it because she looked different in her hippie dress from the straight-looking people sitting around her? I thought I knew the real reason. Any girl who didn't do what her parents wanted had clearly been brainwashed. Now that she was eating garbage, it wouldn't be long before she'd be in some courtroom singing in Latin with an *X* carved into her forehead like the Manson girls.

Though I hadn't realized it till now, whenever I thought of Miranda's ex-husband, he always had the same wild eyes and long auburn hair as Charles Manson—Charlie, as the girls called him, who could handle rattlesnakes without being bitten and bring dead birds back to life. I walked up the stairs, pushed Eddie's door open, and stood in the doorway watching his little chest rise and fall a few times, his hair so white it glowed in the dark like the tail of a comet. With one arm he clutched his Dapper Dan doll, the thumb of his other hand in his mouth. I went into Sandy's bathroom. It was still damp from her shower, and the humid air was scented with musk.

I pulled the neck of my T-shirt over to look at my white strap marks, then lifted up my shirt and stared for a while at my stomach. It was a golden brown, the fine hairs white. Then I examined several darker hairs I'd found earlier that day under my left arm. One of the things I liked best about babysitting was that I had time to look at myself as much as I wanted. Each new hair meant I was moving closer to the Danger Zone. Once my body flooded with hormones, I'd become vulnerable to the whims of men. Men, it wasn't hard to see, ran everything, and once a girl got breasts and all that went with that, men had wizard power over you, they could make you do anything they wanted.

Sandy had left her bathing suit hanging on a hook on the back of the bathroom door, and before I even realized it, I had pulled the bikini bottoms up over my jeans and fastened the top over my T-shirt. I decided to practice a move I'd seen Sandy do when she bent down to tie Eddie's shoe. It was a small gesture, but I'd been fascinated by how she'd collapsed her skeleton to the ground with concern and focus. I broke the movement into parts. First there was the noticing of the thing that needed your attention. Your face showed a sudden focus as the knees began to bend. The next part was the hardest to do smoothly: you floated downward without any effort, gentle as a flower petal. With my fingers I simulated tying a shoelace before releasing back up into the regular stream of time. As I stood up I tried to look satisfied in a small-time way, but my face in the mirror looked *deeply* satisfied, as if I'd just prevented World War III or something.

Maybe if I put on a little eyeliner. I pulled the tiny brush out and moved it along the edge of my eyelids. The black made my eyes look separate from my body, as if they had a different destiny from my nose or my mouth. I tried a sort of chaotic walk that Sandy used as she moved over the lawn toward her lounge chair. I walked back and forth in front of the mirror, slopping my body around as if it were liquid in a bucket, but the bathroom was too narrow to get a real feel for the full sequence, how she opened the duplex door, moved across the grass, dropped her butt over the lounge chair, and swung her legs up, centering her face into the sun.

I went down and got a beer from the refrigerator and Sandy's sunglasses and looked at myself in the mirrored wall.

"I don't know why I keep fucking him," I said to myself in Sandy's high voice. It was no use: no matter what adjustments I made, I never really looked like anything other than a boy dressed up in girls' clothes.

I was getting sleepy but I knew I needed to stay awake so no harm would come to Eddie or me. At the window I saw that all the lights were off in my own family's unit across the street—even my dad who usually stayed up late was asleep—and I started to wonder if I'd ever lived there. Maybe I was the one who had betrayed Eddie's father and was now pining for a sleazy oral surgeon. Though I tried to push the story back, I thought about the babysitter who'd gotten The Phone Call, a man's voice at the other end laughing. The man kept calling until the babysitter finally called the operator, who told her the man was calling from the phone upstairs! If that one wasn't scary enough, there was the one about the babysitter who saw a man standing outside looking in the window, only to realize the man was actually standing behind her, and what she was seeing was his reflection in the glass. The scariest of all, though, was the babysitter who had called the parents to ask if she could throw a blanket over the creepy life-size clown statue that stood in a dark corner of the living room. I saw the bloodshot eyes surrounded by white grease paint, the red painted smile and rainbow wig. After a long pause the father said, "We don't have a life-size clown sculpture!"

I heard a tapping sound and got worried Miranda's evil ex-husband had cut the phone line. My heart boomed in my ears. I couldn't stay in the unit; I had to wake Eddie and we'd go out into the yard, just up in the tree line, and wait for Sandy to get back. But just as I was slipping on my tennis shoes, I heard a car come up the street blasting the Allman Brothers. It wasn't the baby-blue Pinto Sandy's girlfriend had picked her up in. It was a white Mustang. As the Mustang parked in front of the duplex, a trail of raspberry embers flew out the driver's-side window and into the weeds. I waited for Sandy to get out of the car, but she didn't. I saw shapes moving in the car's back window like koi swimming sluggishly in murky green water.

+

When I finally got home my father was up and sitting in the dark, listening to his jazz records with oversize headphones. I watched his reflection in the sliding glass doors that led out to the deck. Roanoke, it was perfectly clear now, was not the Sun Belt. There were no landscaped parks. No fountains. Things at

my dad's job had already gotten weird. It all started when he told the guy who thought he was Speed
Racer *Good luck in the big race,* and then at group he
suggested to the lady who was afraid of her washing
machine that *form is no form.* As a pastor he'd reas-
sured parishioners that they rested inside the heart
of God. But he didn't believe any of that anymore.
Now Dad tried new ideas on the patients. Ideas
he'd learned in his Trungpa book: that there was no
such thing as a self separate from the rest of the
universe and that all dualities were delusion. These
ideas freaked out his patients: the washing machine
lady had to be sedated, and Louie, the man who wore
rain boots over his hospital slippers because he was
afraid of floods, figuring his body was the same as
the bricks, walked right into the wall. Dad was on
probation now. At first he'd taken to bed as he always did when a job wasn't going well; I brought him
a crustless grilled cheese sandwich. My mom gave
him a pep talk: he'd have to make his job at the VA
hospital work, since we'd only just gotten here and
we couldn't afford to move.

✦

The thermostat by the side of the house read 103
degrees. I could feel the heat through the soles of my
tennis shoes. The duplexes shimmered and swayed
in the silver light, made of fish scales rather than

brick. One trick of the light and all of Bent Tree would flicker and then disappear. I went inside to the refrigerator, got an egg, and walked out to the sidewalk. I cracked the egg and let it drip out onto the cement. There was a half-hearted sizzle and the bottom turned white, but the top was still gelatinous and runny.

Eddie opened his window and yelled out.

"You got to do it on a car hood."

I nodded but decided to retreat into the air conditioning instead and read about mummification. I was interested in how the Egyptians pulled the brains of dead people out through their noses with a hook and then held them in jars shaped like cats. I wanted to tell somebody about the cat jars, which were shiny black obsidian, with whiskers cut into the stone and emeralds for eyes, but I knew my mother would just shake her head and say I was morbid. I used to be able to tell her anything, that at times I felt I was a snowy owl, or that I wanted to be a cash register. Not anymore. My dad might be interested, but he was working. I held my View-Master up to my eyes and turned toward the light of the window. Chief Red Feather greeted visitors at the entrance of Knott's Berry Farm. Click. A stagecoach parked in front of the Old Saloon. I set the View-Master beside me and lay watching the light move over my perfume bottle collection. I liked how it glittered the edges of the glass, how it moved incrementally toward the wall, illuminating the grains in the paint and the strands of the carpet below. I closed my eyes and started to say the days of the week, waiting for the sun to make the inside of my eyelids red.

At some point I heard a car stop on the street. At the window I saw Sonny get out of a taxi and walk over to Sandy's car. Her front door flew open and she ran over the grass barefoot in her mini-kimono. I ran down the stairs and swung open the door, the heat hitting me as if from an open oven.

"It's my car. You gave it to me!"

She was up on her toes, the tendons in her neck defined.

"Well," Sonny said, not even bothering to turn, "I'm taking it back." He wore a pale blue golf shirt and white pants. Though it was hot, the material hadn't wilted. The clothes hung on his thin frame as if on a hanger.

Sandy wobbled down the driveway, her bare feet unsteady on the gravel. He swung around and put his hands on his hips; she moved her fists up and I was sure she was going to beat against his chest, but instead she clasped them to her own heart, her knees swung sideways, and she fell onto the gravel.

Eddie ran down from the duplex in just his white underpants and tennis shoes.

"You killed her!" he said.

"She's just being dramatic," Sonny said as he stood staring down at her. I walked over to where she lay, her long eyelashes closed, her perfect breasts pointed to the sky. Eddie put his cheek down next to his mother's and her eyes flew open like a doll's in a horror movie.

"You fucker!" she said. "That car is mine!"

Sonny waved his hand, disgusted by her theatrics.

"Don't do this," she said. "DO NOT TAKE MY CAR!"

He got into the Porsche and cranked up the engine. Sandy leaned into the open window and grabbed the car's steering wheel.

"What are you doing?" Sonny said, trying to pry her fingers off the wheel. "Stop this!"

"No."

I was by the edge of the driveway holding Eddie's hand.

"Mommy," Eddie yelled to her, "let go."

The sound of her son's voice woke Sandy up a little, and she looked back at us, her kimono fallen open so we could see her black bra and purple panties. Her hair was wild, flying around her head.

"Let go of the wheel," I said. I wanted to say she was making a fool of herself, that she didn't need Sonny, that she and I could live together and I'd watch Eddie while she went to night classes.

Sonny put up the automatic window so the glass edge pressed into the skin of her elbow, but she still didn't budge, so he released the emergency brake and the car jumped forward. Sandy was yanked a few feet until the car picked up speed and she lost her grip and skittered into the grass by the side of the road.

We ran over to where she was getting up.

"Oh Lord," she said, "what a fucking jackass."

She brushed the grass off her hands and we watched the car snake through the subdivisions and head toward the highway. Now that it was over, she seemed to find the whole encounter hilarious.

"I'm going to borrow Woody's car," she said, retying her kimono around her waist. "I need you to come with me to Sonny's. I need a witness."

"I can't," I said. "My mom is still mad I got home so late the last time I watched Eddie."

Sandy turned to me.

"You want me to just let him get away with that?" she said. I could tell she was getting mad and this time it was at me. "Some friend you turn out to be," she said, as she walked away.

"I'll do it," I said, "but I have to be home before Mom gets back from the grocery store."

The car Sandy borrowed from the guy in 9B smelled like cigarette smoke and turpentine. An empty fast-food cup with a straw sticking out of the top lay side-ways on the floor.

"I really appreciate your support, Jesse," she said, glancing at her face in the rearview mirror. Her lips were outlined in red pencil and filled in with gloss, and she'd changed out of her kimono into a white lace blouse that showed both her tan skin and the black material of her bra. Between us on the front seat was a brown paper bag, the cuff of a blue oxford hanging over the top as if trying to escape.

"That shit actually thinks he can take my car," Sandy said. "How am I supposed to get to work?"

"Don't say *shit*," Eddie said.

"Sorry, honey," Sandy said. "I mean, he brings his laundry over, I wash that man's underwear. Once I even pulled a tick off his ass."

"Gross!" I said.

After the tight way the Porsche drove, Sandy was having trouble keeping the Dart in a single lane. I wasn't sure if she deserved the car or not. I wasn't sure what women deserved for being mothers and taking care of men, but I had to say something.

"Sonny is mean," I said.

"I hate old Sonny," Eddie said. "He never got me that Matchbox carrier he promised."

"He is terrible at keeping promises," Sandy said. We drove past a chain of fast-food restaurants like charms on a giant bracelet. I'd been ready to declare that it was over between Sandy and me. But now that I sat beside her I wondered again if I should offer to move in.

"Sorry you had to see that mess," she said, turning to me.

"I saw it too," Eddie said.

"It's not your fault," I said.

Sandy's face came apart, her chin dropped, and she wailed and held a hand up to cover her mouth.

"But it is!" she said. "I did all kinds of bad stuff."

Eddie climbed up on the back of her seat, hugged her head and grabbed her ears. His shirt was on inside out so all the seams showed.

"How you doing, buddy?" she asked, trying to keep the car from running off the road.

"Not that good," Eddie said. He had been sick over the weekend and he was still pale.

"Why don't you sleep some?"

He curled his body into the car's backseat and folded his hands under his head.

"Tell me," he said. "Why didn't I bring a pillow?"

"Use this," she said, reaching into the bag and pulling out a cotton sweater.

"I don't want Sonny's old sweater," he said and started to kick the back of my seat.

We turned into Hunting Hills. So far I'd avoided driving there with my mom, though I had heard her talk about the houses. They had private verandas, butler pantries, and sunrooms made completely out of glass. We passed a stone house with a circular drive and one built to look like a Spanish hacienda. My mother had pointed out the styles to me in her home design book.

"I just want my car back," Sandy said as she pulled into the driveway in front of a brick Georgian. Her sports car was parked in the open garage.

"I won't be long." She walked up to the front door and swung the brass knocker. The door opened, though we couldn't see who stood in the darkened hallway.

"This is old Sonny's house," Eddie said. "We came once to swim in his pool."

"Does his wife live here?"

"How should I know?"

"How was the pool?"

"OK."

We watched the house. In one of the top windows I saw the edge of a peach-colored chair beside a pale blue ceramic lamp. The sprinklers were on and spray hit the side of the Dart, throwing droplets up on the passenger-side window.

I wanted Sandy to drop off the bag by the front door and run back to the car so we could go get ice cream and talk about Sonny. I really enjoyed hearing what a jerk the guy was, how he had never done a dish at her house or even scraped his own plate. How he would say she was getting a little chunky and how she had to listen to his same goofy jokes over and over.

Eddie handed me a bunched-up piece of newspaper.

"Open it," he said.

Inside the paper was a good-looking rock, granite with flecks of mica.

"Thanks," I said.

He'd been giving me presents lately, including a handful of acorns and a bracelet made of buttercups.

"Don't mention it," Eddie said, hanging his freckled arms over the seat.

"In a battle," he said, "do you think a lion could beat a moose?"

"I'll say yes."

"What about a skull? Could it beat a karate man?"

"Unsure about that one."

He set his cheek down on the top of the front seat.

"Does your mom ever say she's going to kill herself?"

"Not in so many words," I said.

"My mom said it."

"She doesn't mean it though."

"How do you know?"

"I just do."

"Can I sit on your lap?"

"Sure."

He squeezed himself into the front seat and onto my lap. His hair smelled like butter and his knees were covered with dirt. He turned the radio dial. All that ever played on the Roanoke radio stations was Lynyrd Skynyrd, with an occasional Little Feat or Allman Brothers song. All day Skynyrd blasted out of car stereos and at night from duplex windows. I twisted the dial down to the far end of the numbers, the one station that played the trippy stuff from the sixties—Jefferson Airplane, the Doors, and my favorite song, "The Lion Sleeps Tonight." Eddie showed me how when you pressed your fingertips against your closed eyelids, colors came up, reds and oranges melting into each other.

Sometime later, Sandy came running down the slate path, her mascara smudged around her eyes. I looked up through the windshield. Sonny stared down at us from an upper-floor window; he had a strange smile on his face.

Sandy swung open the door.

"What happened?" I said.

"Same old shit," she said. "At first he said he'd give me back the car but then he said he wouldn't."

She made Eddie and me get in back and put on our seat belts.

"Hold on," she said as she jumped the sidewalk and ran over a row of rhododendrons and up onto the lawn. Eddie and I looked at each other and he gripped my hand. She spun the car around the fountain in the middle, shards of grass and dirt flying up outside, before the car bumped over the curb and ran right through a patch of petunias.

"I believe that's called a donut," she said, once we were back on the road. She moved the dial to the Skynyrd station and turned the volume up loud.

✦

It rained the next day, and I stayed in my bedroom arranging my school supplies into different configurations, putting pencils into my new puppy pencil case and sniffing my new erasers. After practicing it many times in different script styles, I wrote my name very slowly on the cover of all my new notebooks. To me the blank white sheets were like photographs of the Milky Way. They gave me a weird feeling of reverence.

Every little while I went to the window and looked out. Sandy's blinds were closed and whenever I went to her duplex, which I did every few hours, Eddie came to the door in his pajamas and told me she was still asleep.

The next morning, just after Sandy had left for work and Eddie and my brother had gone off to their hooch in the woods, a van pulled up and parked in her driveway. It was still raining. Two men, one short with a fringe of hair around the side of his head and the other a surly-looking high school kid, used a key to open the door of her duplex. At first I thought Sonny, in an effort to make up, had sent guys over to paint her place. In a few minutes, though, the men carried her couch out to their truck.

I ran down in the rain to get Mr. Ananais.

I told him what was happening at Sandy's and he followed me up the hill. I stood by the doorway while he talked to the older man, who showed him a pink slip of paper.

"Are they breaking in?" I asked when he came out.

He shook his head.

"They have Sonny's keys," he said. "The lease is in his name."

"What about the furniture?"

We watched them carry the geometrical print down the driveway and slide it into the truck.

"It's all Sonny's," he said. "What kind of a man would take away a woman's furniture?"

The younger man carried the afghan that Sandy kept on the back of the couch and the wicker fan that had hung over the television. I knew for a fact that one of the residents in the nursing home had crocheted the blanket for her.

"That's Sandy's," I said.

He stopped and turned his head.

"It's on the list," he said flatly.

"Well it's not Sonny's," I said, grabbing it out of his hands.

"Hey," he said, "give that back."

"It's OK," the older guy said, coming up behind us carrying a lamp in each hand. "Let her keep it."

Mr. Ananais pulled me away.

"You have to calm down, *koukla*," he said. "The ladies in Bent Tree are sometimes a little crazy. I had a girl come out of her unit naked and go around door to door asking for a cheese sandwich. These ladies will have arguments about anything, how to cook a chicken, or if rain is rain or if it's drizzle."

We watched the movers pull the metal door of the truck shut. I copied the number off the license plate and Mr. Ananais went down to his duplex to call Sandy at work. He promised me he wouldn't evict her, that he'd give Sandy a chance to pay her rent herself. After the movers drove off, I sat on the curb in front of her duplex under my black umbrella with the blanket over my lap. The light faded like a lamp being dimmed by slow degrees. The sky was green, then white, the air smoky with raindrops and the trees on the mountains darkening. When the rain stopped, steam came up off the asphalt and the cicadas started to pulse.

My dad came out to talk to me. I could tell my mom had sent him. His beard had grown in and he'd lost weight; his hair was pulled back in a ponytail. Before we got kicked out of the rectory my dad would have told me not to worry, Sandy was a child of God. He'd insist that all people and animals, even snakes and crocodiles, were connected at the root, a solid blob of life. At the end too, when we died, we'd be connected once again. It was only in life that we *seemed* like separate beings.

But now he wasn't sure what to say.

"I guess you're not hungry?"

"No."

I thought he might point to the trees swaying in the soft wind and expect me to get all goose-pimply, because the Holy Spirit was moving in the world. He used to do it all the time, and while now it was rare, he sometimes still held his hand up, out of habit, to show that the spirits' enchantments were not completely dead.

Instead he pulled a cookie wrapped in a napkin out of his pocket.

"Just in case," he said, setting it beside me on the curb.

I watched him walk back into the duplex. I was mad at him. Without God to protect us, I had to watch over

Sandy and help her the best I could. I saw my mother doing the dishes at the sink through the kitchen window and I knew Phillip and Eddie were inside watching television. It got darker. The streetlight came on and moths beat against the glass. Clouds blew sideways and a few stars came out. I was afraid that when Sandy came back, she'd see her empty apartment and swallow a whole jar of aspirin. If I didn't wait up for her, she might not make it through the night.

CHAPTER TWO

JILL

On my first day of seventh grade, I waited for the junior high bus by the row of mailboxes down on the main road. I had chosen my outfit only after setting all my options out on my bed and trying on each one. I went through various movements in front of the bathroom mirror before settling on the wide-wale corduroys and the green blouse with the large pointy collar.

I crossed my arms in front of my chest and angled my head. From practicing, I knew the pose I wanted to present when I stepped on the bus. My chin had to have a delicate look and my lips had to be relaxed and slightly parted. I wanted to look mysterious like a Victorian heroine, with pale cheeks and sunken, glittering eyes. In Philadelphia I'd blown the first day of sixth grade by acting friendly and wearing a shirt I'd tried to sew myself out of calico fabric. I swore I would never let that happen again. I had a new persona I'd been planning to introduce the first day of school: a girl wise beyond her years who was not at all nerdy or spastic or prone to crying jags. When people asked me where I was from I was going to say Northampton or Old Lyme, as if my life were resplendent with rope swings and sleeping porches. But now that I was out on the bus stop I realized nobody really cared.

Sheila was the only one I wanted to meet. I'd watched her from our deck, lying out with her girl-friends on towels in her small backyard. She was fully developed, as grown-ups liked to say, and dressed like Julie from *The Mod Squad*. She wore a choker around her neck, a floral blouse with lace at the wide cuffs, and rose-colored corduroys.

I was convinced there was a direct connection between breast development and the way girls lost interest in playing jacks and singing along to John Denver songs. In the sixth grade, my friend Kelley had been happy to jump rope with me until her chest began to swell and the creases around her nose got greasy. After that she drifted to the back fence where the boys hung out. I had noticed that once a girl went over she was impossible to get back unless you your-self went over too. Then you could be friends again and talk about pop idols and blue mascara.

Besides Sheila and Dwayne—a sullen older boy in tight bell-bottoms and a Skynyrd T-shirt—the only other kid at the bus stop was Jill Bamburg. She lived in the duplex next to ours. She looked exhausted, with gray pouches under her eyes. During her mom's parties, I'd watched Jill and her little sister, Beth, in white nightgowns, and her older brother, Ronnie, use homemade wands to make bubbles the size of small dogs. After the liquid soap ran out, they dropped objects from their second-story window and timed how long it took them to fall.

I moved closer to Sheila. She smelled like musk oil and Eve shampoo. She jumped away as if she might catch geekiness from me, so I sunk back to where Jill stood. I spoke to her, hoping, idiotically, that it might make Sheila jealous.

"What a drag school's starting," I said.

Jill looked at me with her flat brown eyes.

"I guess so," she said, looking past me up the road to see if the bus was coming.

Finally the bus pulled up and the double doors swung out with a loud metal click. I got on last and saw Sheila sitting next to a red-haired girl wearing a Tweety Bird T-shirt. Dwayne sat with the boys in the back who were singing a Doobie Brothers' song. Junior high went from sixth to ninth grade, but Dwayne looked much older; he must have flunked and been held back. Jill sat with a friend in the middle of the bus. Only one girl was alone. She sat by the window, her white-blonde hair long in the front to hide a port-wine birthmark that stained her cheek. She looked up at me hopefully but I decided that sitting beside her was too big a risk.

I took an empty seat near the front instead. I knew that proximity to the driver offered a certain amount of protection. This period of grace lasted only for the first few days, though. After that, being close to the driver became a liability.

✦

In school Sheila moved among a flock of shiny-haired girls in colored corduroys, cheesecloth shirts, and Earth shoes. They were like jewels dropped in the muddy hallway waters, with their bright fingernails, glittering eye shadow, and peacock-feather earrings. At lunch they sat together and talked about lip gloss flavors and whether patchouli oil smelled better then musk. They looked so alike it was hard to tell one from another.

I knew, with my short haircut and knobby knees, that I would never join their group. If I were a boy I would have escaped into a football obsession, comic books, or *Star Trek* reruns by now, but girls, girls had no such escape hatches.

I hadn't always been like this. Before we moved from the rectory I rode my bike everywhere and all the neighborhood kids loved me, because I was the best at making up games. We often enacted scenes from the Bible. My favorite was the raising of Lazarus, where

I'd make my brother rub dirt on his face and lie down on the grass. I'd stare at him with my glowing eyes as I commanded *Rise!*

But that period was over. In Roanoke nobody cared if you had a good imagination, if you knew everything about mummification rites or had acted out every detail of the burial rituals of the natives in Timbuktu. The teachers at Low Valley Junior High were mostly female, with thick Southern accents, heavy makeup, and carefully teased-up hair. At lunch I saw my homeroom teacher, Mrs. Remsly, eating deviled eggs out of a Tupperware container. The only men were the grim-faced janitor, the young AV guy wearing bell-bottoms as he rolled his overhead projector down the hallway, and the principal, whom so far I knew only as a deep baritone coming over the intercom, leading the Pledge of Allegiance and asking us not to throw food in the cafeteria. I darted from class to class like a small stunned fish. Nobody was particularly unfriendly, but nobody was nice to me either.

I needed a guide to help me negotiate the local customs, and that guide had to be Sheila. She had the power. At lunch, I saw the birthmark girl, whose name was Pam, sitting alone at a table in the middle of the room. Pam had a Holly Hobbie lunch box and thermos and she ate while she read, not caring if she had milk on her upper lip or a smear of mustard on her chin. She invited me to sit with her, but I pretended I didn't hear. Instead I sat alone and stole glances at Sheila, who sat with a bunch of girls, laughing and nibbling her sandwich.

After lunch I watched how expertly Sheila rolled her combination, swung open her locker, glanced at herself in the little mirror she'd taped inside, then pulled out her math textbook. When I walked behind her I wanted to place my finger on her delicate collarbone. I wanted to ingest her like one of my father's communion wafers and let her instruct me, like Jesus, from the inside.

✦

One afternoon when I got off the bus, I walked behind Sheila. It was still hot. A warm breeze blew through my hair and in front of 3B I saw the leaves of the ratty sunflowers dropping, the dirt around them dry and red. I'd been rehearsing what to say to her. Saying I liked the braids in her hair sounded too intimate, but complimenting her clogs didn't seem personal enough. All day I'd weighed which part of her perfect body to concentrate on. Finally I decided to tell her I liked the birds stamped into her leather belt. It showed my eye for detail without being creepy. But before I could say anything, Sheila swung around.

"Are you following me?"

"No!"

"Why are you walking so close to me then?"

"I'm not," I insisted.

"And why did you touch my hair in health class?"

It was true. During the menstruation movie, while the soap opera music blared and the egg made its way down the fallopian tube toward the uterus, the projector light had been so silver on Sheila's head that she had not looked real. That's when I reached out beyond the edge of my desk and set the pad of my index finger gently against the back of her head.

"I was brushing away a spider." It sounded lame even to me.

Sheila looked at me. She had her hands on her hips and her head tilted sideways.

"Yeah. Right," she said. "You should just admit that you're a lezzbo."

Jill ran up behind us.

"Leave her alone," she said. "She's just trying to be nice."

Sheila looked from me to Jill.

"Freaks," she said. "Go off to freakland and do your freakazoid things!" She hurried down toward her duplex, her clogs sounding on the asphalt.

"Don't mind her," Jill said. "She's a double-dutch bitch."

I felt as if my brain had been scooped out with an iced-tea spoon. As Jill talked about Sheila her words moved around the empty space inside my head. True, I was walking up the incline, but I had no sense of my legs moving, just a floating feeling, like a dust mote careening around in an angle of light. I watched Jill's mouth move.

She had a painfully long, pale face and hair that fell limply around her cheekbones. At her mother's parties, men with mustaches drank beers. Along with watching Jill and her sister make bubbles, I'd also watched them play badminton, hitting the birdie back and forth. As the night wore on, their games got more surreal. I'd seen them volley both an ice cube and a banana.

While her mother didn't allow after-school visitors, Jill said if I agreed to hide in her bedroom I could sneak inside 11B. But we'd have to be quiet. We slipped through the screen door into the living room and I was confronted by a number of smells: sandalwood, beer, and some third thing I'd never smelled before. The couch sagged and the coffee table was covered with puddles of dried wax. An Indian-print bedspread hung behind the TV and there was ivy dangling from a macramé holder in front of the window. It was identical to the hippie crash pads I'd seen on TV and in movies, but different because instead of grown-ups in tie-dye shirts and macramé belts, it was filled with children. Beth, Jill's third-grade sister, sat on the floor surrounded by math books. Ronnie, her older brother, was slumped on the couch watching *General Hospital*.

Neither of them looked in our direction. Upstairs, Jill had the same room as mine, though hers was decorated more sparsely, with a mattress on the floor and a cardboard dresser. She'd taped pictures from magazines up on the wall, mostly baby animals and photographs of sunsets. In one corner, a giant stuffed panda, whose name was Barnabas, slumped over as if he'd been shot in the back.

"I didn't talk to you at first," Jill whispered, "because I wasn't sure I could trust you."

"Why are you whispering?" I said.

Jill pointed to the wall.

"My mom is sleeping."

She told me how in sixth grade Sheila had pretended to be her friend but once Sheila got her braces off she'd told everyone at school that Jill was a dirtbag.

"She announced that I had leg spasms, which was true, but it only happened once. And she said my farts smelled like dog food."

"Whose farts smell good?"

"Hers," Jill said. "They smell like cinnamon."

She shook her head.

"She's just the worst sort of person," Jill went on, "two-faced and a bitch."

Jill cast her eyes down to her blanket, a nubby afghan of triangular blue and pink strips.

"Were you planned?" she asked.

This was a common question. If you were planned it meant your family wanted you, you'd come into a friendly spot, you were loved. But if you weren't planned, that was a whole other story.

"I was," I said. "But my little brother wasn't."

My parents had never actually admitted this, but my mother had implied it a few times.

89

"None of us were planned," Jill said. "Not a single one."

It was hard for me to figure out how this could be true. But before I could ask Jill more about it, her face got very serious. She was suddenly *deadly* serious.

"Before we can be friends," she said, "you need to know that the Bamburgs are a tragic family."

"In what way?"

"In just about every way you can imagine," she said. "You name it, we're tragic."

She pulled out a drawer.

"For instance—"

She took out a black comb with dandruff lodged in the teeth and a key chain with a Harley Davidson medallion. She laid both on the bed.

"That's it, that's all I have left of my daddy."

"What happened?"

"Motorcycle wreck. He's buried in that graveyard on 419 next to the Taco Bell."

"That's terrible," I said. I never knew what to say when people told me sad stuff. Jill took the comb into her open palm and looked at it as if the thing had the power to transport her back to the sixties when her dad was still alive. I wanted to change the subject.

"Did you know the lady who lived in our unit?"

"Miranda? She had a Dolls of the World collection."

"What about her ex?"

"He's a freaky hippie guy. He threw her clothes off the deck once. But for around here, that's nothing. Did you know a lunatic roams the woods at night?"

I shook my head.

"I heard from a kid in 4A that he loves the taste of children's pinkies. Eats them like chicken wings."

We heard her mom get out of bed. Jill put her finger to her lips as she left the room. It was her job to get her mom a bowl of cereal and bring her the black pants, white blouse, and apron she had to wear to waitress at the Western Sizzler. While I waited, I poked around Jill's room. In her closet a dress hung sideways off the hanger and a metal back brace lay on the floor over her shoes. On the shelf above, there was a line of dirty stuffed animals. The pink kitten had a lazy eye.

After her mother left the house and I heard her car head down the road toward the highway, Jill called up the stairs that the coast was clear. By the time I got down, she had thrown the couch cushions on the floor and Ronnie had pulled the bedspread off the wall and tied it around his neck. He was repeating the lines of Barnabas Collins from a recent episode of *Dark Shadows*. Inside the mausoleum, Maggie was questioning Barnabas about a sheep that had been killed. The creature had been found drained of blood. I watched until the scene changed to Parallel Time and Jill dragged me up to the bathroom, made me get into the tub, close my eyes, and grub through the bathroom shower curtain. I had to close my eyes tight and push through the plastic until I'd moved into another dimension. Once I was there she informed me in a solemn voice that Ronnie and I were now married and she was dying of a brain tumor.

At five o'clock I told them I had to go home for dinner. Jill seemed to take this as an insult. She cast her eyes down and I thought she would now confide a grisly detail from her father's death, that his arm had been ripped off in the crash or that his eyes had popped out of their sockets. Instead she asked if I'd follow her into the basement.

In the dark laundry room she pulled the string that turned on the overhead bulb and reached into the space between the washer and the dryer. She brought out a towel, unfolded it, and lifted up an elongated string bean. I recognized the long green pod as one of the ones that grew on a tree beside the empty foundation up the mountain. It was a big tree with huge ragged leaves and long beans growing down like sci-fi fringe.

"When they dry out," she said, "we can smoke them in the French Quarter."

✦

Tanglewood Mall, off the highway and about ten miles from Bent Tree, had a special section in one corner called the French Quarter. I'd seen the ads in the paper for the Tennis Villa, where rich ladies bought little white tennis dresses, and Mrs. Smith told me that the port-wine cheese at the Gourmet Shoppe was the most divine thing she'd ever tasted. There was a rumor that when Little Feat came to the Civic Center, the lead singer got a trim at The UpperCut, the French Quarter's unisex salon.

Twice my mom had taken us to the mall, but both times she'd only wanted to shop for bargains at J. C. Penney, and I had had to run after Phillip, who had a terrible habit of wandering off in department stores.

At the end of the first week of school, Jill persuaded her mom to drop us off at the mall. I told my mom that Mrs. Bamburg would be shopping with us, even though I knew she planned to go off to the Ground Round across the road and drink beer with her friend.

✦

The bean pods, wrapped in tinfoil and stuck in Jill's Mexican shoulder bag, made a muted rattling sound against her hip as we moved through the mall.

"They have samples in the cheese shop," Jill said, "the sweetest cheese you've ever tasted."

"What kind is it?"

"How should I know? What I'm trying to tell you is that it tastes good."

We walked through Penney's and into the mall. So far Tanglewood was the only Sun Belt part of Roanoke. Under a cathedral ceiling, a fountain bubbled beside soaring palm trees. I actually felt like I'd been transported to one of the planets I was always reading about in science fiction novels. We passed Chess King, Jeans West, Merry-Go-Round, where a whole carousel of suede fringe vests were on sale. I was still confused as to why we couldn't just smoke the pods up in the woods in back of Bent Tree.

Jill was on a mission, leading me toward the French Quarter, the mall's soft, sweet center. Under a brick archway lay a darkened expanse of small shops with thatched roofs and gold windows. We roamed the dim corridors past the window of the Tennis Villa, where a white dress shimmered, smelled fresh-ground coffee wafting out the door of Lock, Stock, and Barrel, and passed the Seven Dwarfs, whose window featured imports from Europe—Hummel figurines, music boxes, crystal ashtrays. The mannequin in the bridal shop had blue glass eyes and long eyelashes. She stared across the corridor to the mannequin in the Hancock's men's shop window, in a sports coat and leather driving gloves.

Jill swung open the door of the restroom in Le Brasserie, the French Quarter sidewalk café.

I'd hoped for gold-leaf walls and French-looking light fixtures but was disappointed. The room was painted an institutional green and the sink was stainless steel, though once Jill turned off the lights, knelt, and lit the candle, the walls turned sepia. She unwrapped the tinfoil and placed one pod after another on a paper towel. Then she passed me the white peasant blouse with red embroidery around the neck that she insisted I wear for the ceremony.

Jill felt all the people in Bent Tree had known each other in earlier lives. All the souls gathered together in the duplexes had always been linked, first in the same Indian tribe and, before that, as members of a royal French family and, before that, as slaves owned by the same Pharaoh. Each time it was different; I could have been her mother in one life and in another we might have been married. My father might have been my son or even my boyfriend! She was hoping to be able to see back into some of the lives, or maybe even get some information that would help us free ourselves from Bent Tree and go into what she called another dimension.

"Are you sure the door is locked?" Jill asked.

I checked again and nodded.

"OK then," she said, holding the first pod to the candle's flame. The tip caught, glowed orange, and, when Jill held it to her lips, a single tendril of lavender smoke rose up in the dark air between us. She passed the pod to me. The wet tip tasted like a dried leaf and the smoke was grainy against my lungs.

"I'm feeling something," Jill said, closing her eyes. "Something like I'm an Indian in the olden times. I can see a bowl of dry corn in front of me and two naked children playing with a hoop."

The scene she described was directly from an illustration in our social studies textbook.

"What about the future?" I asked.

Jill clenched her eyes tighter, and the candle sent an angle of underwater light over her face.

"I see a fish," she said. "It's staring right at me!"

Jill opened her eyes.

"Go on, take another puff," she said. "Maybe you'll see something."

I sucked on the end of the pod and held the smoke down in my lungs. I expected to feel light-headed and see a lava-light show, but instead I saw a ranch house made of red brick with green shutters. There was nothing remarkable about the house, but something about its very normalness bothered me. When I opened my eyes, Jill was staring at me, her eyes wide and sad in the dark.

"I see myself sitting at a desk," I said.

"Are you writing?"

"I don't know," I said.

"Try to see," she said. "It's important."

I closed my eyes and imagined black letters against white paper.

"It's a story about a walrus."

"A walrus?" she said.

I laughed a little and I saw Jill's face pinch up. Her features rearranged themselves and her cheeks got red.

"If you're not going to take this seriously," she said, "then we should just forget it."

"What?" I said, trying to hold back my laughter. "You don't like my story?"

"You're making fun of me!"

"You saw a fish!"

"It was a catfish with whiskers." Jill shuddered. "And it looked a little like my daddy."

"Black fish are often the bearers of terrible news," I said. "Sometimes they even come to warn sinners about the apocalypse."

Jill stood up and threw the bean pod into the toilet, where it sunk with a sharp hiss. She jammed the un-lit bean pods into the trash can. Then she unlocked the door and ran out into the French Quarter.

I searched the mall for an hour. I looked in the arcade, Orange Julius, even the girls' section of J. C. Penney, before I finally found her downstairs in the back of Spencer's Gifts looking up at an oscillating black-light poster, green and orange diamonds shift-ing round and round. The colors were not comforting like the golden images of my View-Master or the em-erald and sapphire hues of the church's stained-glass windows. Neon-pink daisies grew out of a skull's emp-ty eye sockets. Above us, the speaker blasted "Free Bird" so loud it seemed we had fallen into a pocket of stillness between the notes of the song.

"My mom says God hates our family."

"That's not true," I said.

"How do you know that God doesn't hate us?"

I just knew, but I couldn't prove or explain. My dad thought God, if he existed at all, was powerless. But Jill felt God was strange, terrifying, and real. Her face in the strobe was pale and eerie. Her eyes were sunken, and all I could think of was how in health class Sheila had told us that if you went to the edge of Tilden Lake at night, threw in three stones, and said the Hail Mary backward, a satanic Mary appeared and threw a dead baby at you. I could see the black lake water and the top of Mary's head breaking the surface, her neon-blue face sliding up out of the dark.

✦

The night before Halloween, I lay in my bed, imagining spirits seeping out of the earth, swirling in the air over Bent Tree. I finally drifted off but I didn't sleep long. It was still dark when I awoke to the sound of a voice calling my name. I wasn't really surprised; I knew it was just a matter of time before creatures from the netherworld tried to contact me. *I . . . hear . . . you*, I whispered slowly. But the voice just kept on saying my name until I realized the voice was outside, and that Jill was standing in the street in front of our duplex, her ski jacket pulled over her nightgown, her feet stuck into her brother's huge tennis shoes.

When she saw me at the window, her face lit up and she motioned wildly for me to meet her down at the front door. I pulled the knob and she shoved her social studies notebook at me, showing me the list she'd written out in pencil. As I read, she leaned over me, her face pale and anxious. Under the heading *Haunted House*, she had written *Dracula's Cave? Mad Scientist Laboratory? Dr. Frankenstein Workshop?*

Under the heading *Games*, she had written *Bobbing for Apples, Musical Chairs, Drop the Clothespin in the Milk Bottle, The Limbo*.

Jill looked at me, her black pupils huge even in the near-dark.

"I couldn't sleep," she said. "In the night I started thinking about sickos that stick razor blades in candy apples."

I was familiar, through my mother's stories, with how hippie drug culture had collided with freaky homeowners to create lunatics who seemed to enjoy poisoning candy in an effort to kill off neighborhood kids. I'd heard about the heroin-sprinkled chocolate-covered raisins, needles stuck into Snickers bars, cyanide in Pixy Stix.

"But what can we do?" I said. I ran my hands up and down over my goose-pimpled arms. The sky was gray and low and branches blew around all over the side of the mountain.

"We'll have a party," she said, "a safe place so the creeps can't kill them."

I was learning that Jill had the spark and intensity of a downed electrical wire. Her notebooks were filled with lists. *Ten Qualities of a Friend. Why Dogs Are Better than Cats. How to Survive in a Blizzard.* She was always the first to raise her hand in class, and even though she'd ended up getting only eleven votes, she'd run for class president, telling us during her speech that she would make chocolate milkshakes available for sale in the cafeteria and that for the winter dance, she and her team would build a Transylvanian castle, transforming the gym into a Gothic wonderland.

During the physical fitness tests in gym, I'd watched her hold on to the metal bar. The narrow muscles of her neck stood out like hot-dog meat, and as she grimaced I saw her skull and collarbone, her skeleton gripping the bar for dear life.

She was determined to educate me about the ways of Bent Tree, as if the place were a country of its own with history and ritual that only she could impart.

First, practical danger. The guy who lived with his mother in 3B might offer to take my picture. He'd say I had a certain look and imply he had contacts in Hollywood. NEVER EVER EVER go into his duplex under any circumstance.

There was an older lady who lived with her sister in 9A. They might seem friendly but it was important never to be seen speaking with them.

"Why?" I asked.

"Because they're Eldridges!"

"What's wrong with that?"

"You don't know?" Jill was incredulous.

I shook my head.

"Their ancestors took in Union soldiers during the Civil War."

"That was a long time ago," I said.

"Not really," Jill said. "Once a traitor, always a traitor."

She told me to watch out for the *Christers* in 2B, 7A, and 20B.

"They have big smiles and they act all friendly," she said, "but the next thing you know they're offering to drive you to their prayer group."

People moved out at the end of every month; August and January saw the biggest loss of occupants. She'd watched and written down lists of the things she saw floating out duplex doorways: a taxidermied cat curled up on its satin cat bed; a giant Styrofoam strawberry; a red, white, and blue life-size cutout of Evel Knievel. In the boxes left behind, you could find treasures: zodiac medallions, Mexican handbags, ponchos covered with dog hair.

She believed that Mr. Ananais had a secret yin-yang method of pairing people in adjacent duplexes so that they balanced each other out. Next door to her family lived an out-of-work brakeman for the railroad, a sweet chubby guy who ate hamburger patties and heated up Tater Tots for dinner every night and who told Jill and her brother stories of ghost trains and haunted railroad stations. Without him living in the building, Jill was convinced the place would rip free of its foundation and float into the sky. And beside Sheila was a lady who was so annoyingly friendly that she balanced out Sheila's bitchiness. I could see Jill was right. Mrs. Smith, who lived next to us in 12B, loved Nixon and was still sad because the South had lost the Civil War. Her duplex was filled with teddy bears and Civil War memorabilia. The year before, she'd been chairwoman of the Daughters of the Confederacy's Civil War Ball. According to Jill, Mrs. Smith balanced out my dad's hippie tendencies. (He now believed Jesus was a real person, a rebel like Che Guevara or Cesar Chavez. God, he was convinced, was as much in the rushing Roanoke River as inside any church.)

The thing that haunted Jill was how once people moved out of Bent Tree they seemed to disappear completely. People claimed they were moving to cheaper apartments like Sans Souci over on Garst Mill Road or Guilford Manor out by the airport. But Jill had never seen anyone after they left. It was as if, after pulling out of the entrance, they entered another dimension completely.

I was learning that when Jill got an idea in her head, it was hard for me to resist joining her. I put on my clothes and we walked to Kroger, where we used our babysitting money to buy mini candy bars, pretzels, potato chips, and a turnip. Jill said her Grandmother Brendy told her that turnips would protect us from evil spirits. Back at Bent Tree, we went to work cleaning up her family's duplex. All afternoon we worked, wiping down the bathroom and the kitchen, vacuuming the shag, and trying to air out the living room.

We let Ronnie choose from Jill's list of party themes. He opted for *Mad Scientist Laboratory*. He boiled spaghetti for guts and twisted apart a few of Beth's dolls for body parts. He wasn't all that interested in looking like a mad scientist with crazy hair and a white lab coat. Instead, he wrapped his mother's boa around his neck, outlined his eyes with black liner, and played his Bowie record on 78 so the music elongated. I had noticed Ronnie's fondness for eyeliner and that around the house he sometimes wore Jill's skinny turtlenecks. As we cleaned, we heard him laughing maniacally into his cassette player.

Beth mixed Kool-Aid in a plastic pitcher and set out Dixie cups. She poured snacks into bowls and arranged them on the table, then retreated to the bathroom to draw dots on her cheeks in imitation of Pippi Longstocking.

Once we finished cleaning, Jill and I lay on her bed making a schedule for the party; our legs were touching and she pressed her shoulder into mine. Jill smelled like muddy rainwater and her breath still had the afterburn from the bag of barbecue potato chips we'd split on our walk back from the grocery store.

Was I a lezzbo? This I considered a very good question. I didn't really know what lezzbos did. When I closed my eyes at night, I never imagined our naked bodies twined together. I envisioned the two of us walking up the side of the mountain holding hands. I thought of myself like a tree or a flower. I had longing, but it was not explicitly aimed at anything.

✦

At four, with his hair gelled back, the boa around his neck, and lipstick blood flowing from both sides of his mouth, Ronnie went to wake Mrs. Bamburg for work.

"Bad news," he said, speaking with a sexy-evil Transylvanian accent. "She does not answer."

"I'll get her up," Jill said.

Jill had a trick to lure her mother out of bed. She put on the Allman Brothers, went to the kitchen, and got out a can of beer.

"It's near the anniversary of Duane's death," Ronnie said. "Hearing that might make her worse."

"Oh, you're right!" Jill said, running back to the stereo, lifting the needle, and putting on the new Thin Lizzy single her mother had brought home from Woolworth's.

I followed her up the stairs. Even though I'd spent as much time as I could with Jill, I'd seen her mother only a few times. She had a frizzy perm and wore wire-rim glasses above her chubby cheeks. She looked more like an older sister than a mother and, like an older sister, she was usually too tired to do anything around the house. Jill did the laundry, made the beds, cleaned the bathroom. Mrs. Bamburg brought home groceries, once a week, but she just left the food on the counter for Jill to unpack.

"Mom," Jill called through the door. I stood in the hallway. I remembered trying to lure Miranda out of her bedroom. Maybe we should sing a song. Jill and I knew the lyrics to several John Denver songs and to "I Got You Babe." She was always Sonny so I could be Cher. I tried to stand very still, so still I could feel my heart pump and my brain hum.

There was no answer. Jill turned to me and motioned that I should stay in the hall. As she opened the door, I saw that with the curtains closed, the room was dark. Her mother had the comforter pulled over her head so her body in the bed resembled a mountain range. Warm air tinged with cigarette smoke spilled over me and into the hallway.

Jill went to the blinds and raised them a few inches, then sat on the side of the bed.

"Please, Mom," she said.

From under the covers her mother gave a grainy moan. Jill tried to pull back the comforter but her mother held it tight over her face.

"I'm sick," she said. "I need you to call in for me."

"But I did that yesterday!"

"I don't feel good," she said. "I can't go in."

"You got to," Jill said, yanking the comforter.

The soles of her mother's feet were chalky. Her toes looked delicate and sad, the baby toe curling into the bigger one beside it as if it were lonely.

"Give me back my blanket!" she said, sitting up and reaching toward Jill.

Jill didn't say anything, just stepped away from the bed so her mom couldn't reach her.

Downstairs Jill picked up the receiver and dialed the restaurant. She asked to speak to the manager.

"This is Jill Bamburg."

She listened, nodding her head vigorously.

"Yes. But. No sir. OK."

She hung up the phone.

"If she doesn't go in today, she's fired."

This news, delivered by Jill through her mother's bedroom door, elicited only a grunt. Her mother slept on as we filled the buckets and dropped apples into the water, rolling and shiny. Jill taped the picture of a pumpkin Beth drew on the front door and we made a list of the children we knew who lived in Bent Tree. There were eleven all together, plus two babies and, of course, Sheila and Dwayne, the older kid from the bus stop. He was what the kids in school called a dirtbag, but all I really knew was how he tortured us on the bus, dared us to lick the seats, and called all the younger boys faggots.

When she finally did come down in her bathrobe, Mrs. Bamburg was holding the beer Jill had brought up earlier.

"What is all this?" she said, blinking at the streamers, the scarves thrown over the two lamps, the chairs set up for games.

"The party," Jill said. "Remember?"

Mrs. Bamburg nodded without enthusiasm and turned into the kitchen, where she picked up the phone and called her friends one after another, telling them that the *little shit* manager had finally fired her. She told the story so many times, with the exact same words, that I felt like the earth might have gotten stuck and stopped rotating.

By seven o'clock, though it was fully dark, not one trick-or-treater had rung the bell. Ronnie had gone down to his room and Beth was doing math problems from his high school textbook. We'd even seen my brother and Eddie, in green fatigues and bleeding ketchup from their heads, walk right by our duplex with my dad. They were headed for the subdivision down the road, where it was rumored they were giving away full-size candy bars.

"It's evil spirits," Jill said, her eyes wide. "They are keeping people away from our party."

"That's crazy," Beth said, pushing her glasses up on her nose. It was funny to see her doing math problems because everyone knew the real Pippi Longstocking would never do homework.

Jill walked into the kitchen, got out the turnip, and motioned for me to follow her around the side of the duplex. We walked next to where the siding met the cement foundation. We circled clockwise three times. I couldn't keep up with Jill. She was upset not only that we'd worked so hard on the party and nobody was showing up, but also that kids right now could be biting into Mars bars filled with razor blades and M&M's sprinkled with angel dust. Abruptly she stopped and swung around. I followed her three times counterclockwise around the duplex, all in an effort to ward off evil spirits.

We sat on the stairs in front of the house, the turnip beside us, the stars splattered above us. I took hold of her hand. Even though it was cold outside, her palm was warm and moist. Holding it was like holding a small, soft animal.

Jill decided that the problem was that we hadn't advertised our party enough. We should go down by the main road and let everyone know. At the edge of Bent Tree, right by the mailboxes, we saw the girls from 4B. The older one was a cowgirl in a red felt hat and matching vest, and the younger one, who threw around a furry tail and meowed loudly, was a kitty cat.

"We're having a party in 11B," Jill said to the mother, a short-haired woman in a yellow trench coat. "We've got all kinds of safe, fun activities."

The woman looked at the handmade poster with a drawing of Dracula in his coffin and then up at us. Unless she was deaf, she'd heard music blasting from Jill's duplex and sometimes men having fistfights on the front lawn; this mother thought we were the sort of people that Jill wanted to have the party to protect the kids against.

"Thanks honey," she said. "But I got to get these kids to bed."

"Please come up." Jill grabbed the woman's arm.

"Maybe another time." The woman moved away and hurried down the path toward her front door.

"Meow," the little girl said, but then grimaced like a mean cat and hissed at us.

We walked across the road into the subdivision with the brick ranch houses. There was a girl in a Cinderella mask with tiny eyeholes jumping on a trampoline. A jeep drove past with a dead deer tied to the top. I thought it was a Halloween prank, but Jill said hunting season had just started and I had to get used to seeing deer sprawled out on the roofs of cars. Most of the ranches were decorated for Halloween with dried cornstalks tied to their mailboxes and jack-o'-lanterns that lit up their front doors. Jill passed fliers to a group of teenagers in hooded sweatshirts wearing zombie masks and carrying pillowcases full of candy and a father taking around his toddler dressed like a lion in brown pj's, black whiskers drawn over the kid's chubby pink cheeks.

When we walked back up and sat on the steps again, I could tell Jill was disappointed; nothing had turned out the way she'd planned.

"Kids might still come," I said. "It's not too late."

I could see now, though, that there were Pintos and Mustangs lining the street in front of Jill's duplex, and I could hear Lynyrd Skynyrd blasting out the windows. No children would be coming to our party. We went back inside, where her mother was slow-dancing with a guy in an Indian kurta. We could see his red chest hairs poking out the top of his shirt. Her mother, who'd been drinking ever since she got up, pressed into the man like a soft stick of butter, her mouth attached to his, and I could see by the way her cheek shifted that his tongue was fully in her mouth.

"That's so gross!" Jill said, pulling me up the stairs. Two women and a man sat on her bed smoking. She told them to get out, that she needed to do her homework, but they ignored her and kept talking, the man explaining how to make dandelion wine.

We wandered back downstairs.

A few people wore costumes. Sandy, dressed like a bunny, in rabbit ears and an aerobics leotard, was talking to a man wearing purple-tinted glasses and love beads. She'd taken on more shifts at the nursing home so she could pay her own rent. Most of the other outfits were half-committed—a guy in a funny hat and a girl wearing rhinestone sunglasses. I saw that my father was in the corner. I'd told him earlier about the kids' party and though it hadn't worked out how we wanted, I was still glad he had come. He wore his wire-rim reading glasses and a surplice from when he'd been a minister. At first I thought he had come as a priest but then I saw that he carried a gold-trimmed book and realized he was supposed to be Prospero from *The Tempest*. I waved to him from across the room and he waved back. He was talking to a man with a mustache.

I didn't like the look of the man. Any guy who looked like Charles Manson even a little gave me the creeps, and I could tell by the way the man kept holding his hands up to replicate a rifle that he was telling my dad about hunting trips. Before we left the rectory, my dad might have come to a party like this to actually minister to lost souls, to tell them they were not alone, that there was a halo of presence around each of us and while you might feel separate from God, this was only an illusion. Now he was more like an anthropologist doing fieldwork. By the way he laughed and shook his head I could tell he was interested and amused by the man's story.

Jill and I pushed through the crowd and went back outside. It was dark and the tops of the trees blew left and then right; nearly all the leaves were off now and the evergreens sat smoky in the darkness. The mountain was above us, wild and unknowable. I was cold in my white leotard and painter pants. I had made myself a unicorn horn out of tinfoil and attached it to my forehead with masking tape, but it had bent sideways and looked less now like a magical horn and more like someone had stuck a knife into the side of my head.

Jill was Victoria Winters from *Dark Shadows* in a black dress with a lace collar.

"This is the dress my mama wore to the funeral."

"Doesn't it give you the creeps to wear it?" I asked her.

"Yeah," she said. "But aren't you supposed to have the creeps on Halloween?"

"I guess," I said. I sounded noncommittal, but what she said hit me hard. She wanted to honor the dead even if it made her uncomfortable.

We watched people moving in the windows like fish in an aquarium.

"Do the speech," I said.

"I don't feel like it," she said.

"Oh come on," I said. "It will make us feel better."

"You think so?"

"Do it!"

"My name is Victoria Winters," Jill began. "My journey is beginning. A journey that I hope will open the doors of life to me, and link my past with my future, a journey that will bring me to a strange and dark place, a world I've never known."

✦

Later, back in my own bed, trying to fall asleep, I heard a voice. This time I knew it wasn't a spirit. Jill stood outside my window in her nightgown. I went down and opened the door. It had warmed up a bit, so the ground sent up a fine bluish mist.

"My mother split to get beer," she said, "but she's still not home."

"Was that before the fight or after?"

As the party was breaking up, two guys had gone at it in the street under the dusk-to-dawn lights.

"After," Jill said.

"Maybe she decided to spend the night someplace else?"

"Maybe," Jill said.

"Do you want to come in?" I said. "I'll sleep on the floor and you can sleep on my bed."

She shook her head.

"Beth might wake up."

"She can come too."

Jill shook her head again.

"She'll come back," I said.

"I hope so." Jill turned back toward her duplex but then paused.

"Do you think I could talk to your father?"

"Why?"

"He's a preacher, right?"

"He was one."

"I need advice on how to remove the curse on us."

"I thought you hated the Christers?"

"I'm desperate!" she said. "Besides, your dad's got *the power*."

It was true. Though he wasn't a minister anymore, his hands still held a sense of holiness left over from when he'd baptized babies and given wafers away during communion. Sometimes I'd watch his hands at the dining room table or as he read the newspaper; his hands reminded me how we'd once been held together inside a circle of grace. He could still calm my little brother by touching his head, and by putting his hands on the two men from the party, he'd broken up the fight.

"You can talk to him in the morning."

"OK," Jill said reluctantly.

After she left, I lay in bed listening to my father snore across the hall and to the occasional truck rattling down on 419. I knew Jill thought if she could break the curse, her mom might come back.

I knew Jill was worried about kidnapping, but her biggest concern, and mine too, was sex slavery. There was a long history of sex slavery, one Jill and I had studied. I had noticed that older boys liked to talk about gory scenes in horror movies, and that Phillip and Eddie enjoyed pretending to shoot people, but Jill and I spent much of our time talking about girls held captive by men. Most horrifying were the Manson girls, particularly the one near our own age named Snake. There was the girl in California chained to the toilet in the day and kept in a box during the night. The crazy thing was, the thing we could not get our mind around no matter how hard we tried, was that even during the trial, she was calling her captor on the phone. We often told each other that David Cassidy wanted us as his sex slave. We wrote this in notes and folded them up in intricate triangular patterns and tossed them to one another in health class.

✦

Jill knocked on our door early, before my dad had gone to work, while he was still drinking coffee. She said she needed a private word with him and they went out onto the deck and closed the sliding glass door.

I knew Jill wouldn't tell him her mother was missing—she was too afraid of social services—but she'd ask about the curse. I felt embarrassed for her because my father didn't believe in spells. When parishioners talked about ghosts he'd roll his eyes. But my dad listened to Jill and when she'd finished, he took both her hands in his own and shook his head slowly.

After he'd gone I asked Jill what he'd said.

"If God exists," she said, "he doesn't hate anybody."

I nodded.

"Actually he wasn't very helpful. I was hoping for concrete things I could do to break the curse."

"Like what kind of things?" I asked.

She looked at me seriously.

"Like throw an egg in a river or search for a bird's feather."

✦

That afternoon we walked duplex to duplex looking in basement windows. Did the inhabitants seem like people who would keep sex slaves? A guy who lived alone in one of the lower duplexes was high on our list of possible sex-slave masters, but when we looked into his basement all we saw was an exercise bike and a poster of Liberace. What about Dwayne? Jill shook her head. She was convinced that the person who kept a sex slave wouldn't risk bad behavior; it would be a quiet guy, a guy who always ordered the same thing every time he went into Long John Silver's.

We walked out into the subdivisions. Under one carport was a large wooden box, but when we got closer we saw that the box held tools and a lawn mower. Another split-level had a row of mums that Jill thought looked suspicious, and I didn't like the lawn jockey, his black face painted beige. Across the street, we spotted a man coming out of his front door, heading for his station wagon. He was wearing a wide tie and a powder-blue leisure suit. I thought the leisure suit alone made him a candidate, but when Jill saw that he carried a Bible she was more convinced than ever that the man might be hiding a sex slave.

✦

After a few days, the Bamburgs grew accustomed to their mother being gone. As Beth pointed out, it wasn't as if they saw her much anyway. Life with parents was unnatural and full of rules, and it was only when their mother was gone that the Bamburg children could live as they pleased, cozy and chaotic as puppies in a box.

Jill nailed sheets to the ceiling, tenting the living room, and spread blankets and pillows over the shag. The television was on day and night. Nixon, who to my dad's horror had won the election, was always on the screen, his huge head smiling down at us like a distant emperor, as we played Operation and Mystery Date.

For the first days, we feasted on strips of bacon and chocolate milk and searched for Mrs. Bamburg in all the subdivisions along the highway. Jill decided that her mom had entered Parallel Time and was running a home for lost dogs in a big house in the country, pulling burrs out of long-haired dogs and giving the small, nervous ones lap time. People left Bent Tree all the time, Jill reasoned; it was in the very nature of the place that souls who completed their trials drifted out and new sinners, like my family, made their way in.

After we ran out of bacon and chocolate milk, Jill heated up frozen pizzas and pot pies. We downed sugar by the spoonful, first granulated, then the confectionary. The Bamburg kids ate through the canned soup, the tuna fish, even the condensed milk, which they spread like jelly on saltines. On the two-week anniversary of Mrs. Bamburg's disappearance, Jill served boiled potatoes covered with corn syrup and passed around a jar of maraschino cherries.

"All that's left," she said, "is this bar of dark chocolate and a half bottle of apple cider vinegar." She sat on the floor with her legs crossed and her back curved, her spine sticking up through the material of her turtleneck sweater. Jill broke the chocolate into four parts. I passed mine to Beth, who looked at me gratefully before popping both squares into her mouth.

"If only we could photosynthesize," Beth said, "all our problems would be over."

"You could go to the food pantry at First Baptist."

"Take food from the *Christers?* Have you lost your mind completely?"

I'd forgotten how much Jill hated the born-agains. To her, taking their handouts was worse than starving.

"I could sneak food from home," I said.

"Would you do that?" Jill said. "It would only be until I start working."

The next day, after we got back from school, I slipped two cans of ravioli and a couple of bananas under my shirt. As I came into the Bamburgs' duplex, not bothering to knock, Jill and her sister and brother gathered around me, looking round-eyed like the possum that ate out of our garbage can. Jill didn't even bother heating up the food; she just opened the can and split the ravioli three ways on the Pyrex plates. They each moved to a far corner of the tent, gulping down the food quick as hungry dogs.

The system worked well enough until my mother noticed a bulge in my jeans. I pulled out the jar of peanut butter and roll of Ritz crackers sunk down my pants. Her eyebrows arched up. I knew if I told her the Bamburg children were hungry, she'd let me take anything I wanted. My mother was funny that way. While she looked down at everybody who lived in Bent Tree, she'd been the first to bring a casserole down to 1B when she heard the old lady who lived there broke her hip. She'd even let Sandy do her and Eddie's laundry in the basement while their machine was broken.

But I also knew if she found out Mrs. Bamburg was missing, she'd call the police.

At first I'd argued for calling the police myself, but Jill told me that the last time their mom left, they'd all ended up at a foster home with a lady who raised German shepherds in her backyard.

I told my mom: "We're having an indoor picnic." It was a lame excuse but better than nothing.

"We don't have money to feed the neighborhood," she said, turning me around and opening the cabinet so I could put the items back up on the shelf.

When I walked in empty-handed, the Bamburgs were disappointed. Beth started to cry. I told them that after dark I'd drop food out my bedroom window. While my mother watched *All in the Family*, I smuggled a loaf of bread and a stick of butter upstairs. Then I made the signal, turning my lights on and off three times. Jill, who'd been waiting in the shadows beside her duplex, ran barefoot over the yellow grass to pick up the bread.

+

Ronnie stopped going to high school. At first Jill nagged him, saying they'd get busted if he didn't show up. But he claimed he'd told the ladies in the front office that his family was moving to Florida and they'd wished him well and taken his name off the register. Jill didn't like him hanging around the duplex all day, and she warned him that if he went outside during school hours, he'd blow it for all of them. Beth, on the other hand, loved school, and Jill had no trouble getting her up, making sure she showered and that her clothes were clean. Jill told me that if a kid came to school for too many days with stained clothes and dirty hair, the guidance counselor called child protection. Jill filled out the free-lunch form for her and Beth. In the cafeteria, she wolfed down everything, even the disgusting Salisbury steak and gross gelatinous gravy.

✦

After the bread was gone, we walked down to Kroger. Jill told me she'd seen a hippie the day before pulling food out of the Dumpster. We went around the back and Jill, holding her nose, climbed inside. Standing on a raft of old cabbages, she passed me expired cans of turkey gravy and TV dinners. She found a bag of apples too rotten to eat but perfectly good for applesauce and several loaves of stale bread. Jill speculated that if the plentitude of the Dumpster held out, they'd be set for food at least through winter. In the spring she could forage for wild turnips and wood sorrel up the mountain and plant tomatoes and zucchini like Mr. Ananais did on the sunny side of the duplex. Every few days, I helped Jill scavenge in the Dumpster for what she called "Dumpster delicacies," which made up the Bamburgs' odd menu. Smoked oysters and week-old cupcakes, tuna fish and crushed pineapple, cornflakes soaked with tomato juice. Her plan appeared foolproof until Beth ate out of a dented can of beef hash and spent the rest of the night hugging the toilet.

After that I snuck over a pound of frozen hamburger in white butcher paper. Our freezer was full of the stuff, and I knew my mom wouldn't notice. But Jill and I both knew I couldn't keep doing this. We lay across Jill's bed, the sides of our heads touching and our bare toes looking so similar we could be a new creature with four feet. Since she wasn't wearing her back brace, Jill had started to hunch, and her face was pale and ominous even in broad daylight. We were trying to figure out how she could get money. The rent was due soon, and while Mr. Ananais would let it slide for a week or two, soon things would get desperate.

"I could make pot holders and sell them door to door," Jill said. "But each one takes an hour to make."

"All that work and you only get a quarter for them!"

"I could babysit more."

I was quiet. It was unclear how Sheila had cornered the market. I'd seen her going in and out of nearly every duplex with children. Nobody wanted Jill and me anymore because Sheila looked so much more like a girl should, with her long shiny hair and baby-blue ski jacket. Even Sandy, who was taking nursing classes at night, used Sheila now instead of us.

"We could have a bake sale!" I suggested.

"How will we get the money for flour and eggs?" Jill said.

"We could shovel snow."

"Oh please," Jill said. "The snow never lasts more than half a day around here."

I hadn't known that, though I should have guessed. It was already mid-November and still warm. Heat came off Jill's body and I could feel her anxiety, as if jolts of electricity were making it impossible for her to relax. I took her hand and squeezed her fingers. We both looked up at the ceiling, and I saw some black spots, dead bugs in the glass shade.

"We could blackmail somebody," I said. "Find out who's cheating on their wife or husband, then write a letter saying if they don't send us a hundred dollars we'll tell all about it."

Jill sat up.

"That would be really low-down," she said. "I hope we don't have to do anything like that."

"I'm saying if it does come to that, I'd do it if you wanted me to," I said. "I'd even break into somebody's house if you asked."

"Now you're just talking," Jill said.

"No," I said. "I've thought all about it."

It was true. Lying in my bed in the dark, I'd sworn myself to my friend. I would do anything, even kill somebody, if she wanted me to.

✦

After school the next day, we walked through the subdivisions toward the strip mall. Jill had decided to get a job, and she'd made a list of businesses along the highway. In front of a brick ranch home, a man raked and Jill watched kids jump and roll in the piles of leaves. She had a weak spot for family scenes: kids in bathing suits dashing through sprinklers, families eating dinner together. Even our Halloween party had been an attempt at a wholesome life. I tried to distract her by asking questions for her job interview.

"Who is your model in life?"

"Cher!"

I thought of trying to get her to say somebody like Rosa Parks or Madame Curie. But Jill was honest, and those other ladies didn't have a chance compared to Cher in her roller skates, multicolored kneesocks, and white leotard rolling along the sidewalk in Venice Beach.

"Do you believe in God?"

Even as I said it I realized it was a mistake. Jill would start up on how God hated her family so much he'd put a curse on them.

She looked at me. To hide the circles under her eyes she'd used her mother's white cover stick.

"Do you really think anybody would ask me that?"

"They might."

Her features came apart a little and I thought she might cry, but instead she laughed and I followed her across the highway, where we waited on the median, cars rushing by on either side.

"Do you think I look all right?" Jill asked. She had to yell above the sound of the engines.

She wore her mother's trench coat with a floral scarf around her neck that made her look like a grandma.

"You look great," I yelled back. "They'd be crazy not to hire you."

We walked up into the Hop-In parking lot, first on Jill's list of possible job locations. The plate-glass window advertised two-for-the-price-of-one corn dogs and cheap gallons of RC Cola. Jill pushed her shoulders back; the ridges of her spine stuck up out of the coat material like beads on a chain.

I followed her into the store, past the rack of magazines that included *Playboy* and *Mechanics Today* and the long row of candy bars and chewing tobacco. Shiny hot dogs rolled in their metal ridges beside the slushie machine. The manager was bent over, getting napkins from underneath the counter. We'd spent time here, playing pinball and watching the manager's girlfriend, a fierce ginger-haired woman, drink free slushies one after another until her tongue was blue. As he turned toward us, we saw one of his eyes was swollen shut.

"What can I help you ladies with today?"

"Are you hiring?" Jill asked.

He smiled.

"You got to be eighteen to sell beer."

"But I guess you don't have to be eighteen to buy it," Jill said.

Everybody knew the manager never checked anybody's ID. Kids on the school bus said he once sold a six-pack to a nine-year-old. It was a bold preemptive move for Jill to mention that. She must have been thinking of my idea of blackmailing someone.

"What's that supposed to mean?" he said.

"What's what supposed to mean?" Jill mimicked.

The manager squinted at Jill.

"What about custodial work?" she said. "I could take out the trash and clean the bathrooms."

He studied Jill the way a cattle farmer might study a cow, looking over her narrow shoulders, her hunched back and arms like pipe cleaners.

"I'm a lot stronger than I look," Jill said. "Once I picked up a cement block and there was another time—"

"I don't think so," he said. "Come back when you're older."

Outside Jill hit herself in the head with her fist.

"Did you hear me in there?" she said. "My mouth just went on by itself."

We stood by the side of the parking lot, next to a stand of sumac trees. Drops of rain ticked on the asphalt and sprang off the parked cars. My legs inside my jeans were freezing and my teeth chattered. Jill wanted to go in again, but I convinced her it was hopeless. I followed her to the two other places on her list, the pizza place and the grocery store where she'd hoped to be a bag girl. Neither were hiring.

We walked under a low haze of clouds back toward Bent Tree. We passed picture windows where we could see people sitting very still, staring at TV screens. Water gathered at the edge of Jill's jawbone and dropped down to darken the beige material of her mother's overcoat. The light was pink behind the gray branches.

In an effort to cheer her up I pointed to a ceramic lawn donkey, his wagon filled with blue plastic roses.

"How adorable," she said at first, looking at it blankly. Then her eyes widened. She ran down into the ditch by the side of the road.

"Look at me!" she said. "I'm the troll that lives under the bridge!"

She ran back beside me and stuck her arms straight out in front of her like a zombie, walking with her eyes closed over the asphalt. The rest of the way she did crazy stuff like opening people's mailboxes and yelling "Is anybody home?" Jill was acting like one of my dad's patients. She taunted a beagle tied up to a front porch and jumped on a Big Wheel that sat abandoned in a driveway.

As soon as we got back to her unit she ran to the record player and put "Indian Reservation" by the Raiders on the turntable. She made Beth turn the overhead light on and off like a strobe.

I jumped up and threw myself against the floor and Jill fell down against me, bumping into my ribs. Inside our skin our bones were sturdy as fat branches; we had weight. With the lights off Jill sprang up again and screamed.

I felt sweat coming up under my clothes and a wildness take hold of me, a craziness that I hadn't felt for years. Once again I could almost believe I was wrestling a wolverine or a hungry little meerkat.

Beth said her arm was getting tired, so she left the lights off, but we still jumped, throwing ourselves down, then jumping up again.

Jill punched her fist in the air and threw herself at the television, knocking it off the stand. The picture collapsed in on itself and the screen went blank. Before she'd been smiling, ecstatic, but now I just saw her white teeth in the dark.

"What now?" I asked.

"Now?" she said, jumping on top of me and speaking directly into my ear. "Now it's time to get serious."

✦

She'd read an article in the *Roanoke World-News* about the massage parlors on Williamson Road. One lady who worked at Petticoat Junction claimed all she did was tickle men with a peacock feather, and occasionally she gave an older man with poor circulation a foot massage. A lady who worked at the Smile

Lounge testified that she gave her clients manicures using clear nail polish and if they asked, she would trim their mustaches. The article also mentioned that a massage parlor worker made ten times more than a waitress.

"How hard can it be?" Jill said.

I was skeptical. When I asked about the massage parlors my father blushed and changed the subject, but my mother warned me prostitutes worked at those places, that they did disgusting things with men for money. I was pretty sure tickling a man with a feather didn't count as disgusting, but I wasn't really sure. I knew sex was disgusting, hard kissing was disgusting, even just pressing your private parts together was disgusting. But the massage parlors, according to the women who worked there, were not about prostitution. Instead men sat on the edge of the bed, just talking with the women or watching them fold laundry or file their nails. Sometimes there were special requests and the women would jump rope or talk about their favorite childhood pets. Jill brought up the girls in *Playboy*. These girls fascinated and bewildered us because on the one hand they spread out completely naked on fur blankets, but then in the interviews where they listed their hobbies, they wrote that they loved to play basketball or ride bikes.

"Just imagine," Jill said. "With all that money I can buy a beautiful pink ham!"

She also wanted to save up so we could all fly to Disney World and stay at a motel that had a pool and a shuffleboard court.

We took the bus down Williamson Road, past the Vagabond Motor Lodge to the Lee Theater. The movie titles, *Girls That Do* and *The Divorcee*, were spelled out in red and black letters with big red triple X's beside them. Next door was a place with blackened windows and a sign that read TODAY'S ADULT ENTERTAINMENT. Music rattled the front door. We stood across the street by the guardrail in our ski jackets. It was so cold that the tips of Jill's ears were red and my nose ran.

Petticoat Junction was a brick ranch house with purple shutters and a large American flag flying from the pole out front. The windows of Miss Renee's Health Club had been cemented over. Jill took my hand and squeezed it hard, then tried to straighten her back. She had lost weight; the bones in her face pressed out, making her features shine. When there was a gap in the traffic we ran across the highway and walked down the driveway to the side door. We stepped over a puddle of muddy water. I tapped my foot in a tight triangular pattern as Jill pushed the buzzer and we waited.

There was noise behind the door and as it opened a man appeared in a waft of warm air scented with sandalwood incense. He wore a bright-red shirt and had dark curly hair. Around one wrist was a leather band and drawn on the knuckles of the other hand were blue tattoos.

"I need a job," Jill said.

"You got the wrong place," he said.

We watched his Adam's apple go up and down.

"I can use a feather better than anybody," Jill said. She reached into her Mexican bag and pulled out a turkey feather she'd found in the woods.

"See," she said, "I even have my own!"

"Little girls," he said, waving his hand. "Go away."

Jill threw her body against the door.

"If I could just talk to you inside!"

"No!" he said.

"Just let me in!"

"Crazy bitches," he said, slamming the door and throwing the lock.

Between the massage parlors was a Citgo and we walked over and stood by the gas pumps under a string of red, white, and blue flags. Jill was wearing her mother's macramé skirt with a safety pin clenching the waist and suede boots with paper stuck up into the toes. She unzipped her ski vest with the rainbow on the back, took a pair of balled-up tube socks from her bag, and stuffed a sock into each of the cups of her bra, tying up her blouse so her belly button showed.

"What are you doing that for?" I asked.

"You know why," she said.

"Let's go back."

She looked at me with a sudden softness in her face.

"I can't go back," she said.

"Why?"

"You know why," she said again and walked away from me toward Petticoat Junction.

I ran after her on the wet asphalt. She knocked on the door and a tall woman in a blonde wig answered. Behind her sat three women, their eyes all outlined in black. Each one wore a different neon-colored baby-doll nightgown with feathers at the hem. One used a mirror to put on lipstick while the other two read magazines.

"Your mother is not here," the woman said. "I already told you on the phone."

"You've got me confused with someone else. I'm not looking for my mother," Jill said, then paused. "Well, I guess I am looking for my mother, but not here."

The woman's brows had been plucked and drawn back in so they formed a semicircle high above each eye.

"I'm a good dancer," Jill said, thrusting out her hips. "If you let me in I could show you."

"Your mother is not here," the woman said, as if she were deaf and hadn't heard anything Jill said.

Jill pulled her feather out of the bag again.

"I have a feather," she said, throwing herself toward the woman, "and I'm not afraid to use it!"

The woman's mouth dropped open and she slammed the door.

"Let me in!" Jill shouted. "You didn't even give me a chance to show you my splits."

✦

When I got home my mother was sitting in her bathrobe watching television. I couldn't be certain, but by the way she was sitting I guessed my parents had had a fight and my father had taken the car out for a drive again. She was at 3 but in danger of slipping to 2. She didn't turn her head when I came into the room, and I saw she was watching her favorite show, *Mary Tyler Moore*.

While my mom usually talked continuously about how important it was for women to stay home and make the domestic sphere beautiful, to be loving wives and attentive mothers, how my grandmother had wanted her to be the valued helpmate of a rich and considerate man, there she was sitting on the edge of the couch in complete thrall to Mary Richards, a working girl. I could tell by the way she didn't acknowledge my presence that a silent treatment was in effect. I knew I should just go to my bedroom and read one of my library books about teenagers dying of leukemia, but instead I tried to figure out what had triggered it. If she'd found out I'd been to Williamson Road she'd be furious, but there was no way for her to know about that. I remembered I had laughed at dinner when my father told the story of the patient who thought he was a telephone pole and I'd yelled at Phillip for stealing Tater Tots off my plate. I didn't think either of those would have set her off. The most likely reason for the silent treatment was that I'd been home so little lately. I thought of telling her I planned to stay home more. I wanted to say how her hair looked pretty pulled back with the pink scarf and that she was the most beautiful mother in all of Virginia.

But I knew neither of these things would work. I always pretended that I was unaffected by my mother's silent treatments, but actually they made me feel like the ground underneath me had lost its solidity and I was swaying inside the terrible dark.

+

The silent treatment lasted days, even though I jumped up after dinner to load the dishwasher and complimented my mom on everything from the way she sat sideways on the couch to how she organized the spice rack. Still she walked right past me as if I were invisible. Even when I got desperate and pretended to have a temperature, she put her hand on my forehead, shook her head, and let her fingers drift off, all without making eye contact.

Finally, after school one day, she spoke to me. She'd seen Beth rooting in the garbage cans beside our house, gnawing at a stale honey bun, then using a stick to shovel applesauce into her mouth.

"Beth is a little weird," I said. "Did you know she was a math genius? She can do problems even God couldn't figure out."

My mother looked at me with an expression I was familiar with—she'd had the same expression when I tried to tell her that tomatoes were giant berries or that the reason I'd gotten a D on a test was that I'd had amnesia. She knew something was off, that what I said was only part of what I actually meant.

"No," she said slowly, "I wasn't aware of that."

"It's very weird," I said.

"I haven't seen Mrs. Bamburg lately," my mom said. She sat on the couch and set her laundry basket beside her. "Her car is always sitting in the driveway."

Now that she was talking to me again, I wanted to confess everything to her. I'd tell her the Bamburg kids were hungry, how they had no money for toothpaste or laundry soap, how Beth had a cough she could not get rid of and Jill was so worried about the rent she was lucky if she slept a few hours a night. But I couldn't betray my friend.

"That's because Mrs. Bamburg got a job as a guard at a warehouse," I said. "She works all night and sleeps all day."

"Those poor kids," my mother said, shaking her head.

I knew she was satisfied for now, but that it was only a matter of time before she found out that Jill's mom was missing.

I ran over to Jill's to warn her that my mother was suspicious. I found her upstairs sprawled over her bed. I expected that after I told her, she would ask me to help her run up into the woods and live off the land. Living off the land was an interest we shared. Jill wanted to build a hut with a moss-covered floor and a hole in the roof so the smoke from our fire could escape up into the night. She wanted to steal the goats from the petting zoo up at Mill Mountain. They looked so miserable chained to the mesh fence. We would let them eat wildflowers, then milk them and make goat cheese. My notebook was full of the furniture I planned to build by weaving together branches with kudzu vines, and I had the ingenious idea of stuffing pillowcases with leaves for our mattress.

But Jill didn't even change positions on the bed. Her head was tipped backward; the ends of her hair brushed the shag. Tented beside her was her mother's copy of *Jonathan Livingston Seagull*.

She was sick, she told me, of using pages of the telephone book for toilet paper and eating stale hot dog buns.

She didn't seem to care that my mom might find out her secret. "Whatever happens," she said, "I'm going to try and be philosophical about it."

I couldn't tell if she was disappointed that I hadn't tried harder to cover up about her mom being gone or if she was just exhausted. I watched her eat one-third of the Little Debbie cake I'd snuck over, carefully leaving some for Beth and Ronnie. I tried to get her interested in a game of Scrabble or Frustration. She just lay there with her eyes half-closed.

Finally, I picked up a safety pin sitting in a bowl next to her bed.

"Let's become blood sisters," I said.

She sat up.

"Let me go first," she said.

She stuck the pin into the pad of her thumb and when she pulled it out a small bead of blood appeared.

I stuck the needle into my thumb, a prick that was cold and then warm as a dot of blood rose up. We pressed our thumbs together and our blood mixed.

✦

I never found out who called social services. My mom denied it. Anybody could have seen Beth eating out of the garbage. Jill warned her to stop, but she was relentless, going from duplex to duplex, picking out pizza crusts and half-eaten peanut butter sandwiches. Whoever called, the result was that early on Saturday morning, the Bamburg children filed out, youngest to oldest, followed by a chubby lady carrying Jill's back brace. Jill had on several layers of clothing, her two favorite sweaters, and both her mom's suede coat with the fur collar and her ski vest with the rainbow on the back. I ran outside in my nightgown, and when Jill saw me her face flooded with a huge and ludicrous smile.

After they drove away, I went back into the house. Phillip was on the couch, watching cartoons, eating Cap'n Crunch one by one out of the box. My parents were still asleep. I went upstairs and locked myself in the bathroom and tried to stare at my face so long it would no longer seem like mine. Then I hunched my back, opened my eyes wide, and ran the water, pretending to do the dishes the way Jill did, with quick mechanical movements of my hands. I pretended to lay the dishes out beside the sink to dry. I did this until my dad knocked on the door, asking about the endless running water. When I opened the door, his hair was hanging around his face and he wore his seminary T-shirt over his pajama bottoms. I slipped past him.

In my room I walked back and forth from wall to wall thirty-three times. As I paced, the light moved incrementally over the shag. I figured if I used Jesus's age any evil spirits in the room would be blasted out the window.

When my mother called me down to lunch, I went, but I could not eat any of my cheese sandwich and potato chips. I just stared at the food until the tiny holes in the bread looked huge and the chips made a grease stain on my paper plate. At first the grease spots looked like the chain of Caribbean islands, but after I stared long enough they looked like the freckles on Jill's collarbone.

✦

In my room I set up all the objects I had crushes on, starting with an empty Avon perfume bottle shaped like a puppy. Always before, when I'd touched it and smelled it, I felt a small expansion, as if part of my heart were warm Silly Putty. But this wasn't working. None of my other crushes—like the silk scarf with huge pale-pink roses or the spoon with the filigree handle—had any effect on me.

Finally I took my book on burial rites off the shelf and stared at the front cover. It was the only thing I had that always worked. I'd checked it out of the library three times in a row and I never intended to give it back. I'd decided if the librarian, a skinny lady who always had red lipstick smudged on her teeth—which made it seem as if she'd been eating live chickens—ever said I couldn't check it out anymore, I would wait until it was checked back in, take it off the shelf, sneak into the bathroom, throw the book out the window, and then go around outside and pick it up. Who else in Roanoke could possibly need the *Big Book of Burial Rites* as much as I did? Who would pore lovingly over the description of widows, sometimes girls as young as sixteen, throwing themselves into the flames of their husbands' funeral pyres?

Now, though, I was afraid to open it. I was afraid that it too might have lost its power to comfort me. I traced the letters on the cover with my finger and lay for a few minutes with the weight of the book on my lap.

I couldn't help myself. I opened it up to Chapter Six and stared at the photograph of the *rogyapa*, or body breaker, who used a sledgehammer to disassemble a body so vultures could freely eat the organs. The caption read: *The rogyapa's cheerfulness makes it easier*

*for the soul of the deceased to move out of purgatory
and into the next life.*

I flipped back to the chapter about the *sokushinbutsu*
monks who spent years trying to mummify themselves.
First they ate only nuts and seeds, then bark and roots,
and then, for the last month of their lives, they drank
poison tea. Finally each monk locked himself into a
stone tomb, barely larger than his body. In the tomb
there was just a breathing tube and a bell. Each day
while he was still alive, the monk rang the bell; when
the bell stopped sounding, the tube was removed and
the tomb sealed. Three years later the tomb was opened
and, voila, there was a tiny mummified monk! The living monks carried the body to the altar and worshipped
it as a Buddha.

I closed the book and went downstairs to see if I
could find some nuts in the kitchen cabinet. I ate a
handful of walnuts. On Monday I could buy a bag of
sunflower seeds at the Hop-In. Roots and bark would
be easy to come by up on the mountain. Only six more
years until I'd be locked inside a crypt in the lotus position, my body so lean and untasty even the maggots
would not want me.

My father came downstairs into the kitchen. He
was on his way to his second job at the psych center.
When we lived in the rectory, I'd often see him walking across the lawn between the church and rectory in
his black surplice and white robe, his silver pectoral
cross swinging around his neck and a smile on his

face. Now he worked not only nine to five at the VA hospital, but also at the psych center most nights. He looked tired out all the time, distracted. He wore his blazer with the frayed lapel, a wide pink tie, and bell-bottom jeans.

"I'm sorry about your friend," he said, grabbing the keys off the hook on the wall and heading out the door.

I got out the Fred Flintstone jelly glass, my hands shaking as I poured the milk up to the top of his hair-do. My beautiful friend was gone. I stared at the green wall phone.

You had to believe really hard to make anything happen. It was like God—you believed in Him to make Him exist.

Call me, I mouthed, shooting out a beam of light to wherever Jill might be now.

✦

All weekend I'd lain across my bed with my head tipped back—exactly as Jill had—staring up at the ceiling, sending out SOS signals from my brain to hers. Several times in the night, I stood in the dark kitchen and commanded the phone to sound. By Monday, as I got dressed for school, I'd convinced myself I would never see Jill again, that she'd been sent to the or-phanage in the country. I'd never seen the actual building, just the metal sign on the highway that read DANDYLOCK GIRLS' HOME. Maybe she'd gone berserk like the runaway girls in made-for-TV movies, cutting off chunks of her hair with a switchblade and screaming swear words. In that case, I figured, she'd be down at the reform school in Richmond.

I'd been at Low Valley Junior High only a few months, but I'd heard stories about girls who disappeared. Kids said one girl was a prostitute now in Atlanta, and another had run away with an old man to France. An eighth-grade girl who'd disappeared the year before had shown up one day in home economics, just as our teacher was going over how to ferment pickles. The girl told everyone she'd spent a year at a private school in New Orleans, but Jill said everyone knew a guy on the football team had knocked her up and she'd been sent down to relatives in Florida while she was pregnant. It was not unusual for girls to disappear, to turn into stories, but it was rare for them to come back, to change back again into girls.

As I suspected, Jill's seat in homeroom was empty, and the teacher, knowing we were friends, asked if I knew where she was.

"No ma'am," I said.

The intercom crackled to life and the principal, Mr. Powers, told us, in his intense Southern accent, that anyone participating in a food fight in the cafeteria would be suspended and that our football team, the Mighty Eagles, were still undefeated and, on a side note, that the new smorgasbord restaurant out in Salem was delicious.

The door flew open while the principal praised the potato salad and there was Jill, waving a note for the teacher. She wore her favorite cheesecloth shirt, blue cords, and a pair of new fur-lined clogs. She took her seat and smiled at me, mouthing *I missed you.* I was so happy I felt I might float out of my chair and up to the ceiling.

She opened her notebook, the one with the to-do lists, and wrote furtively, every now and then glancing up to smile.

"We got split up!" she said to me once the bell rang and we were out in the hallway. "I don't even know where Beth is!"

"That's terrible," I said.

"I'm with a brakeman and his wife out by Tilden Lake. I sleep in their dead daughter's bedroom!"

Everyone knew Tilden Lake was haunted.

"Is that the girl who comes out of the lake asking why the fish ate her eyes?"

Jill shivered.

"I have to sleep in her room!"

"That's creepy."

"She was a cute little girl, I have to give her that. There are pictures of her up all over the house."

In our first-period class, Jill asked so many questions about Chairman Mao—*Did he have false teeth? What was Mao's opinion on foot binding? Did he believe in dragons?*—that our social studies teacher had to tell her to let somebody else have a turn. In health class she seemed idiotically interested in the five food groups. Even in English, which was her most hated subject, she wrote a poem about a girl waiting for a soldier in a bus station.

Little girl. Little girl.
Who will catch you?
You sit on
the bench beside the mother
with her baby
and the black lady
reading her Bible.

She seemed to be set at a higher speed than usual, fluttering her fingers, cracking her neck, pulling her legs up under her body. At lunch, she quickly lifted out of her bag a ham sandwich, an orange, and a homemade brownie wrapped in plastic. I could tell by the careful way she set each item on the table how much the food meant to her.

"Now that the police are searching," she said, "it's only a matter of time before they find my mom."

It was pretty clear to me she was using words to make a little ledge for her to stand on. I nodded, but I didn't think her family would be coming together anytime soon. If her mother hadn't come back by now, she was probably out in California. Or she might have passed out of her human form into a small mummy sitting lotus-style in a cave someplace.

Jill's eyes kept sliding down the length of the table to where Dwayne sat with some of the boys from the bus. Dwayne was talking about sacrificing frogs to pagan gods and using black magic to communicate with Duane Allman. On the bus that morning, without Jill there to protect me, he'd dared me to pull up my shirt, and when I refused he called me a lezzbo. He called poor Pam "Kool-Aid face" because of her birthmark and dared her to French kiss him. I had no idea why Jill would have any interest in him, but on her way back from the trash can she slowed in front of him and jutted out her skinny hips.

During gym, we played volleyball, the girls' class against the boys'. Jill stood in the front by the net, across from Dwayne. He stared at her, and I could tell that Jill was discombobulated. Something about his gaze made it impossible for her to think. Midgame, after he'd spiked the ball so hard it knocked off Pam's glasses, he spoke to Jill, but I was too far back to hear what either said. The girls' gym teacher, Mrs. Popsic, kept squatting down, clasping her hands together straight out in front of her, and shouting, "Got it!" whenever the ball came near where we both stood. Mrs. Popsic was the cheerleading sponsor, a middle-aged lady with short hair. On game days she helped the girls decorate the football players' lockers, taping construction paper signs—GO GET 'EM EAGLES—to the painted metal and placing candy bars on top of the jocks' textbooks.

After the volleyball game, the locker room rang with girls' voices. I hated the large white-tiled room with the multiple shower spigots because: (a) I hated to be naked in front of anyone but myself, and (b) I'd once seen a prison movie where inmates got stabbed in a room that looked exactly like that one. Blood clinging to white tile was not an image I'd ever forget. The only way you got out of taking a group shower was to go up to Mrs. Popsic and say *P*. This meant you could use one of the half-dozen private showers. I said *P* once a month because I didn't want the other girls to know that P had not visited me yet.

After we showered—which for Jill and me just meant running into the room, sticking our butts into the spray, and then running back out into the locker room—Jill pulled on her four-leaf-clover underpants and white bra. She was the slightest bit ahead of me development-wise. While I had the smallest swelling around my nips, as Jill called them, and a few stray black hairs between my legs, Jill had a puff of hair under each arm, and her breasts, while small, were definitely there. I worried that Jill was going away from me, transforming from a girl who was willing to listen to my Disney records and even occasionally play with my dolls into a teen-ager who wanted to read *Tiger Beat*, talk about Bobby Sherman, and write the names of boys over and over in her notebook. Her eyes would deaden and she'd be another zombie girl roaming the hallways of Low Valley with shiny hair and an add-a-bead necklace.

Jill hummed and stared down at the floor where the metal bench support bolted into the cement.

I turned to my locker, pulled up my jeans with the raindrop pockets, and started to button my shirt.

"Get dressed," I said with my back to her. "We'll be late for the bus."

I saw Mrs. Popsic in her office, the walls covered with Eagle Pride posters and black-and-white photographs of sports teams. I sat on the bench to pull up my socks and, as I sat there, Jill took a step—still in her bra and underwear—out into the middle of the locker room. At first I thought she was going to the fountain for a drink of water. Instead, she ran out the double swing doors and into the hallway.

The girls got quiet and watched the door swing back inside. I ran to the door and pushed it open a crack. I saw the boys' faces. One in a striped short-sleeve shirt let his mouth fall so far open I could see his silver fillings. Dwayne, in his beige corduroys and big Confederate flag belt buckle, had an expression on his face I can only describe as gratitude. At first Jill just stood there, like a deer caught in the headlights of the boys' stares, but then she twirled, her eyes closed, her arms swinging at her sides, her bare feet moving over the linoleum tiles. Jill's back was white in the bright hallway lights, her spine like a string of pearls running down under her skin.

✦

Mrs. Popsic dragged Jill into the locker room and stood beside her while she dressed, asking her over and over: Had she lost her mind? Did she think a prank like that would get her anywhere? She yanked her toward Mr. Powers's office. When Jill came out, her face was red and wet. She told me later that Mr. Powers had threatened her with his fraternity paddle, then picked up the phone and dialed her foster mom, Mrs. Swenson. Jill begged me to ride home with her on the bus.

I couldn't say no. Jill's new bus had a driver who was so fat he had to enter through the back emergency door. Jill said that when he died he'd have to be buried in a piano box. The kids on bus 22 were quieter than the ones on my bus. They sat in groups talking softly to one another. We got off by the side of the road in a wooded area near a mailbox with a red reflector, and Jill took my hand as we walked up the long gravel driveway toward the black lake. The wind off the water was cold and damp. My legs goose-pimpled under my pants.

The single-story house had a wreath made of plastic flowers on the door, an American flag flying from a pole in the yard, and, on each side of the porch, silver balls sitting atop concrete pedestals. Mrs. Swenson, a woman with short frosted hair, answered the door. She was wearing a Christmas sweater.

She told me to wait in the living room while she and Jill talked.

+

I called my mom and told her I was at Jill's, then I sat on the colonial couch and stared at the spinning wheel in one corner of the room. A big picture of the dead daughter hung over the fireplace. She was definitely a cute little girl, sitting on Santa's lap with her uneven bangs and lopsided smile. A glass-fronted cabinet held a collection of teacups. One had a handle shaped like a lobster claw. Through the wall I heard voices, but for all the sense I could make the sounds might as well have been water. When Jill finally came out, her smile was wide and idiotic.

"That was awful."

"I bet," I said.

"Mrs. Swenson told me she'd been upset enough for several lifetimes and if I ever do something like that again, they'll give me back."

"Did you promise to do better?"

Jill nodded her head vigorously.

"I am so going to do better! I'm going to study more, really study, not just fill in the blanks of my workbooks, but try to actually learn something. I'll find Beth and Ronnie, I'll make a million calls if I have to. I'll even go door-to-door with their picture. I decided while I was sitting in Mr. Powers's office that even if God does hate our family and he has cursed us for all eternity, I'm just going to beg him for help."

I wasn't sure if I should advise Jill to beg God. What would my dad say? He didn't seem to care if my brother or I said our bedtime prayers. Used to be he'd sit on the edge of the bed and recite along with me, *Now I lay me down to sleep*, and then I'd ask God to bless my family, my doll Vicky, the old peach tree in the yard. He'd let me go on and bless anything I wanted.

"Beg him," I said. "It's worth a shot."

It was all a crapshoot, as Jill used to say. I knew you could find a certain relief in begging God—it had helped me—but on the other hand, God never answered directly and that was always depressing.

"That's not all, either," Jill continued, almost breathless. "I'm going to write Mrs. Nixon and ask her to help seals and whales. I'm going to visit sick children in the hospital, the really sick ones that freak everybody else out, the ones with brain cancer and leukemia. Whenever I see old people I plan to go right up to them and ask if I can help carry their groceries, or help them up the steps. I am going to do a lot around here, too. I'll start doing the laundry and maybe even cooking."

We sat on the chilly floor and played Yahtzee, Jill jiggling the dice around in the leather cup much longer than was necessary. With all the odd smells and the calico couch, it felt like we were visiting some older relative, a great-aunt we hardly knew. The pictures on the walls were prints of barns and farm animals ,and the only books the Swensons seemed to have were a book on building your vocabulary and another one on knitting. Mrs. Swenson eventually went out to her Bible study at church, instructing Jill that there were cold cuts and cans of Coke in the fridge and that we could watch television in the basement. She said she'd drive me home when she got back. Her voice was a little weary; she was not a mean person, it said, she was trying to be reasonable.

Downstairs two La-Z-boy recliners sat in front of a big television in a wood console. Jill switched around the channels but the static was too bad to really see much of anything. In the corner was a dry bar with brown leather stools. On the bar sat a bamboo container of plastic swizzle sticks like the ones they gave out at the Fiji Island. A stack of small rooster napkins sat beside glasses with images of Easter Island.

Jill went behind the bar and lifted up a bottle filled with gold liquid.

"Don't you think we deserve a drink?" she said, that nutty smile spreading across her features.

"I thought you were going to do better?"

"I'll do better after we have a drink," she said, pouring a few inches of the liquid into two of the Easter Island glasses and filling them up the rest of the way with Coke. The Coke hissed and spit, sending up a tiny wisp of steam.

"Do you really think this is a good idea?"

"Probably not," Jill said, "but let's do it anyway!"

After our first drink, Jill began to sing in fake French, a sort of goofy lullaby. The Coke was sweet and warm. I'd only ever had a glass of spiked eggnog, and another time, I'd snuck one of my dad's beers, but now as my glass emptied and Jill went back to talking about how much she hated Mrs. Popsic—in her tennis skirt and sweater with the school emblem, an eagle, on the pocket—I felt something inside me shift. It was like I was finally able to lie down after years of standing. I felt a peace I had not felt since we'd left the rectory. I understood why grown-ups drank. The stuff was like a potion in *Alice in Wonderland*, the bottle marked EVERYTHING IS ALL RIGHT.

After our second drink, Jill decided it was time to walk around the lake. She got a flashlight from a drawer and we walked out into the dark.

At first the cold felt fantastic and the lake shimmered behind the house—black, with purple and a line of silver here and there. The cold wind off the water was the Holy Spirit; it did not just flow over us, we were caught up in it. Jill walked too close to the water; once her foot slipped on the frosty dirt and she nearly fell in. I told her to come back up to the path, but she just stepped rock to rock. It was so cold I couldn't feel the tips of my fingers, and the warm feeling in my stomach was turning into nausea. In the circle of light I could see foamy brown pond scum and sticks that had gathered against the muddy edge of the lake.

"What's the worst thing you've ever done?" Jill asked me.

"I don't know," I said. "I'd have to think about it."

"My mother told me when my dad had his first wreck, the one before the one that killed him, I wouldn't kiss him in the hospital."

"You were probably just scared."

"Maybe," she said, "but I still feel awful about doing my daddy like that."

Wind rushed off the water and into my ears. Everyone believed Tilden Lake was haunted. It wasn't just the Virgin Mary; some said a little dead girl lived at the lake bottom in a cave made of amethyst. She ate raw catfish, biting the heads off first and then peeling back the skin with her teeth. Others said they'd seen her around the lake's edge wearing a little pink bathing suit. Jill was going out farther on the rocks, which were slick with algae and unsteady under her. She didn't seem to care that her shoes and her pants were wet to the knees.

"Let's go back!" I said.

Jill swung around.

"You're not going to like what I am going to tell you," she said. "But promise you'll go along anyway."

"OK," I said, figuring she'd tell me she wanted to try to sleep in the woods, build a lean-to and start a campfire. This spot had a lot of potential. There was a fairy circle of birches and a soft patch of moss. Finally we would live off the land.

"Dwayne is going to meet us."

"What?"

"He's waiting at the other side of the lake."

"Are you crazy?!"

"We'll just say hi and come right back."

"No way," I said. "I'm not going."

"Fine," she said, "I'll go by myself."

She took off down the path, running. I followed her, but I was terrified at the thought of meeting Dwayne. What if he killed us, and we went down to the lake bottom and had to live with the little dead girl in her cave? I hadn't come to a lot of conclusions about the afterlife but I didn't want to spend it with a ghoulish toddler. The trees around us were made of black ice, and when they moved in the wind, the sound was as delicate as a dozen chandeliers. The tiny chimes had made me feel that Jill and I were changing into unicorn girls, moving through a black glass forest toward our mysterious fate. But now that it became clear that our fate was to meet Dwayne, it all seemed pointless and pathetic. Dwayne was the perpetrator of Indian handshakes and wedgies, the boy who was the best in the school at making fart sounds with his hand shoved into his underarm.

We came out of the tree line. Dwayne held up his lighter so we could see his long greasy hair and hunched shoulders encased in a circle of muzzy light. In Bent Tree I'd seen him sitting on a lawn chair in his duplex living room, watching a black-and-white television balanced on a cardboard box. His dad, a skinny man with a red nose, sold used cars at a lot out in Vinton. One time on my way to the bus stop in the morning I'd seen his dad asleep in his car, his face pressed into the glass and his legs hanging out the passenger-side window.

"You've come a long way, baby!" Dwayne yelled.

"It was totally dark," Jill said. She waved her flash-light over the lake surface, showing the jagged moving water.

"Shit," Dwayne said. "We didn't have nothing but this lighter." When I heard him say *we,* I realized there was someone behind him. I could make out a large expanse of shoulder, square head, creeping side-burns. He wore a black nylon jacket with a fur collar that made him look like a cop.

The mountain above us was big and black. I could just make out the tips of the tree branches where they seemed to melt into the sky. I wanted to go home; my parents would be worried. Now that we were here, what exactly was supposed to happen? This new Jill was different from the old Jill. Even though it was dark I could see her eyes had enlarged, and she was standing with her hands on her hips in a way I'd never seen before. She was like the girls on *Dark Shadows,* all smooth hair and cheerfulness at first, but pretty soon black circles would appear under their eyes and they'd lie around all day, dreaming of blood.

"Should we walk out to the middle?" she said, mo-tioning to the dock with the diving board at the end. I was worried she was planning to do something dra-matic, take off her clothes and jump into the water. I knew this would be more suicidal than dramatic, be-cause the water was freezing and Jill couldn't swim.

"What do you say, Julio?" Dwayne asked in that voice boys used exclusively to tease each other.

"Yeah, man," Julio said, though I was pretty sure his name was not Julio. Dwayne walked beside Jill and Julio walked next to me. I kept my hands deep in my pockets as if they were attached to my hips. I did not want to chance random hand contact. When I looked at him sideways, I saw that his face was solemn, and I realized this was not easy for him either. Dwayne had probably promised that I was tall and beautiful. I was tall, that part was true, but I was not beautiful. I was sure when he first saw me a few moments ago, he was disappointed that instead of looking like Julie from *The Mod Squad*, I looked much more like Huck Finn.

My heart struggled like a trapped sparrow. Between the boards of the dock, I saw the water pitching. At the dock's end we stood and looked up at the stars, pinpricks in black paper, their reflections smashed up in the moving water. I felt we had entered the firmament that my dad had told me about, that vast black nothingness before God made the earth and the sun and all the animals. He'd also said that in medieval times, people thought mice and rabbits were made out of the extra bits left over after God made the bigger animals like lions and bears.

I thought of saying this aloud—it might be interesting to the others—but the wind was loud in the branches and on the water. We turned back in silence and walked off the dock and toward the overhang with the picnic tables.

Once we were out of the wind, Dwayne pulled Jill away from me, and Jill raised her arms as if it were impossible for her to stop him. They went to the corner, where I couldn't really see anything but the light reflected off the zipper of Jill's ski jacket.

Julio sat on a picnic-table bench. He hooked his hand into my elbow and pulled me toward him. I would have pulled away, but I lost my balance and fell onto his lap. I sat there, panicky and teetering like a porcelain figure on the back of a whale. To be polite, I felt I had to sit there for at least a few minutes.

"So what's your real name?"

"Guess!" Dwayne yelled from his corner. Boys always talked only to each other, no matter who else was around.

"Harold?" I guessed.

Dwayne snorted.

"Harold is a perfectly good name," I said.

"If you're a faggot," Julio said.

Dwayne laughed.

I tried to pretend I was the unicorn girl talking to Mr. Brown Bear about the taste of violets and how we missed the porcupine who lived behind the gas station. But Julio's lap was nothing like the bear's and my fantasy did not hold; I started to panic.

"What are you all doing over there?" I yelled to Jill.

"You're like a rabbit," Julio said. "Just settle down."

I was afraid if I leaned too close to his face, I would be blotted out completely.

"I have to go," I said. I pulled away from him, jumped off the platform.

"Just relax," Jill yelled to me. I didn't look back. I was already on the path.

As I got near the road, two cones of light passed over me and I realized Mrs. Swenson was back early from Bible study.

I turned and saw that Jill was behind me. We ran faster than I thought two girls could run, branches smacking our bodies as we hurled ourselves through the woods and around the lake.

By the time we got back, the car lights were off and Mrs. Swenson was just a dark figure standing on the porch. I could tell she'd been inside already to look for Jill. She was now gazing at the dark water. I heard Jill trying to regulate her breath as we hid behind a stand of trees close to the porch.

"It's me," Jill said.

Mrs. Swenson turned toward Jill's voice, trying to make out her shape in the darkness.

"Don't you know me?" Jill said.

Mrs. Swenson stood there quietly before she went back into her house and closed the door.

✦

Jill didn't show up at school the next day. When I got home that afternoon, I called the Swensons. Mrs. Swenson answered and said Jill was gone. She'd run

away and nobody knew where she was. Her grandmother hadn't heard from her and Dwayne claimed
he hadn't heard from her either, but by the way the
corners of his mouth turned up I knew he might not
be telling the truth. Rumors went around the school.
Stories about how Jill had run away with a pot dealer,
how she'd been kidnapped by a bunch of bikers and
taken to Mexico. These, while horrible, bothered me
less than Sheila's story: she claimed that Jill had fall-
en into Tilden Lake and drowned.

+

CHAPTER THREE

JULIE

Mom glanced up now and then from her photo album to watch the new tenants moving into the Bamburg duplex. I still thought of it as Jill's place even though I hadn't seen her or the rest of her family for three years, since I was twelve. A single guy had lived in 11B since the Bamburgs moved out, a pale young man who worked at the Jiffy Lube on 419. Last week, without warning, he'd packed up his beer-can collection and left. My mom and I watched the new woman carrying boxes and her daughter coming in and out of the living room. The girl cradled something white and round in her arms that I assumed was a stuffed animal.

Mr. Ananais told us the woman, whose name was Julie, was a former Miss North Carolina and that she owned a dance studio out in Salem. She wore a wraparound skirt over a white leotard. On her thin wrists hung big silver bracelets, and her long brown hair spurted out of a ponytail at the top of her head. I assumed my mom would say she was just like Sandy, who, since she'd broken up with Sonny, had a different guy sleep over every month. But my mom wasn't ready yet to render her verdict; Julie's possessions confused her. Chrome lamps, a crystal champagne bucket, a sheepskin rug—all too glittery for my mother's taste, but she had to admit the stuff was expensive. After unpacking, Julie hung a mirror over her beige leather couch. It reflected the wires flowing out of the back of our television set and my mom sitting at the table in her bathrobe.

+

Nixon had resigned and I'd gotten my period, but not much else had changed besides my bra size. The world went on: Patty Hearst got kidnapped, Evel Knievel tried to jump the Snake River Canyon, and the Weathermen bombed the State Department. Though time had passed and I was now fifteen, I felt trapped like a bug in amber. I was stuck in place while my dad kept seeking. Over the years he'd had many phases. First he got interested in past-life regression, convinced that all his current problems were connected to unresolved problems in his past; in one life his father had beaten him and in another his little sister had drowned. After that he'd joined a group that practiced rebirthing. Birth, he explained to me, was traumatic. The baby learned the world was hostile. But through rebirthing the participant felt a saturation of *divine love*. I sat in the car and did homework during one of those sessions. The screams that came from the Unitarian church basement scared me. When he came back, he seemed flushed and a little crazy, his eyes darting around the road. He told me the woman who'd been reborn had *really gotten into it*. She'd even, like a baby, peed her pants.

"Yuck!" I blurted out before I could stop myself.

I thought he'd be mad, but he just laughed. Currently he was going to a dream-therapy group and reading Alan Watts. The books lay piled up on the coffee table. When I walked by he'd look up and say, *"Get this!* You are an aperture through which the universe is exploring itself." God, if he existed at all, was just as much in the Long John Silver's as inside any church. He told me Christianity was a sort of playacting. He didn't need scripted prayers or creeds to reach divinity; he, like everyone, needed to find his own route. When he looked back at our time in the rectory—a time that was to me as precious as it was remote—all he felt now was regret.

✦

My dad had no interest in Julie, but I studied her, watched her sit on her plush couch, drinking white wine. I assumed she was too glamorous to be interested in us. But one night, after my dad went to his second job, my mom came down in her good dress, a burgundy linen number with a boatneck and high heels. She smelled slightly of mothballs and wore red lipstick. Julie was coming over for a drink!

I went back to my science notebook, filling in the names of the trees beside different-shaped leaves. When the bell rang she ran to the door. To my mom, every aspect of a woman's appearance translated into particular information. Womanhood for her was a cult with hundreds of secret symbols. A turquoise ring meant one thing worn on the index finger, something completely different on the pinkie. When Mrs. Smith wore a red scarf tied sideways around her neck it was OK, but when Sandy wore a red scarf as a belt my mother called her a Gypsy. I was afraid my mother would not approve of the way Julie's white enamel necklace hung around her neck or the way her toenails were painted orange, but she welcomed her and thanked her for bringing wine.

"Git!" Julie said to me as my mom opened the bottle and poured the clear liquid into wineglasses. "I want to chat with your mama."

I retreated upstairs, but only to the top step. Julie had a movie-star Southern accent. The accent implied that sure, she was living in Bent Tree, but for her it was a choice rather than a jail sentence. I listened to my mother. I couldn't make out her exact words, but I was more worried about her tone. When she was intimidated her default mode was condescension.

Phillip wandered out of my parents' bedroom where he was setting up a Lincoln Log complex—a large fort and several outbuildings all filled with plastic farm animals and green army men.

"It's stuck," he said, holding up the canister of Lincoln Logs.

"You must have spilled chocolate milk in there or something."

His eyes were slick in the dark hallway as I used my thumbnail to level the tiny log up.

+

To me dancers were like angels or fairies, but better because they were real girls. I loved the movies about the girls who spent all day practicing, practicing so hard beautiful beads of sweat broke out on their faces. They stayed up all night dancing until the sun came up. They had the intensity of nuclear reactors. Julie had been one of those girls! One of the lucky ones who turned into a story, a fairy tale. Yet she'd landed in Bent Tree, and that's where the mystery lay, that's why I couldn't sit there any longer; I had to go downstairs, open the cupboard, take a long time picking out the jelly glass, finally choose the one with Fred Flintstone, open the refrigerator door, look dramatically from the orange juice to the pink Kool-Aid to the milk, finally pick the milk, tip the glass container of milk, get two Oreos from the package on the counter, and arrange them first on top of each other, then like wheels, side by side.

Unfortunately, the whole time I was in the kitchen my mom was talking about the singing career she had before she met my dad. I knew all the lines by heart, how she sang Cole Porter songs at a jazz club. She was both playing it all down, like *no big deal, I was a jazz singer*, but also hinting that if she had not gotten married she would have been a *superstar*! I opened one of the kitchen drawers; inside were instructions on how to use the washing machine, tacks stuck into cardboard, a clay ashtray Phillip had made in kindergarten, a jagged piece of linoleum. I had no idea what I was looking for, but when my mom asked I said a pencil eraser.

"Honey," Julie said, winking at my mom, "go over and check on Kira for me."

"I have a lot of homework," I said. "I think I'll just stay here."

"Get your butt over there!" my mom said.

I could tell she was a little bit hysterical, but in a different way than usual; she was at 3, but giddy.

"I'll go," I said, "but if I fail my math test it's on your head, not mine."

Julie laughed. I heard them both laughing as I walked over the flat dirt and onion grass to the Bamburg duplex.

I knocked. It took awhile, but eventually Kira opened the door. She held a real white rabbit in her arms.

"Hi," I said, "your mom sent me over here to check on you."

She looked at me without any expression.

"I'm thirteen," she said. "I'm not a baby."

I didn't say anything. In her footie pajamas she looked like a fat baby who'd taken too many vitamins and had grown a hundred times its normal size.

"You might as well come in," she said. I followed her through the living room and up the stairs. Her room was like the girl's room in the furniture store at the mall: white dresser with gold detail, a white canopy bed covered with pink pillows, plaques of pink-cheeked girls in patchwork frocks, porcelain-headed dolls held on pedestals, and a collection of kitten figurines. But she was not the sort of little girl who should be sleeping in the bed, who sat on the rosebud spread carefully changing the clothes on her delicate dolls. She looked more like a frog-girl. I felt sorry for her—she was like Pam at school, somebody I pitied.

"Nice room," I said, sitting on the edge of the bed.

"It's a little cramped."

"You had a bigger place?"

"A house," Kira said. "But we lost it."

"How can you lose a house?"

"The bank took it."

"Oh," I said. "I'm sorry. That's a mean thing for the bank to do."

"It's OK," she said, throwing an arm up. "Who needs property!"

Her imitation of her mom was spot-on. She dropped her hand back to her rabbit's silky ears. His eyes were pink and sinister but I still wanted to hold him. I'd always wanted to be like the girls in books who partnered up with serious cats to solve crimes. On the days we weren't solving crime, I imagined, the cat would lie on my lap while I read. In Philadelphia I'd put a salamander in a shoe box with a rock and some grass, but overnight on the porch he was attacked and killed by giant red ants. I kept a cricket in a jar with holes nailed through the lid and another time a caterpillar. I'd named the cricket Herman and the caterpillar Fuzzy Woo, but both got so limp and depressed I eventually let them go.

"Can I hold him?" I asked.

Kira looked at me carefully.

"I'll be real gentle," I said.

"I don't think so," Kira said. She began telling me Snowball's life story. She and her mom were on their way back from the beach in North Carolina when they stopped at a bar to use the bathroom. It was one of those dark places that smelled of BO and cigarette smoke. Right away Kira saw the glass aquarium by the popcorn machine. Inside was a huge snake, and shivering in one corner was a baby rabbit! Kira burst out crying and begged her mother to buy Snowball. At first Julie said she was being ridiculous, but Kira screamed so loud that Julie finally said OK. It took Snowball a year to get calm enough to listen to music, and he still couldn't sit through the reading of a whole bedtime story.

"You can just set him in my lap," I said. "I won't even touch him."

Kira shook her head.

"He's extra twitchy because not only did he end up in the tank with the snake, but the whole reason he got there, this is what the bartender told my mom, was that his mother was ripped out of her rabbit hutch and eaten by a German shepherd."

"That's terrible," I said.

Snowball twisted in her lap as if he'd heard her talking and was reminded of his near-death experiences.

"It's OK, bunny boy," Kira said, going into a higher voice. "You are King Bunny, aren't you, yes you are. And all the chipmunks, the squirrels, the mice and the moles, they all come kneel down to Snowball, that's right, Snowball, Prince of the Forest."

I looked up at the ceiling and saw a few brown dots in one corner. I remembered how Jill and I had shaken a bottle of Coke and then let it fly all over the room. This was after we'd lit a *Vogue* magazine on fire on the deck and then walked across the first floor only on raised surfaces—kitchen countertops to the dining room table to the arm of the couch, all the way out the sliding glass window to the deck rail, where Jill had lost her balance and almost killed herself.

"There's a man in the woods who eats children's fingers," I said. "He lurks around Bent Tree at night looking in the windows."

This got her to stop talking.

"What kind of man?"

"A crazy man," I said.

"Did he escape from jail?"

"No," I said. "He's the ex-husband of a lady who used to live in our duplex."

She looked at me.

"He killed a girl in 16A by eating off her pinkies."

"Why didn't he eat the other fingers too?"

"Pinkies taste like chicken wings."

"You know," she said, "I can sort of see that."

✦

It was late when Julie came back. Kira hadn't wanted to play Mystery Date or get down her Ouija board. Snowball was her only real topic of conversation. I ran down the stairs where Julie gave me a sloppy hug, her small, tight breasts pressing into me; she whispered in my ear that I should come over whenever I wanted.

At our duplex, my dad still wasn't back. In the last few weeks he'd been meeting with his dream-interpretation group out in Fincastle. At each meeting everyone related a dream and then they'd discuss it first in Freudian and then in Jungian terms. The leader, who had Gestalt training, felt that every person in a dream was the dreamer. To hear my dad talk about the group made me miss Jill. She had insisted that while she dreamt her soul slipped out of her body and actually visited the places and people she saw in her sleep. She flew to the ocean floor and then toward a person who looked like both her daddy and Abe Lincoln.

In my room, I stuck my transistor radio between my mattress and pillow. I'd learned I could still hear the music, which came up through the feathers, traveled mysterious as smoke into my ear canal and spread like dark glitter inside my brain. I was hoping to hear Cher. Her voice was best at night. Jill had told me that birds sang different songs in the night than in the day, and it was the same with Cher. To hear "Half Breed" at night was like a religious experience. But no such luck. "Cat's in the Cradle" was on and then "At Seventeen," two songs so sad they made you want to kill yourself. "Jackie Blue" after that, not a bad one but not what I had in mind.

I heard my dad come in the front door. I liked to hear about the dreams. While some were boring, others fascinated me. I ran down the stairs.

"How was it?" I asked him.

He was sitting on the couch taking off his shoes.

"How was what?"

"The dreams!"

"There was a good one about a bird flying out of a baby's mouth."

"What kind of bird?"

"Sparrow."

"What about Jude?"

I liked Jude's dreams best; in one a fish asked him for a piece of chewing gum, and in another a white tulip turned into a kitten head.

"He wasn't there."

He lay down on the couch and picked up his Alan Watts book, throwing his bare feet up on the cushions and pulling a blanket up to cover himself. I said good night and went back up to my bed. I reached my hand under the pillow, turned the dial, and the sound—static mostly—came back up. At first I was worried it was Gregg Allman. But as the static cleared I heard Elton. I loved Elton. He was like Bowie, if Bowie were less fantastic and a whole lot chubbier. You couldn't worship Elton like you could Bowie, but what he lacked in star power he made up for in desperation. His voice soared up into my brain; he was talking about the princess perched in her electric chair and how sugar bear had saved his life.

✦

When I woke up the next morning my mother was already out of her bathrobe, and when I got home from school the shag had been vacuumed and the kitchen counter swept of crumbs. She'd put away her photo albums, set candlesticks on the table, and placed a tapestry—given to us by a Chinese missionary— over the back of the couch. She set out on the coffee table *The Family of Man*, a book of photographs that showed, among other things, a just-born bloody baby, and *Surfacing*, a book my father told me was about a woman who went insane.

Phillip was running the vacuum.

"What's all this?" I asked.

"Who knows?" he said. "But at least she seems happy."

After my dad left for the psych center and my brother settled into my parents' room to watch the portable television, my mom changed into a good dress, the polka-dot one with the full skirt, put on lipstick ,and arranged cheese cubes on our nice serving plate. She put *A Funny Thing Happened on the Way to the Forum* on the stereo and turned on our lamp with the brass base and linen shade. She sat sideways on the couch, looking through *Town and Country* magazine. She tried to act cool, as if she set herself up with hors d'oeuvres and paged through magazines every night. But I could tell by the way she kept glancing over to Julie's apartment, staring at a tiny version of herself in the mirror over Julie's couch, that she was a little unhinged. A 4 moving to a 3.

I'd spread my notebook, graph paper, and pencils all over one corner of the living room in an effort to mark the territory as my own. But once Julie arrived and my mom opened a bottle of wine and they sat down on the couch, laughing and smiling widely into each other's faces, I was banished to my usual spot at the top of the stairs. From this vantage I could see down the stairwell, which was covered with the same gold shag, now matted flat. At the foot of the steps lay my brother's sneakers and on the hook above hung a baseball cap and a black umbrella.

I could hear best if I leaned in between the bars of the wrought-iron railing.

Julie complained about her last class of the day, an exercise class for what she called "old fatties," many of whom couldn't even, God bless them, touch their goddamn toes. My mother laughed and complained about how boring it was to fold towels and make beds, how she hated the mangy shag. I got bored listening to them trade complaints back and forth. I crept back down the hall to my room and read for a while about the Zoupee people and how they buried their dead in blankets woven out of fern fronds.

By the time I came back to the steps, Julie was deep into her life story. Now this was more like it! After her reign as Miss North Carolina, she'd gone to New York City, where Eileen Ford herself told her she would never make it as a model and the girl she met in the waiting room at Wilhelmina had turned out to be a lesbian. A lesbian! I leaned farther between the black metal poles.

Phillip came out of my parents' room and interrupted my eavesdropping. He pointed to a picture in the back of his comic book of a man flying through the air with a jet pack strapped to his back.

"I want this," he said.

If he talked too much my mom would hear us.

"I'll get it for you," I whispered.

"Really?"

I nodded, and he ran back into my parents' room.

After New York, Julie had come to Roanoke and worked as a bank teller, doing occasional local commercials for beverage distribution centers and car dealerships. In a moment of weakness and insanity she'd married her high school sweetheart, a beefy guy whose family owned the local supermarket. They moved into a split-level over in Windsor Terrace. This was the largest subdivision in Roanoke, with hundreds of houses, all on small lots, saplings tied to stakes in the yards and silver TOT FINDER stickers on the upper windows.

Her husband and his friends spent weekends in the basement drinking beer and eating mixed nuts. It didn't take her long to realize she had made a mistake. She tried to tell him that the house depressed her. He said that in time they'd have a bigger one, in time they'd have everything they needed. She felt like she was drowning. When he was at work one day, she took the car and started driving. She was hours out of Roanoke when she realized she was going to drive all the way to LA.

Right away things were magic out there. She found a cute studio apartment and got an agent; small TV roles were offered to her within the week she arrived. Parts playing receptionists, nurses, waitresses—all of them, she had to admit, were dumb blondes, but heck, she was in fucking Hollywood. She even played a tennis bunny in a film starring a famous comedian, a guy with one blue eye and one brown eye who was very into spiritualism. It was on the movie set, sitting in her trailer, that she realized how late her period was and that she was pregnant. When she called her husband to tell him, he was thrilled even though she had left him without writing a note. He told her to come on home.

My butt was sore and I could feel parts of my brain, in the back somewhere, turning in for the night. I peeked into my parents' room where my brother was sleeping sprawled out on the bed, holding a plastic saber. I pulled the bedspread up to cover him and turned off the light. In my room, moonlight came through the blinds and I pulled down my corduroys, pulled my turtleneck over my head, and put on the oversize T-shirt I had taken to sleeping in. I kept my door open and listened. I wanted Julie to go back to her own duplex, to hear my mom wash the dishes, set them in the rack, then climb the stairs, go into her bedroom, undress, and get into bed.

But it was not until much later that I finally heard the front door close. I jumped out of bed and saw my mom walking Julie to her front door. As my mom walked back, Julie called out to her and blew a kiss. My mom pretended to catch the kiss in her fist and push it down into her pocket.

Every night my dad worked, Julie came over. She and my mom drank wine. When Julie was around my mom seemed like a different person, as if she had been kidnapped and replaced by a glamorous imposter. It was all just too much. Julie was coming over in the morning, too, after we left for school. When I'd get home in the afternoon, all the signs would be there: cigarette butts in the ashtray, mugs with coffee residue, and jelly glasses that smelled of wine in the sink.

On Saturdays, after Julie taught her morning classes, she and my mother went around to the open houses in the new subdivisions. They were gone into the evening, so that most Saturday nights we now ate toaster-oven pizzas. I took the English muffin from the bag, cut it in half, spread tomato sauce over the top, sprinkled it with garlic salt, and laid the American cheese on top. I stood by the counter watching the red coils to make sure the cheese softened but did not burn.

+

On the last Thursday of the month, after Dad got paid, he took us out to Pizza Hut. We all agreed that Pizza Hut pizza was terrible, a distant relative to pizza, as if pizza had been murdered and come back to life as a pizza zombie. But over the years the greasy ground sausage and sweet tomato sauce washed down with a huge pitcher of root beer had become, if not delicious, then at least addictive. As we ate, Phillip told us how during the fire drill a kid named Dougy had peed himself and that a girl in his class had gotten caught with a lollipop in her cubby.

Our waitress, an older lady with an unusual shade of orange hair, asked how we were doing, and we all nodded fine. My mom had not yet mentioned Julie, though I could tell by a sudden change in the air that she was about to. I wanted to head her off. I'd made a mental list of conversation subjects: (1) What did she think of Jimmy Carter? (2) What did she think of the fire hydrants painted like minutemen for the bicentennial? (3) Would she reconsider our request for a CB radio?

But before I could ask my questions she started up about Julie, saying that Julie had told her the Pizza Hut owner was a sleazebag.

I looked over at the middle-aged man with the mustache who was taking checks at the cash register. He looked friendly enough, though his shirt was unbuttoned a few too many buttons so I could see his sprouting chest hair.

I took a long drink of my root beer and imagined the sweet liquid floating over the seaweedy tentacles of my taste buds.

"And how would she know?" Dad asked.

At first, Dad was glad Mom had a friend. He'd explained to me how impossible it had been for my mom to make friends as a minister's wife. And besides, he'd continued, using the same tone he used to speak about patients at the psych center, since they'd moved around so much in the last few years she'd had no time to befriend anybody.

Now, though, my mother's constant talking about Julie was wearing him down. She wasn't just telling you things about her, but also implying she was divine.

"Julie knows everybody in this town."

She began reciting the details of Julie's story, which were as familiar to me now as the stations of the cross: after she'd gotten her break in LA, the brilliant comedian had taken her aside on the movie set and told her he would help her make it in the big time. If only she hadn't gotten pregnant, if only . . .

My father wiped his mouth with the paper napkin, took out his wallet, opened it, and pulled out two ten-dollar bills.

"I think I'll walk home."

"You're going to walk home?"

"That's what I said."

He slipped out of the booth and moved toward the door.

"I want to go with him," I said.

"I won't have you walking down the side of the highway," my mother said tightly.

"What about Daddy?" Phillip said.

"He's a grown man. If he wants to act like an idiot that's his business."

"You're going to just let him go?" I said.

I jumped up and ran after him.

"Jesse!" my mom yelled. "Come back here *now!*"

In the parking lot, the asphalt glittered and my dad was nearly to the foot of the Pizza Hut sign when I caught up with him. COME ON IN! was spelled out on the sign in removable black letters.

"Come back," I said. "She doesn't mean anything."

He looked at me and then down at his shoes.

"It's a beautiful night," he said.

It was true. The air was deep purple, and all around the parking lot, petals flew off the trees like confetti, banking on windshields and in little piles on the asphalt. I could see the blue light inside the bank across the street. He would be fine. No matter what happened he would be fine. I was more worried that rather than walk home, he'd start walking backward, hitchhiking like Guy, and then we'd never see him again. To me, my dad was on loan to us, and sooner or later we'd have to return him like a library book. What would happen to us when we lost him? That was the real question.

"You won't come back in?" I said.

He shook his head.

"I'll see you at home."

I turned back toward the Pizza Hut. A black dog slept on the backseat of a station wagon next to a stack of old newspapers. The dusk-to-dawn lights flicked on, and inside the restaurant I heard Cat Stevens singing "Peace Train."

+

All the way home, my mom drove like a maniac, switching lanes without signaling and driving up on the shoulder. She'd had just about all she could take of our father. He was a man-child, and she was fed up with his selfishness and immaturity. She was at 3 moving fast toward 2. During 3 she ranted and it was, to be honest, sort of amusing, but at 2 she got quiet and a desperation set in that was unbearable.

When we got home my mom went directly to Julie's duplex. I ran Phillip's tub and told him to wash the pizza sauce off his chin. When he got out, he begged to sleep in my bed and because both my parents were gone and the duplex felt, even to me, a little spooky, I let him. I got the extra blanket from the hall closet, the plaid one with the silky edge, and the bedspread with the ink stains that had been my dad's in seminary, and made myself a bed on the floor. He told me how he and Eddie had had a fight over Spiderman's superpowers. Eddie said Spiderman had the web spray and could climb up walls but that was it, while Phillip believed Spiderman could also think like a spider. The fight had ended badly, with Eddie throwing dirt clods.

After that he fell asleep. Phillip was famous for sleeping, having once leaned over the arm of a sofa and fallen asleep in an upside down U-shape with his butt in the air. But his allergies made him snore and the floor was hard. Dad was probably gone for good, run away with a lady from his dream group. What kind of job could my mother get with just a high school education? I wasn't stupid. I knew why so many duplex complexes were going up along the highway. Families were breaking up like crazy and they had to have split houses for the half families to live in.

My heart throbbed and I felt sweaty under my T-shirt. I tried to settle myself down by going through burial rites: the laying of coins on the dead's closed eyes, the filling of their mouths with instant rice. You might think this would be creepy, but at times like this, the only thing that calmed me was thinking of a Dylo woman carefully washing down the body of a dead person with a sea sponge soaked in goat's milk.

✦

The High Style Dance Academy was behind the Citgo gas station over the town line in Salem. My mother drove me around the gas pumps and a pile of tires to the aluminum building. On the drive over she talked about what a great opportunity it was that Julie was letting me take lessons for free. I was sick to my stomach and had the beginnings of one of my headaches. While I worshipped dancers, my relationship to dance was complicated. At the elementary school talent show every year, no matter which school I was in, mothers brought in glittering costumes covered in dry cleaner plastic and certain girls got to perform on the stage in the gym. A girl named Amber had danced so passionately to "Rockin' Robin" in an aquamarine leotard and black fishnet tights that she got overheated and threw up. For months though, vomit or not, she ruled the playground, teaching us the routine. In Philadelphia, the music teacher had asked me and another girl to do an interpretative dance while the guitar choir played "Morning Has Broken." This had more to do with how terrible I was on the guitar than any talents I had for dancing. I think the teacher figured that there was no way I could be a worse dancer than I was a guitar player.

The other girl was a doctor's daughter with long blonde hair, a ballerina who often got out of school early to perform at nursing homes. A week before our performance, I went to her house to choreograph and practice our act. In her living room she put the Cat Stevens record on the stereo and explained to me what she had in mind. She wanted us to *slowly* lift our left legs, then *slowly* lift our arms, then *slowly* turn our heads up to the gymnasium ceiling. *Pretend your arm is full of cotton. Concentrate only on your leg, your leg is the only leg in the entire universe!* I tried to move my arm as slowly as possible. After it became clear I was hopelessly clumsy, she got sullen. At the dress rehearsal, with both of us in white leotards with white scarves tied around our foreheads, I messed up so badly on the leaps, crashing into a music stand, that afterward she wouldn't even speak to me. The next morning I wrapped my foot in an Ace bandage and told the music teacher that I couldn't go on because I'd sprained my ankle.

That should have cured me of my fascination with dance. But I was like a member of a spaceship cult: when the spaceship does not come, a few members quit, but the core group is more sure than ever that the mother ship will come.

"I guess this is it?" my mother said, pulling into the dance-school parking lot.

She was teary-eyed, a 4 moving into a 3 because I was finally going to gain the grace I needed to enter the World of Rich People. My mother was ambitious for me, but she saw my future only in terms of whom I would marry. Her parents—a housemaid and a chauffeur—had spent their careers in service to the rich and, while she had not fulfilled their hopes, there was still the chance that I would marry money.

She parked the station wagon in front of the dance studio and squeezed my arm. She thought she was looking at me deeply, but I knew her eyes had flipped and she was gazing inside her own head to some old memory. Before she could speak I told her I would meet her outside afterward.

Inside, girls chattered to one another as they hung their coats on hooks and slipped off painters' pants and corduroys and traded clogs for ballet slippers. This was a jazz class, rather than ballet, so the leotards were in every color. One girl wore multicolored leg warmers and a few had on headbands. I recognized several faces from my junior high, but most of the girls were from the high school.

I followed the other girls into a cavernous room floored with gray linoleum. The walls were covered with white wood paneling and posters, one of a tiny girl in a tutu that read DREAM at the bottom and another of giant toe shoes. On the wall that surrounded the window into Julie's office were photographs of recitals from earlier years: groups of girls in sequined outfits with wide, intense smiles.

Julie was at the rail by the mirror, her leg up on the barre, her pale arms bent forward so I could see the back of her long, elegant neck. She didn't look up or smile at the girls, who all seemed to know to sit on the floor with their legs spread wide and stretch. Everyone was limber enough to lay their bodies down against their legs. I could lean forward only slightly. There was still a good ten inches between my chin and the floor. I hoped nobody would notice.

The girls moved sideways, a few did splits. One girl, limber as a wet noodle, leaned into a back bridge. The phone rang in the office, and Julie walked over and picked up the receiver. She glanced at me, so I knew it was my mother calling, already checking up on me. She laughed, hung up, and walked over to where I sat on the floor, squatting down beside me. Soon I felt the pressure of her fingers against the bones of my spine,

and I straightened my back and strained to move closer to the ground. I thought of Jill's shoulders. I knew
nobody wanted a girl with a hunchback.

✦

Every time Julie came to visit my mom, I was sent
over to play with Kira. She did not take dance lessons at her mom's school, she told me, because she
didn't like to sweat. At first, I'd tried to get Kira to do
the things I'd done with Jill. She could be Barnabas
Collins and I could be Victoria Winters. Or I said I'd
teach her the bump or the hustle. But no matter what
activity I suggested, Kira got grumpy and red-faced
before we even started, and said she wanted to quit.
Then she retreated to her spot under the canopy of
her bed with her rabbit on her lap like a girl in a sad
storybook.

One night in January, when the air had warmed
enough for me to wear just a sweater, Kira let me in
and I followed her into the living room where she was
watching *Starsky and Hutch*. Beside her on the couch
was a saucer with a nibbled carrot and a limp lettuce
leaf. I could tell by her sour look she was planning on
turning down any game I suggested. She stroked the
whole length of Snowball's furry body. But tonight I
had an idea that she would not refuse.

"I'll be Patty," I said, "and you can be the girl with
the short black hair."

Patty Hearst's trial had just started and footage of her robbing the Hibernia Bank was playing again on the television.

"I want to be Patty," Kira said.

Kira, Patty? Impossible! I had all Patty's moves down. I'd locked myself in the bathroom to practice, putting on my dad's long trench coat and holding Phillip's BB gun, shuffling jerkily and moving my head around, then stretching out my arm and glancing at my wristwatch. The watch glance was a motion I wanted to get just right, so I'd repeated the sequence at least a hundred times, pushing out my arm, then bringing it closer and tipping my head.

"I want to be Patty," Kira said again.

"I see you more as a character actor," I said. "What about the security guard?"

"Patty or nothing."

I really wanted to be Patty and act out the bank robbery. It's a hard feeling to explain—wanting to act something out. I used to have it all the time. I wanted to play mommy and baby dolls, I wanted to be the cat who marries the chihuahua. But that was a long time ago. Lately, I felt the urge only occasionally, but when it came, like now, it was powerful. I watched Kira stroke Snowball. She wore a candy-cane-striped nightgown with eyelet at the cuffs. I'd known other unplanned kids, like Jill, for instance. But Kira was the most extreme case I'd ever seen. Not only had she been conceived by accident, but her mother seemed to feel she was an accident still. I decided to do the *Christian thing*, as Mrs. Smith was always saying. But I had to get a little something out of it.

"I'll let you be Patty if I can hold Snowball?"

Kira looked at me with interest. Until that moment she had not realized I was a ruthless negotiator. I knew she did not want me to hold Snowball. Whenever I asked, she always gave some excuse: Snowball had a cold. Snowball was suffering from a bout of nerves and had twitched all night with flashback nightmares of the German shepherd and the snake. Snowball was her binky, her blanket, and her nightlight all mixed up together. I sat slowly on the edge of the couch to show how gentle I could be.

"OK," she finally said, "but don't squeeze him."

I picked up Snowball, surprised at how loose he was, as if he were filled not with bones and organs but with water. He sniffed my hand and I started to pet him, moving my hand dreamily through his fur.

Kira clomped upstairs. I heard her overhead in her mom's room opening drawers. After a few minutes she ran down the stairs and burst through the doorway wearing a black beret and a long coat, and carrying a bent clothes hanger. I was impressed with her getup.

"Stick 'em up!" she yelled.

Snowball twitched and struggled. I clamped down with my hand on his back and he swung around and bit my thumb. I was so surprised I let him loose and he took a flying leap off the couch and ran under the stereo console.

"Now look what you've done!" Kira wailed.

There was no blood, just tiny teeth marks on the pad of my finger.

Kira knelt beside the console and tried to reach him, but her arms were too short. She sat back up and got his favorite storybook, about a bunny mother and her little bunny baby. She lay flat on her stomach, reading to him and showing him the pictures. Snowball was unresponsive. We played him records, Elton John and Kris Kristofferson, but it wasn't until the B side of the Marvin Gaye album that the rabbit hopped out from under the console and hesitantly sniffed Kira's SLA coat.

+

By the end of January, I had learned the full routine to Elton John's "Philadelphia Freedom." In class on Saturday mornings, Julie never corrected me in front of the others. She just moved near, using her hands to reposition my knee or elbow. She kept me after class every week and broke down the flick kick and the jazz drag, the snake and the layout. After she helped me, she turned off the lights and locked the door and I walked with her across the parking lot to her car.

Julie moved with her back straight, her skirt floating around her knees. Inside she let me pick an eight-track from her case; I always chose Cher. So far on the drive home we'd talked about LA, Mexican food, Peggy Fleming skating to "Ave Maria" in blue light, the pros and cons of mascara. She sipped from a thermos filled with white wine and when a song came on that she liked, she sang along loud.

In the dashboard light Julie's face was greenish and I could see how she filled in her eyebrows and dusted glitter on her cheekbones. She lit a cigarette and blew smoke out the window. Like my mom, Julie drove fast, sometimes even blowing through red lights. The strip-mall windows reflected the car, as if we were racing a ghost.

✦

Maybe I was crazy, but when I locked the bathroom door and practiced the pivot step and catwalk over the tile floor, sometimes throwing in a few Patty wristwatch glances, I thought I looked good. I was, as they said, developed now. Everything was more or less where it was supposed to be. Sometimes I'd talk to my reflection, saying *Hey, foxy lady* or *Hey, hot mama.*

Mostly, though, I'd move in the mirror like I was Julie's daughter. Whereas Kira was a hopeless case, Julie could be proud of my grace and composure. We'd go to the Brasserie in the French Quarter, get our hair trimmed at the UpperCut, then shop for lace underwear.

In mid-February, Julie dragged the cardboard box out of her office and passed out our costumes. I held the bag on my lap as we drove home after class. Julie didn't want to chat; she was preoccupied. During class she'd gotten one of the older girls to lead while she retreated into her office to talk on the phone and sip wine from her thermos.

"Tell your mother I can't make it tonight," Julie said as she dropped me off. As I walked up the sidewalk to our front door, Julie turned the car around in a wide, jerky U-turn and headed back out of Bent Tree.

Inside, my mom was all set up as usual with her cheese plate, *The Music Man* on the stereo, wearing her best fifties shirtwaist dress. When I told her, her eyes filled up with water. She was a 4 going down into a 3. Maybe I should make an excuse for Julie to comfort my mom, but I was sick of her misery being at the center of every moment. I was well on my way now to making my own glittery and glamorous life.

I ran upstairs into the bathroom, locked the door, and tore the plastic off my costume. The color was neon red with one long sleeve sewn with navy sequins. The other side was sleeveless, a daring design but one I considered fantastic. I pulled down the leotard I'd worn to class. I had hairs now down there but I was still so skinny my ribs stuck out. I pulled on my costume, and I have to admit I was starstruck. I'd had Halloween costumes, the bumblebee hand-me-down from a girl at church and a princess one my mom had made for

me. But this was my first for the stage. My exposed
arm looked pale against the red, but I hoped that, like
a space suit, the Lycra would propel me into another
dimension.

I looked at my reflection carefully. Did this girl
have that special something? Was this girl ready to
begin her slow climb to stardom? I adored the way
the girl in the mirror did the snake, jerked forward
into a lunge, checked her watch a few times, and
then froze, grinning into her reflection like her life
depended on it.

✦

Usually Julie had left for her studio by the time I got
home from school, but one day I came in the door to
see her and my mom on the couch together, two bottles of wine on the coffee table between them, both
flushed and serious. Julie's eyes were red and she
held a clump of tissues in her hand.

"Is jazz canceled?" I asked.

She didn't answer me, just put her hands over her
face and gave a loud, dramatic sob.

Phillip stood in the kitchen with the fridge door
wide open. My mom had promised to go to the store
while we were at school and get chips and Little
Debbie cakes.

"Is there anything to eat?" he asked, slamming the
door and opening the cupboards.

"How should I know?" my mother said.

We glanced at each other. It was like he'd asked for food from a stranger who happened to be visiting our house.

Phillip rolled his eyes, grabbed a can of Coke, and went up to his bedroom. I got out the cocktail crackers. There were a few at the bottom; I decided to eat them with margarine, preparing them slowly as if I were the queen and the crackers my subjects.

"My life is shit," Julie said, struggling to get the words over her tongue and out of her mouth.

"That's not true," my mother said, grabbing her hand.

"I lost my house!" Julie said. "And look at my daughter!"

Julie picked up the bottle of wine and poured what was left into her own mug. I opened a kitchen drawer and they both looked up at me with the same distant, loony expression.

"Don't you have homework?" my mom said.

I nodded and started up the stairs, the crackers on a Pyrex plate and a jelly glass of cold milk in my hand. I set the plate and the milk on the top step and walked down the hall to my parents' room where Phillip was lying on the bed watching the small black-and-white TV that sat on the dresser. I opened my bedroom door and slammed it hard so they would think I was inside.

I sat in my usual eavesdropping spot at the top of the stairs. All I heard was Julie crying softly over the noise of the needle hitting the end of the record. Julie told my mom how the school had called to say that Kira had fallen while carrying her tray in the cafeteria. When Julie picked her up Kira was fine but had food all over her dress, even in her hair. I put a cracker in my mouth, let the margarine melt against my tongue.

"How will she ever make it?" Julie said. "Every girl needs a certain amount of grace."

"She's just in an awkward phase," my mom said.

"You really think so?"

"With your genes she's bound to snap right out of it."

"I guess you're right," Julie said. "It's not like your daughter has much to work with either."

I set the milk down on the carpet and looked very hard at the strands moving this way and that around the base of the jelly glass.

My mom laughed. *She laughed.* And said if they ran out right that minute they could get to the Hunting Hills open house and see both the one with the cathedral ceilings and the one with the veranda off the master bedroom. I walked into my room, threw myself down on the bed, and lay there with my face pushed into the quilt.

I'd never claimed to be beautiful. I wasn't stupid enough not to see that my arms and neck were much too long for my body. My head seemed to hang over my shoulders like a wobbly marionette. My eyes were gray-blue. Unremarkable. Dirty-blonde hair. There was nothing about me you could really call attractive. I had always known this in a vague way. But now I knew for sure.

✦

That night I slept in my clothes, and in the morning I didn't change or shower. I just got on the bus wearing the same outfit. This was a sort of small-time suicide. "Didn't you wear that same thing yesterday?" Sheila asked me in homeroom. Rather than answer I grabbed her wrist and twisted her skin into an Indian handshake. Sheila's face got red and she called me a *stupid bitch*. My English teacher's reading of an Emily Dickinson poem made me sick. The way she overarticulated each word felt like a knife stabbing me in the eye. I called the Belle of Amherst a morbid bitch under my breath and got sent to the principal. Lucky for me he wasn't there; he was probably off at the smorgasbord restaurant in Salem eating a huge plate of potato salad.

I just sat in a chair, waiting and watching the secretaries move around the office like fish in an aquarium. The dark-haired one answered the phone and told parents about teacher conferences. The red-haired one told the others about a burger, fries, and soda special at McDonald's, and the oldest lady, with the bouffant, said, "I don't know how you girls keep your figures." The principal called to say he was held up.

The gray-haired secretary told me it was my lucky day, I was free to go.

I didn't go back to class. I wandered out to the smoking block. Dwayne leaned against the building with the heel of his Dingo boot propped up against the brick wall. He was talking to one of the dirtbag girls.

"Well, look what the cat dragged in!" he said.

Through the oblong window I saw a teacher with a terrible haircut standing in front of his class. I saw the backs of kids' heads. Round my feet were cigarette butts and in the sky a warmthless sun. I watched a small beetle crawl over the asphalt and when it got near me I reached my leg out and killed it with my tennis shoe.

✦

That night my mom set out the cheese and crackers and was dressed as usual. I went right to my room. Now I was giving *her* the silent treatment. She didn't notice. She just ran to the door whenever she heard a car on the street.

It wasn't until late in the night that Julie finally came back. I watched her from my bedroom window, falling out of her car and wobbling down the stairs of her duplex on her high heels. When she got to her front door she rooted around in her pocketbook for keys. I heard our door slam and saw my mom run over to Julie.

Julie looked at my mom like she did not know her, then her face twisted up and she must have said something mean, because my mom spun around, ran across the dirt, and came back to our house.

I heard her crying in the bathroom. But really, why should I feel sorry for her? She was a 3 moving to a 2. I was fed up with her. I'd spent most of my childhood trying to cheer her up, and now I was exhausted. So exhausted I could not sleep. No matter which way I turned, my back was stiff and my eyes speedy and wide open.

I heard my mother go into the bedroom and yell at my dad, who was in bed, as usual, reading. My mother screamed at him and my father came rushing out of the bedroom, ran down the stairs, and walked over to Julie's duplex. I ran out onto the front yard, barefoot in my long T-shirt. The grass was cold under my feet and the stars above were like specks of ice.

Julie swung open her door wearing a pale-pink nightgown and holding a glass of white wine.

"How dare you talk to my wife like that?"

"This is between the two of us, pastor."

She spit out the last word, as if it were a curse.

"You're a wreck," my dad said, grabbing her glass and flinging the wine out on the sidewalk.

"You're the wreck," Julie said, furious now, coming at my dad and pointing her finger into his chest, "with your dream-therapy bullshit."

My father's face stilled; my mother must have told Julie, complained to her, about his spiritual floundering.

She put her hands on her hips.

"Clean up your own mess, pastor," Julie said, "before you tell me to clean up mine."

My dad swung back around toward our duplex.

"In the house, Jesse," he said to me. "Now!"

✦

My dad was downstairs smoking his pipe; I could smell the sweet tobacco. He didn't want to talk. He'd told me to go to my room where I now lay staring up at the ugly overhead lampshade with the black dots of dead bugs. I felt like I was in a fairy tale that was running backward, like in school when the teacher wound the film strips the wrong way. The church with the eternal light on the dark altar, the expanse of grass between the church and rectory, my room with the diamond-pane window, and the deep organ chords moving into my room and around my bed, that place and time was a sort of heaven—the end, not the beginning, of the fairy tale. Ever since we'd been thrown out, our life held no purpose; it was like riding in a driverless bus, careening ever closer to the guardrail. I'd had enough. I was getting off.

I loaded a pair of corduroys, my smiley face T-shirt, a sweater, several pairs of underwear, and the *Big Book of Burial Rites* all in my black patent-leather suitcase.

This wasn't the first time I'd run off.

At six, when I'd heard we had to leave our first rectory, I'd packed up my dolls in this same suitcase and run to an old barn on the church property. At eight, after hearing we had to move again, I'd run to my friend's house. Even though her family was not home, I spent six hours waiting in their backyard. In Philadelphia, when my dad first told us we were moving to Virginia, I'd set out with my school backpack full of apples to the graveyard at the end of our block. I planned to wait until my parents and brother moved, and then I would sneak back into the house and sleep on the wicker furniture on the side porch.

The other times I didn't have a plan, but this time I intended to hitchhike to New York City. If I couldn't find any other job, I figured I could always work as a prostitute. Maybe I wasn't beautiful, but I was young, and I knew that, as sick as it was, creepy guys liked young girls to tickle them with feathers.

✦

I dropped my suitcase out the window. Unfortunately the lock gave and my clothes scattered over the grass. I crept down the stairs. Phillip stood in the kitchen in his pajamas staring into the fridge. In the dark, the radiating light made him look divine.

"Where are you going?" he said, letting the door suck shut; the light extinguished and he was my brother again.

"For a walk," I said. I wanted to be candid with him, but it was too risky. Nothing would sabotage my freedom.

"Now?"

"I need some air."

"Can I come?"

"You go back to bed."

"What about the guy who eats little kids' fingers?"

"I'll take my chances."

"Remember you promised if you ever ran away you'd take me with you."

"I'm just going out for a walk."

He headed up the stairs with his handful of Oreos. I felt bad about lying to him now, but I'd come back and break him out too once I got settled someplace.

Outside it was chilly, the grass crosshatched with frost. Light moved at a slower pace at night, outlined objects in silver-lavender. I ran around the side of the house and gathered my clothes back into my suitcase. A dog slept on an old ski jacket behind 2A, and Mr. Ananais's cat, Hector, looked up at me briefly, then put his head back on his paws on the window ledge.

I was trying to figure out what my new Social Security number should be; I knew I had to keep the first three digits the same, but I intended to change the rest and my name too. I was thinking of Veronica or Agnes. To be honest, I didn't want a name but a number, like 99 on *Get Smart*. I liked the sound of 72 and also 68. When I got to my crash pad in New York I would dye my blonde hair jet-black, like Cher's.

I wanted to run out of Bent Tree, but I knew that would look even more suspicious than the already suspicious fact that I was walking around at 2:00 AM. So I walked fast down the incline toward the highway saying good-bye. Good-bye, mountain with your dark pine trees and white-ridged mushrooms growing on dead trees in a way that was both cool and creepy. Good-bye, luna moth with the Mardi Gras–mask wings. Good-bye, Sandy's underwear drawer with the zebra-skin panties and blood-red lace bra. Good-bye, Snowball. Good-bye, Dwayne. Good-bye, Dwayne's chewing tobacco. Good-bye, fat lady in 15A who exercised in front of the TV on a bath towel. Good-bye, hoarding guy in 5B with newspapers piled up to the second-floor windows.

Hello, adventure!

+

I would have to walk along 419 for a while before I got to the 81 ramp. I'd decided it was too risky to catch a ride from anybody on that strip. How terrible would it be if my principal picked me up? Or Dwayne's dad on his way back from the bar? Not that many cars passed anyway.

When I finally heard an engine, I ran and hid behind the bushes on the little woodchip island in front of the Texaco gas station. I worried it was my dad driving around looking for me or, worse, the police. I decided to get off 419 and walk lot to lot.

First I crossed the lot in front of the Allstate Insurance building. It was like running up onto an empty stage. The asphalt glittered under the lights. Then a few yards of bare trees and on to another lot in front of the courthouse, then the lot in front of the post office. All the buildings, private or municipal, looked pretty much the same: two-story, nondescript structures in brick and glass. In the black glass I looked like a girl made of smoke. I would slip into the night and become one with everything, like my dad was always talking about. I'd be the same as a fern frond or a Styrofoam cup on the side of the highway.

I moved through another patch of woods into the lot of the Hardee's; then the Long John Silver's; then the McDonald's, almost to the highway ramp. The shining yellow-and-red building looked like a piece broken off from the sun. When I was five, a McDonald's had opened down the street from our rectory, and for a long time I thought it was the best place God had created, with the sweet fries and the strawberry milkshakes. I'd included it in my prayers, after my immediate family and before my grandparents.

When I was almost across the lot I heard a car moving behind me and ran for a bush in another woodchip island floating between the highway and the lot. The car slowed and turned. I was afraid it was my dad, his overcoat pulled over his pajamas. But as the car moved past, and I saw the teenagers in the front seat, I remembered that behind the McDonald's Dumpster was a path that led to a spot where kids laid down blankets and had sex. I clenched my fists and stuck my fingernails into the palms of my hands. The slight prick of pain reminded me that I was substantial, that I wasn't blowing away into the dark.

Finally I walked up the ramp.

Part of me wished my dad would come get me, but he was too preoccupied with whether the snake in his dream meant renewal because it shed its skin, or whether it meant he needed to face the evil side of his personality. Maybe I could run to Jill, we could paint our toenails, regroup, and then set off together. But though I wanted to see her, I had no idea where to find my friend. My dad had told me not to worry, that the universe would care for Jill, but I'd found, so far anyway, that the universe was not so reliable. *We are as much continuous with the physical universe as a wave is continuous with the ocean*, my dad read out to me. But I wanted to love Jill and have her love me back. I wanted people to love me and I wanted to love them back. I didn't want to give Jill over to the universe. I wanted to love her myself.

I looked down the highway, hoping that before too long a car filled with flower-power hippies would pick me up. They'd be long-haired, smiley, wearing floppy hats and love beads. They'd have names from nature, like Snapdragon, Leaf, Bear. They'd drop me off in New York City before heading upstate to their goat farm. I'd seen a lot of hippies on television but only a handful in Roanoke. When you did see them, because they were so rare, they looked out of place, as if you were hallucinating. Once I'd seen two girls playing tennis topless, hitting back and forth and laughing, their long hair swinging as they lunged for the ball.

But no hippies came. Only a few trucks and a white Cadillac. Out here, kudzu covered the trees and the air was cold. Nobody stopped. I sat on the guardrail and ate a few of my Fig Newtons, looking up at the tent caterpillar's old nests, spread gauzy white all over the trees. I thought of my family sleeping in their beds in the dark duplex. Phillip slept in the small room off my parents', a walk-in closet really, with just enough space for his twin bed. He slept sprawled out in his toolbox pajamas like a drunken sailor. My parents had spooned in the old days, my dad wrapped around my mom, but now they each stuck to opposite sides of the bed. My dad slept on his back, his head propped up with pillows in a way that seemed baronial. My mom slept on her side, her arms around a pillow, her face taut; even in sleep she was a 5 moving toward a 4. I thought of Kira and Snowball, of Julie in her silk sleeping mask and how Sandy slept with Noxema on her face. I even thought of my old unicorn girl, up above Bent Tree, curled on a soft patch of moss.

I wondered where I'd next lay my head. I had thought I could get at least to DC sometime after daybreak, but I'd obviously miscalculated. Maybe I should get off the highway and find a spot in the woods to sleep. I thought of the variety of crash pads available to a brave wayfarer like myself: the teepee, the geodesic dome, the shack constructed entirely of old car parts.

My shadow rose up in front of me and I turned to see a car coming around a curve. I regretted not having a sign like that guy we'd picked up when we first got to Roanoke. My sign could say RIDE WANTED BY FREE SPIRIT or NEW YORK CITY-BOUND. While I was thinking of this, the car pulled off the highway and I watched its lights through the woods till they disappeared and it was dark again by the guardrail. The stars overhead were both loud and silent.

I remembered Jill telling me a story about a hitchhiker her family had picked up, a skinny girl in a sundress. The girl was shivering so Jill's mom had lent her a sweater. She asked to be dropped off at a graveyard, saying her house was at the back. When her mom realized she'd forgotten to get the sweater back, she went back to the graveyard where she found it draped over the gravestone of a girl who had died the year before. I started to worry that maybe I was dead. That maybe my whole family was dead. That we'd died in a car wreck on the drive down to Virginia and that Bent Tree was actually limbo, that every single person in Bent Tree was dead. Or maybe that everybody else was alive and I'd died in my sleep; I was the ghost girl walking along the highway looking for a ride.

✦

I finally got a ride with an old man in a baby-blue sedan with a bobblehead dog in the back window and a pine tree air freshener hanging off the rearview. I lied and said my grandmother wasn't feeling well so I had to hitchhike back from a youth group meeting, a lame excuse but one he seemed to go for. I was worried about him trying to touch my thigh or ask me some obscene and terrible question about my private parts. But he was sweet, offering me a butterscotch candy and saying we didn't have to listen to his oldies station, we could switch to one with rock and roll. He told me his granddaughter was hoping to go to Africa on a mission for the Baptist Church.

"They live like animals over there," he said.

I knew this was not true from the missionaries who used to come to our rectory and show slides, but I decided not to say anything.

"How will she help them?"

He laughed.

"Tell them about Jesus for starters," he said.

Great idea, I wanted to say. *That's definitely going to help.*

He asked me what I thought of CB radios because he was thinking of getting one. I was disappointed that he was sort of ordinary. I watched his profile; his thick glasses reflected the dashboard light. Maybe I was supposed to strangle him and take his car to New

York City myself. It was evil, but then my life would finally have a trajectory. I looked down at my hands. Did they look like weapons?

"I need to get out," I said suddenly. "I can walk from here."

He would not let me off on the side of the highway, insisting on taking me to my "grandmother's house." I pointed to a big white colonial, thanked him, and jumped out, walking as quickly as I could around to the back. I stood in the dark yard beside the picnic table and sandbox. Inside I could see the glow off the back of the stove. I stood there thinking of sleeping underneath the picnic table. Then a light clicked on in an upstairs window and I watched a man walk to a crib and pick up a baby. I ran back up the driveway and toward the highway.

I was still nowhere near New York City. I passed a gas station and started back up the ramp toward 81. I looked into the trees. If I were in a story, now would be the time for my guardian angel to show. I was hungry, tired, and, most important, heartsick. The beautiful girl with white swan wings would give me advice. Or maybe it would be the unicorn girl with Jill's huge glittering eyes, wearing her puka beads, her horn changing colors with her emotions like a mood ring. Bright lights came up behind me and I turned, blinded by blues and whites.

✦

In the backseat of the big Plymouth patrol car, I cried so intensely snot ran out of my nose. The trooper handed me a box of tissues and glanced at me from under his wide-brimmed hat. The mountains were dark, a sort of deep blue-black that was darker than black and more mysterious. The trooper took off his jacket and passed it to me. I lay my head down on the seat and listened to his radio go on about a car accident in Lynchburg.

I cried because I didn't want to go back to Bent Tree, then I cried because my mom was always at 3 going down to 2 and also my dad was a space cadet, hanging off our life together like a man suspended from a window ledge. But after a while, the car moving along the highway calmed me and my eyes closed; I felt light, light enough that God could carry me around in a dream. I was at the old church standing on the lawn among my neighbors from Bent Tree. It was cold and everyone was bundled up in heavy coats with hoods. We were staring into the little woodshed that had always held the light-up nativity. But the figures of Mary, Joseph, the wise men, the cow, the camel, and the sheep were all missing. There was just the manger, a raw wood trough filled with straw. Everyone was angry because my dad, who stood beside the trough holding the plastic baby Jesus, could not get the baby to light up. He tried different things—fed the baby with a dropper, carried it around the barn three times one way and three times the other. *Let me hold it*, I said. At first my dad shook his head but eventually he handed the baby over. I cuddled the little thing to my chest and while it didn't light up completely, I saw, inside its chest, light showing murky and faint through the hard plastic.

"Miss!"

I sat up.

"You all right?"

"Yes sir," I said. We were heading up the mountain toward Bent Tree.

"You're taking me home?"

He glanced at me in the rearview mirror.

"I found a girl about your age in a ditch a few years ago."

"She was dead?"

He nodded.

"She was hitching just like you."

"I am never, ever, ever going to hitch again," I said. "I promise."

He turned his head to glance at me in the backseat. "You look like a smart kid."

"I am," I said. "I just lost my head this one time."

"If you swear to me you'll never do this again, I will leave your parents out of it."

"Thank you, sir," I said, relieved. "From now on I will be the most law-abiding person in the universe."

I tried to sound as sorry and believable as possible.

He let me out at the Bent Tree sign and I walked up the hill with my suitcase. Julie was asleep inside her car, her cheek pressed into the driver's side window. I crept past her, into my duplex, and moved slowly through the dark. What a joke. I couldn't even run away. In about a half hour my family would be up, Dad getting ready for work, my brother for school; they wouldn't even know I'd been gone. Even if I told them, I'd get accused, as I often did, of being melodramatic. Nobody would even believe me.

The couch, the lamp, the gold shag, even my dad's stack of books, looked strange and sad. In the duplex I lived in front of things, but outside, in the greater world, I could just be with them. The light coming on in the dream had snapped off. I was no longer connected to my family; the knot had come loose and I felt myself floating off.

I grabbed an apple from the kitchen and went up to my room. I couldn't be on the highway in daylight, so I'd have to wait until it got dark to try again. Next time I'd ride with truckers and when I saw any car that resembled a state trooper I'd hide.

I lay across my bedspread. Out the window, mist floated over the mountain; I imagined that a dinosaur's head could rise at any moment from the tree line and look around.

Julie was lying out on the sidewalk; she must have gotten out of her car and tried to walk to her duplex. She was all twisted up, her arms in a tangle underneath her, and I had a terrible feeling that she'd bumped her head and was dead.

✦

I woke my mom and she ran out and helped Julie inside. Though I pretended to have a stomachache, my mom made me go to school. On the bus Dwayne came over and sat in the seat behind me. "I was wondering when she'd fall off the wagon," he said. "That woman is the worst drunk in Roanoke!"

"How do you know?"

"Everyone knows," he said. "She dances up on the tables at the bar at the Fox's Den, and she got arrested for breaking every window of her boyfriend's house."

"She's not drunk all the time."

"She's drunk enough," Dwayne said. "And mean. She called my dad a cocksucker."

In school I kept nodding off through my first few periods. Then in algebra I put my head on my desk and fell asleep. The teacher woke me up and sent me to the nurse, where I lay down on one of the cots and slept. She woke me just in time for the bus.

I walked to the back, plopped into a seat, and bunched my jacket under my head. Dwayne ignored the fact that I'd closed my eyes and began talking to me as if our conversation from the morning had never ended.

"And she's a slut too," Dwayne said.

"Whatever you say."

"Whatever I say?" he said. "Just ask all the guys she's been with."

As I walked up the hill toward my duplex, I saw Kira standing out front in her yard.

"Snowball is sick!" she yelled at me.

I followed her up the stairs and she told me her mom hadn't even looked at Snowball. Kira had the lights off and the blinds drawn, a candle lit on the table beside the bed. Snowball lay on his side at the bottom of the cage, panting.

I knelt beside her.

"Rabbits hide their sickness," Kira said, "because they are at the bottom of the food chain."

Kira picked him up. Snowball's ears were indeed cold, and his head tipped to one side as if it were hard for him to keep even. There was a milky film over his eyes and, under the matted fur, his skin was blue. She plugged in a string of lights that she'd strung around his cage.

"He loves Christmas," she said.

She told me she'd stayed home from school just to care for him—already she'd spread out carrots and lettuce, held him in the steamy bathroom, let him sleep with her up on her bed. Every few hours he seemed to perk up, but then his head got wobbly again and the fur of his belly heaved up and down.

"If anything happens to him," Kira said, "I'm going to kill myself!"

I had an idea. I ran over to my room and got my tape player. In Kira's room I set up the player beside the cage. I pressed the button down and Cher's voice, thick as syrup, came out of the speaker. At first Snowball just lay there, but eventually he picked up his head and hobbled over to the side of the cage, leaning dreamily into the metal mesh.

✦

My mom was at a 4 moving toward a 3 as she spread foundation over my cheeks and put glitter on my eyelids. She'd insisted on doing my makeup. Eyeliner too, even false eyelashes that made my eyes look like they'd gotten lost and just ended up by chance on my face. She took out the small curlers and tried to comb the short strands into a ponytail. She told me Julie had dumped out every bottle of liquor into the sink. I wanted to say *big deal, big fucking deal*, but I just nodded. Why was I looking up to her, anyway? I remembered one night a few weeks earlier, I'd come down to find my mom and Julie playing Mystery Date, Julie teasing my mom for getting the Dud while she got the Dreamboat.

I wondered if I should tell her what I'd heard about Julie. I knew, no matter what I said, my mom would just get mad. I had not planned to tell her. I wasn't sure I wanted any of her hope on me. I knew my mom felt close to me when we did girl things together, like shopping or putting on makeup. But weren't these the exact things that got you started down the road to becoming a sex slave?

"Look at you," my mom said.

I turned to face the mirror and for a minute I did not recognize my features.

"You look beautiful."

Now she thought I was beautiful. She should make up her mind.

"I think you look pretty," Phillip said. He took my hand in his own and kissed the back of it.

At the high school auditorium the mothers were flushed and the little girls overwrought and heavily made up. All the outfits were red, white, and blue. The kindergarten tap class wore tiny sailor costumes, with white caps and big red ribbons on their tap shoes.

Kira sat backstage against the wall on a crate, reading a Nancy Drew mystery. I walked over to her. Snowball had been sick all week.

"How is he?"

"Not good," she said. "All day I had to feed him water with a dropper."

A Revolutionary War drumroll started up over the PA and a boy marched onstage in a tiny minuteman costume. He beat on the drum a few times before the red velvet curtain opened to show a giant American flag. Julie came out in a long white dress and welcomed the audience to the Bicentennial Revue. The tiny sailors shuffled to "You're a Grand Old Flag" while Julie stood by the side of the stage directing. As the girls got older, the outfits, while still patriotic, got skimpier. The advanced jazz class wore denim short shorts and red tube tops. The girls on pointe wore red, white, and blue tutus and pirouetted to "The Stars and Stripes Forever."

As we took our spots on the dark stage my heart roared in my ears. This was it; fairy dust would rain down and I'd change in an instant from the mess that I was into a Real Girl. Over the PA system the first few words of the Elton John song sounded distorted. I kept my eyes on the girl in front of me but got behind a step and then two and before long I heard my name hissed from the side of the stage. I looked into the curtain to Julie, her pale face floating in the dark like the wicked stepmother in *Snow White*. I'm not really sure what happened after that. I must have run for the stage door because the next thing I remember, I was walking in the cold drizzle down the highway, caught in a string of headlights. The expressions on the drivers' faces were mostly amused. I could feel the gravel beneath my ballet shoes. One car honked at me. A high school boy leaned out the window and yelled, "I've seen better heads on a glass of beer," then threw a wax cup at me. The lid flew off and ice hit my cheek. I wiped my lipstick off with the back of my hand and pulled off the red and blue feathers my mom had attached to the back of my head with hair spray and threw them into the ditch by the side of the road.

✦

I assumed my family would be home when I got back to Bent Tree, but the car wasn't parked out front and the duplex was black. Julie's door was unlocked and I went right up the stairs to Kira's room. The tape player hissed and the Christmas lights hung around the cage. Inside Snowball slumped sideways against the mesh. I opened the door and reached in. His fur was warm, and when I got him on my lap I saw that his eyes had cleared. I got the dropper and squeezed water into his mouth, his small pink tongue sucking on the nib before he settled deep into my lap, and I ran my hand through his fur again and again.

✦

CHAPTER FOUR
SHEILA

I was not a 5 but a 6 moving toward a 5, and I decided before I dropped any lower I had to do something. Ninth grade was almost over. Before I finished junior high I had to get myself together. I did not want to end up stuck, anxious, miserable. I had to take myself in hand, not wait around, like my mother, for someone else to save me. I walked down to my personal cultural mecca, Loving Expressions Hallmark Cards, by the highway in a strip mall between the bathing-suit outlet and the Christian bookstore. In the back of the long rows of birthday and sympathy cards was a rack of magazines. That's where I found my three textbooks: *Mademoiselle, Harper's Bazaar*, and *Vogue*.

I studied the pages until my legs were numb. I finally bought a *Vogue* and brought it home, ripped out the pictures that captivated me—the way hair floated around a girl's face, the way the cloth clung to breast and waist. It was a phantom lightness, a haunting delicateness. From scrutinizing the pages, I narrowed down the types of women I was interested in emulating:

Natural: This species wore very little makeup and dressed casually, in peasant blouses, often with embroidery. They wore jeans and sandals from India and seemed to have a lot of picnics. While they never played instruments themselves, they often sat on the grass beside a man playing a guitar. In their spare time they filled terrariums with tiny plants and layers of colored sand.

Hippie: This type was related in genus to the Natural but was more extreme. They wore jeans with rainbows embroidered on the pockets, see-through eyelet blouses and halter tops, and leather platform sandals. While the Natural might not be having sex, the Hippie girl both had sex and smoked pot. She sometimes wore leather vests with fringe. I'd seen a few contenders at Jill's mom's parties.

Disco: These girls were smooth, with long shiny hair, and wore sleek nylon dresses with ruched sleeves in Prussian blue or dusty rose. They drank and sometimes snorted cocaine in the bathroom. They could be spotted only at night. On 419, the Quonset Hut disco was filled on the weekend with wannabe Disco Girls, but to see the genuine article you had to go to Maxim's or Studio 54.

Preppy: This was the only species I had seen up close. Once, in Tanglewood Mall, I'd observed a Preppy in her tennis outfit running into the Tennis Villa in the French Quarter to pick up her restrung racket. Outside of tennis whites, the Preppies wore cotton dresses in madras or bright green or pink. Preppy girls were closest to Good Girls. Good Girls did not have sex until they were married, and even then sex was a sacred event. Having sex was very meaningful to men who were having sex with Good Girls, almost like a church service. Sex with a Good Girl, unlike with a Disco Girl or a Hippie Girl, was never what I heard a boy in school describe as a "fuck fest."

Of course, even among these types there were endless variations and mutations. Older women had categories as well. Mrs. Smith with her cowboy scarf and bouffant hairdo was in a completely different category from the poor lady in 10B, who was shaped like a barrel, had only a couple of teeth, and wore her gray hair pulled back in a tight ponytail. At any age or within any variety, a woman could, as my mother said, "go to seed" and end up as a slut. Sluts, as far as I could tell, had only one category. That was why they were sluts—only one thing defined them.

I was not in danger of "going to seed" because I did not have any flowers. And it wasn't that I really aspired to be a Preppy or a Hippie, I just wanted that quality, ephemeral as it was, that I sometimes saw in photographs. Some called it femininity, others beauty, some said sexiness, but to me it was a form of magic.

Like a crazed scientist in search of the rarest butterfly, I might go mad in my search. I'd seen older women this had happened to. Roanoke was filled with them, in wigs or dyed blonde or red hair, eyebrows drawn in, lips lined. Bone-thin and taking awkward steps on wobbly high heels, they were like devotees of a religion that no longer existed. And while they were experts in the procedures and rituals of womanhood, the magic I speak of was no more likely to inhabit them than was a bolt of lightning.

I tried in a variety of ways to emulate the types I'd distinguished. I spent a few weeks wearing the peasant blouse Jill had given me and sitting out at lunch on the grass near the smoking block. Then for a period I wore a denim shirt my grandmother had embroidered for me, but instead of peace signs and rainbows, she'd sewn kittens on the collar and a baby in a bonnet on the back. In my glam-rock period, I ran into the bathroom right after I got off the bus and circled my eyes with black liner until I looked, as I heard a boy say in the hall, like a zombie. When I finally got the rust-colored nylon dress with the ruched sleeves off layaway at J. C. Penney, I was excited. The night before I wore the dress to school, I could hardly sleep, and as I walked down the hall, while there wasn't much of a reaction, I felt a little more real. I considered the look a hit until lunch, when a boy flipped up the hem while I was carrying my tray and exposed my big white panties. Preppy lasted the longest: a white Lacoste shirt and a pair of khakis.

I realized none of these measures moved me any closer to the other humans in my grade. I saw that my experiments had served only to make me seem odd and pathetic. I was at sea. My childhood was over. I'd pushed off from the Isle of Kidville and I was now in deep water, without any sign of Adultville in sight.

I decided I needed a role model, and I didn't mean my dad, who was on a health kick, drinking ten glasses of water a day and eating only stewed onions. I needed a girl to study and emulate. At Low Valley there were no Discos or Hippies, only girls in baseball shirts, clogs, and multicolored toe socks. I needed information not on the types in the greater world but on the types in my own world. I had always considered Cher my guru. My black-haired goddess. She instructed me sometimes through ESP, but now I needed somebody I could worship in the flesh.

Sheila was the obvious choice, as I could examine her on the bus to and from school; in my health class, where she sat a few rows over from me; and at lunch, where we sat at different ends of the same long table. For years she had been in a golden, untouchable realm that made making contact impossible. But just recently Dwayne had spotted Sheila's dad coming out of the gay bar on Williamson Road. This was not as unusual as it sounded. Nearly every month some father came out of the closet. The tiny girl on the gymnastic team had a gay dad. So did the chubby boy who'd worn lederhosen on Halloween. When your dad came out of the closet, your status didn't suffer outright. It was subtle. Sheila sat at the edge of the girls in her group in the lunchroom instead of in the middle. And while they had roamed Tanglewood Mall together every Saturday, now she walked alone.

But even with Sheila's dad being gay, there were no assurances she'd be my friend. I had a lot of work to do. Moving through the hallways, I listened carefully to her complain about hot rollers, saying that Herbal Essences shampoo smelled good but made her hair flat. I heard that round brushes were better than flat ones and that once you sprayed your hair, you should never ever comb it out, though the urge might be overwhelming.

Once my hair grew out of the dreaded pixie cut, I bought a set of hot rollers, and every day before school I got up at five thirty. First I washed my hair, then I did the blowout, finally rolling long strands around the hot curlers. I secured each with a metal pin. While I had the curlers in my hair, my head was heavy and hot, the hard plastic edges sticking into my scalp. After I took them out, I combed my hair and made a few adjustments with my curling iron. I'd burnt myself twice, on both the wrist and hairline, each scar shaped like a beetle. At first I made the mistake of using the smaller curlers in the front so my hair resembled that of one of the desperate-looking permed-hair girls who hung out on the smoking block. Another day I used so much hair spray that my hair was a solid block and smelled like cheap cologne. Whenever I caught a glimpse of my head, I judged my hair harshly. Flatness or dullness was like a splinter in my heart. My hair had a different agenda than my mind; it had ideas of its own.

After much practice I started to get it right. In the bathroom mirror, the height and shine were perfect, wavy but not too curly, and lush. Sometimes I felt like my hair was bigger than my body, that I was just a stick figure underneath a sheath of luxurious hair.

Once I'd mastered my hair I moved on to my clothing. I wore the same few items: a pair of corduroys, a pair of plaid pants, a white blouse or a green one, both with pointy collars, and—on cold days—a green acrylic sweater. My mother, trying to help me, bought me other items—a floral top and even a dress. I'd wear these once or twice, then revert back to my uniform.

Occasionally, someone made fun of me for wearing the same thing every day, but mostly my clothes seemed to make me invisible.

In Phase Two of Project Improve, I started keeping track of what Sheila wore every day in the back of my

221

social studies notebook. I had a chart with clothing items on one end, days of the week at the top. She sometimes wore the same corduroys in one week, but never on consecutive days, and she never wore the same top in a single week. She wore only brand-name pants, Lee or Levi's, which stabilized her outfits. It was important, I learned from her, not to lean too much on any one of the acceptable looks.

It wasn't only clothes that I had to worry about. I also had to follow the accessory trends. Since I'd begun paying attention, there'd been a plastic belt fad, a color barrette fad, and a toe ring fad. These fads could not be dismissed, and not only did you have to participate in them, you also had to be at the right place inside the fad, not the trailblazer who showed up first in jeans with teardrop pockets or striped toe socks, but around the fifteenth or twentieth person. If you waited, you could be made fun of for jumping on the bandwagon. Then the items might actually hurt you instead of helping your status.

I was in a state of constant anxiety over how I would get the fad items I needed. Most recently, I'd seen a few girls, Sheila included, wearing oversize combs stuck into their painter-pants pockets. Though nobody said anything, I sensed this would be the next trend. I made the mistake of asking my dad while he was reading if he'd take me over to the drugstore to purchase one.

"To buy a red comb?" he asked.

I nodded.

"Why?"

"It's hard to explain."

"You're on your own then," my dad said.

So I walked in the rain down to Revco, only to find they didn't have large colored combs, just white ones. Though the white girls never admitted it, I knew the trend had started with the black girls wearing Afro combs in their back pockets. There were only a handful of black kids at Low Valley, living in old farmhouses on bits of land between gas stations and subdivisions; their families had been here long before the subdivisions and strip malls started to surround them. Though their numbers were small, they had a lot of power dictated by their fashion sense, which was, as far as I could tell, flawless.

It was important never to acknowledge that they were the source of the trends. To wear a white comb would be suicidal. So even though it was getting dark and freezing, I decided to walk up the highway to the next strip mall, which had a beauty-supply store. Several cars came so close to me that I had to jump against the guardrail, and my skin under my clothes was chilly and goose-pimpled. I was aware of how stupid it would be to die in search of a giant red comb. The store didn't have red, but they had yellow. I paid and walked out into the rain, ripped the package open, and stuck the comb into the side pocket of my painter pants.

✦

It wasn't only my hair and my clothes. I knew I also had to censor the things I said. I'd worn the same outfit throughout junior high, but I'd also carried around the *Big Book of Burial Rites* and a few times tried at lunch to begin discussions by asking people if they'd rather be buried or cremated. And it wasn't only in the lunchroom; in history I'd demonstrated Lido burial by lying out on the floor with my arms crossed over my chest and my face and feet covered with torn leaves I'd brought from home in a Ziplock bag. I'd tried out some of my dad's ideas, saying trying to define yourself was like trying to bite your own teeth and asking if anyone had heard of the Theosophical Society. For a period I also carried the unicorn girl notebook around and tried to tell the kids who had lockers near mine about the unicorn girl's antics. I had told a girl in my gym class that the mole on our teacher's upper arm looked like a flower bud.

Once I had my hair perfectly curled and my painter pants and cheesecloth shirt combination down, and I'd understood what it was OK and not OK to talk about (burial rites: no; television: yes), I decided I needed practice. To try to approach Sheila and her friends was too risky, so I selected for my dry run a group of girls who sat together at the front table at lunch. They were a clique of no-man's-land types, a few volleyball players and a girl who made her own clothes. They accepted me right away, even inviting me to a sleepover.

I arrived at the split-level, my black suitcase packed with a pair of cotton sweatpants and a pink T-shirt. We danced to 45s and made ice cream sundaes. I was doing well until later, when a girl lit a candle and said she wanted to tell ghost stories. None of the stories were new to me, but when the girls started to talk about Tilden Lake I felt myself heading into the danger zone. I held my tongue until I could no longer control myself.

"When a child dies in the Vinto tribe, they wrap it in leaves and send it down the river in a basket woven from dried flower stems."

The girls stared at me; now I had their attention. I wondered if I should move on to the later chapters, which deal with contemporary burial rites, embalming, and cremation.

"And exactly why are you telling us this?" the chubbier of the volleyball players asked.

"Last year in civics she went on so long Mrs. Reynolds had to tell her to stop, that she was making us all sick."

"I'm sorry," I said, "sometimes the oddest things come out of my mouth."

One girl whispered into the other's ear and then they both laughed.

I'd blown it. It was going to be a long night.

✦

So I was back to square one. Clothes and hair were simple compared to conversation. Talk hovered around boys, eye shadow, and KC and the Sunshine Band. All the girls thought KC was adorable, but a few also thought he looked gay. Every subject had to be current. You couldn't talk about foot-binding or Abigail Adams, or how candles were made of animal fat. These were in history and considered weird. Also no talking about whether communism was better than capitalism or if there could be a planet out there identical to our own. Even simple philosophical questions—*Do cats have imaginations? What is the greater significance of déjà vu?*—should be avoided.

The best topics were something you'd seen on television, particularly *Welcome Back, Kotter*, or *The Carol Burnett Show*, or maybe something funny one of the DJs on WROV said. You could say anything you wanted about your morning hair preparation or how annoying your mother was. You could talk about movie stars and hippies, and if you acted removed, you could also mention suicide, sex, and civil rights, but your tone had to be disapproving.

At night I stuck my radio underneath my pillow and listened. I had noticed that with my eyes closed, the songs made colors underneath my lids: "My Love Is Alive" a silvery blue, and "Fame" a sort of magenta. Bowie songs were the best, making not just a single color but a whole spectrum of silver, blue, and purple light. But it wasn't just the notes that were like shining beads; every noise—the rain against the window, the car tires on the main road, even my dad's snoring—swirled into a kaleidoscope of sound and light.

✦

I'm not sure why he asked me to come to the VA hospital with him. My dad needed help, he said, with a play a few of the veterans were putting on. I had been to the VA before to drop him off. It was a huge three-story brick building with steep stairs up to the front doors. If the weather was warm there was always a handful of men in wheelchairs out front. Often some guy yelled out a third-floor window.

Inside the VA my dad was loose-limbed and happy, very different from how he was at home, where he was always lying on the couch, reading. The play, he told me, was based on an oral history project he'd been working on. He took down the men's stories and typed them up. By telling their stories the men were supposed to get control over their symptoms. The common room, where the play would take place, was already filled with a dozen men. The walls were painted bright blue, and there were vinyl couches against either wall, a wood console television, two strips of fluorescent overhead light, and a cardboard box cut into a trench, pasted with green construction-paper foliage.

Louie, my dad's favorite, wore, besides his rain boots, gray pants with large side pockets and a khaki jacket buttoned up to the neck. A red felt cross was sewn on his armband.

"You're late!" he said.

"I'm sorry, Louie."

"Do you smell burnt rubber?"

"No, Louie," my Dad said. "Nothing is burning."

There were a few men in wheelchairs, one young man was missing both legs, and another had a fleshy stub sticking out of his shirtsleeve.

A guy on the couch jumped up.

"We're making a movie!" he said.

"It's a play, Richie," my father said, "and you're in it. You're Stretcher Carrier Number Three."

Richie nodded. He stood too close to me, and I could smell the scrambled eggs with hot sauce he'd had for breakfast.

"I'm having a problem," Louie said to my dad. "I need to talk to you privately."

The two of them went into the corner. My dad put his hand on Louie's back. I watched a nurse walk down the hallway carrying a tray covered with paper cups.

My father came back.

"Louie is upset."

I glanced over at him; he seemed to be wandering around in a small circle.

"He'll act, but he doesn't want to say the lines."

The four men who were going to carry the stretcher all sat together on one couch. They all wore khakis and white T-shirts with red cross armbands.

"Where's Tom?" my dad asked.

"He's not coming," the youngest of the stretcher carriers said. "He doesn't like his part."

"Was he a Nazi?" I asked.

"No," my dad said, "he was going to play a wounded soldier."

My dad glanced at the clock on the wall; in just ten minutes hospital staff and a few visitors would be arriving to watch the performance.

"Listen up, everybody," my dad said. "It's getting close to time. We need one more actor."

Richie jumped up.

"Fuck all of you!" he said. "This is bullshit."

My dad had told me some of the men were easily angered. I knew too that while the younger nurses loved my dad's ideas, the older ones worried that his play might upset the patients.

"Will you do it?" my dad asked me.

"Sure."

He got me a white lab coat and wrapped my head with an Ace bandage.

"All you have to do is lie on the floor and wait."

Louie moved closer to me. He had a round face; his pupils were dilated and his forehead was shiny with sweat. My dad told me he had seen a lot of people die in the war, that he had terrible insomnia and sometimes cried for hours at a time. He reached his hand out to me; he had only a pinkie and a thumb.

"Don't worry," he said, "we're going to patch you up."

People gathered and my dad narrated the story of Louie running through the water on D-day up onto Omaha Beach, and scratching out a hole to lie down in to protect himself from bullets.

I lay on the cool linoleum staring up into the light and moaning.

"Aid man!" my dad yelled.

As he called out the numbers one through four each man took his place on the sides of the stretcher. Louie cupped my head and moved me onto the canvas. I was lifted up and carried through the audience and out into the hall.

✦

It wasn't until April, when all the fire hydrants in town were painted to look like tiny freakish minutemen, that I got the courage to actually speak to Sheila. I'd had a dream the night before that she and I were holding hands and singing John Denver songs. I would ask her if we were going to have our hygiene quiz in health today. I knew it wasn't until Friday, but I thought this was the best way to make contact.

My plan was to stop and ask about the quiz as I walked to get rid of my trash in the cafeteria. My hair looked good, and I wore my beige corduroys and a gauze blouse that had been Jill's, along with a leather bracelet stamped with roses. The problem was that between me and Sheila was a wasteland of chubby band girls and a whole pack of sixth-grade boys with huge eyebrows and gigantic feet. Then there was Pam, the birthmark girl from my bus, who was reading a fat biography of Eleanor Roosevelt while spooning fried rice out of a Tupperware container into her mouth. The beige foundation she used to cover up her birthmark just made her look pathetic. None of the others were likely to say anything to me, but Pam often tried to start a conversation when I passed, telling me that Mrs. Roosevelt was so serious as a child, her mother had called her Granny. Sometimes I toyed with the idea of talking to Pam, but I was only holding on by a thread myself and I couldn't risk any interaction.

I got up and kept my head down to dissuade Pam from speaking to me. All went well partly because I'd practiced in my room the night before. As I came near, Sheila turned her head and spoke into her friend Heather's ear. My timing was off, so I passed by, threw my garbage in the trash can on top of a half-eaten hamburger and empty milk containers. On the way back I paused near where they sat, and Sheila looked up at me, but my vocal cords constricted and I just stood there until she shrugged at her friends and went back to telling them how her curling iron wasn't heating up the way it was supposed to.

+

On the bus ride home, I decided to shoot for a less glamorous guru. Sheila sat a few seats in front of me; even after a long day at school, her hair fell perfectly on her shoulders and she smelled like powdered sugar. Her aura was so wide and thick I would have needed a chain saw to cut through. I decided to consider second-rung gurus, such as the drill team captain. She sat with a few drill team members at a middle table in the cafeteria, and as I got off the bus, I made a resolution. The next day I would sit, if not beside her, at least a few chairs down.

Sheila got off the bus first, as always, and was walking over Mr. Ananais's lawn. I was already halfway up the hill when I heard Sheila say my name. I turned, waiting for her to call me a lezzbo, but instead she asked if I wanted to watch *General Hospital*. I knew she was asking because Heather, who had always ridden the bus home with her before, didn't anymore, not since everyone found out that Sheila's dad was gay. No matter the reason she'd asked me, I almost blacked out with joy. It was all I could do to act like it was no big deal. Too much enthusiasm left you open to ridicule. I'd seen what the other kids had done to Pam when she talked about Eleanor Roosevelt.

I followed Sheila to her unit along the main road. All the units in her stretch had trees in the yard, and the large boxwoods were well manicured thanks to

Mr. Ananais's electric hedge clippers. He'd told me that when these units had been built, the owner had been flush and so each had a room-to-room intercom and a wet bar.

Inside Sheila's unit, the couch and chairs were pale pink. The glass-top coffee table sat on a white area rug and on top, like a cherry on a sundae, sat a conch shell. Over the couch was a painting of a lighthouse. The ocean motif was carried out on pillows printed with starfish. The room was as dust-free and uncluttered as a model room in a furniture store. No photos of her dad or her family before her parents split up. No photographs at all, only a white vase filled with sea oats and a crystal candy dish shaped like a clamshell.

Our duplex smelled of tennis shoes and pipe smoke. There were always dishes in the sink, unfolded laundry on the couch. Whenever I walked past the living room, my dad, who could sit still for hours, would look up, his pupils like blots of ink, and read something trippy out of his book. *The game is not about being someone, it's about being no one.*

But at Sheila's everything was perfect. Even the kitchen, which had our same avocado stove and refrigerator, had been softened by the creamy toadstool cookie jar and the pale-yellow dish towels. Sheila pulled out a real plate, not a paper one with a wicker holder like the ones we used, and shook crackers out of the box and squirted Cheez Whiz on each one. She told me to get Tabs out of the refrigerator. We set the couch cushions against the coffee table, the plate between us, and got ready to watch *General Hospital*.

So far I hadn't explained how, in ancient times, people thought birds migrated to the moon. I hadn't farted, though at one point I smelled cinnamon and I wondered if Sheila had.

After commercials for Kool-Aid and Lux fabric softener, we watched Laura walk down the hallway of the hospital. Sheila had a face not unlike Laura's: pug nose and round cheeks, with long, shiny blonde hair. On the surface Laura was like us. She was a teenager, a few years older than we were. She was sweet and pretty but underneath she was conniving and selfish. In every situation she always let her desire lead her, though she pretended to be innocent. The amazing thing was, nobody seemed to catch on. In fact, everyone loved Laura.

During the commercial, Sheila got the can of Cheez Whiz and we ate the stuff off our fingers. Sheila's fingers were long, her tongue pale pink like a kitten's. After *General Hospital* was over she led me upstairs. Over her bed, which was covered in a baby-blue corduroy spread, was a poster of Gregg Allman. She still liked him, she said, even though he'd gotten busted for drugs and ratted out his whole band.

Leaning against the wall was a poster board covered with cut-out Playboy Bunnies. One Bunny held a gigantic key and another posed at the Playboy Club in front of backlit photographs of naked girls. Below the collage on her dresser was a lighter with the Playboy Bunny logo and a pair of satin ears.

"Walt brought these back from New York," she said. "He's my mom's boyfriend and kind of like my stepdad."

"Cool," I said.

I had watched "Bunny of the Year" on television last year. It was impossible not to know about *Playboy* magazine and the Playboy Clubs in Chicago and New York. I'd seen pictures of Bunnies dancing on top of the piano. Everybody knew about Hugh Hefner and the orgies he had at his mansion.

"Walt says I'd make a great Bunny," Sheila said.

I thought this was a strange thing to say, but I could tell how the comment had given her hope.

"You would," I said.

I was worried she would take this the wrong way and accuse me of being a lezzbo, but she just started to tell me that at the clubs there were many varieties of Bunnies: Door Bunny, Hat-Check Bunny, Table Bunny. Each Bunny wore a satin bodysuit that matched her ears and high heels.

She told me that when they had open auditions, hundreds of girls showed up.

"Walt is a Number One Key Holder," Sheila said. "That means he can ask the Bunnies out."

"But he's with your mom, right?"

"He doesn't do it because he loves her."

This was so romantic we just sat there a minute until Sheila opened a drawer and pulled out a big ball of white yarn.

"I'm making myself a tail," she said.

Sheila passed it to me. I saw how she'd cut all the yarn into same-size pieces and tied them in the middle. But I wasn't sure if I should say I liked the tail. Should I act indifferent? Sheila's mouth was in a neutral position but I knew if I messed up, her lips could easily slide into a snide smile and she would say something to humiliate me. When I was embarrassed, the tips of my ears got as red as bell peppers.

Sheila turned on the radio that sat on her nightstand. "Black Betty" blasted into the room. I was trying to like the song but the lyrics reminded me of how the health teacher warned us when we menstruated we smelled. Sheila sat against the wall on the gold shag, her eyes open, but behind her eyes she was asleep.

"Ziggy Stardust" came on the radio next. I knew not everyone liked David Bowie, so I kept my expression neutral. You couldn't like anything that was too weird because then that weirdness jumped onto you.

"I don't like David Bowie," Sheila said. "He can't decide whether he's a boy or a girl."

I nodded without looking at her. If I looked at her face I knew she'd see I loved Bowie. Instead I concentrated on Sheila's feet: her toes were long and thin, her nails a lovely pink lavender, and her baby toe was so perfectly formed it looked edible.

✦

My life was now divided into two categories: time away from Sheila, which had that odd combination of dullness and anxiety, and time with her. Together we had our routine: Cheez Whiz, Tab, *General Hospital*. Laura was sleeping with an old guy who had seduced her only to get back at her mother. Sheila wouldn't let me talk during the show, only when the commercials came on. The thing about Laura was that even when she was sleeping with older guys she still looked, with her big wet eyes and golden hair, as innocent as a baby. Nothing she did ever stuck to her, or diminished her. She never seemed to learn anything from her mistakes either, but this was a small price to pay for going through the world doing whatever you wanted.

After *General Hospital*, we did the problems in our math workbook, and then answered the lame questions at the back of the chapter in our history textbook. They seemed designed for people with brain damage. The history class was taught by Coach Carter; all he did in class was tell us to read our textbooks, while he sat at his desk looking at pictures in *Sports Illustrated*. The brazenness of his lack of interest appealed to me. And I loved how he threw a Nerf football, which he kept in his bottom desk drawer, at the boy in the back who always fell asleep.

Only once did I make the mistake of mentioning Sheila's father. I asked where he worked. I could tell by the way her eyes blanked that I'd made a huge mistake. The way the words came out made it sound as if I suspected he was a prostitute and, to be honest, I had speculated, in the privacy of my bedroom, that he *might* be a male prostitute. I thought of him in his sad little apartment with a collection of sex toys, painting his toenails while he wore girls' underwear. I waited for her to say something mean about my own pathetic family, but she just sat perfectly still, as if I had not said anything, before walking into the kitchen to get us another can of Tab.

After our homework we went into her mother's room and Sheila read from either *Sybil* or *Fear of Flying*. Sybil had twenty-three personalities. Two were boys and one was a prostitute. Sheila read how Sybil's evil mother shit in the neighbor's yard and then hung Sibyl upside down from the kitchen ceiling. In *Fear of Flying*, Sheila always read the part about sex being like Velveeta cheese. I was fascinated with Velveeta, how if you melted a slice on top of an English muffin pizza, it melted more like plastic than cheese. I often found myself thinking of the odd texture during my last class. Now I had to wonder if all this time I had been actually thinking about sex. When we got to the part that said *His penis . . . is the tall red smokestack of an ocean liner*, we'd laugh so hard Tab came out of our noses. But it was the part about the *zipless fuck*, which Sheila always read last, that really appealed to me. Instead of worrying about the mechanics, the male part going into the female, you could just lie like two people in footie pajamas, next to each other on a couch.

After *Fear of Flying* we practiced our Bunny moves. We approached the table, pivoted carefully, and "tailed." We practiced asking customers for their keys and then responded when they showed them, *Thank you, Mr. Pochucknick*. We did the Bunny dip: while serving drinks, instead of bending over the table, exposing our breasts, we placed our right foot behind us and swayed our backs to set down the flamingo with the orange slice wrapped around a cherry and stuck with a tiny red plastic sword. We also practiced the Bunny stance, backs arched, hips tucked. We did this only if key members were watching. We practiced "perching" on the back of a chair or sofa, tipping our heads and giving the Number One Key Holders sly smiles.

✦

At exactly 6:15 every weeknight, Sheila's mom came home from her job at the makeup counter at Leggett's. She was violently cheerful, asking me, as she moved around the kitchen, if I had a boyfriend or if I was going to the spring formal. She asked where my dad preached and she didn't approve when I said he'd given up church. She wore several shades of eye shadow that blended into one another like the tiered colors on a bird's wing, and her eyebrows were drawn in with black pencil. Walt called at exactly seven, just as she was setting the plates down for dinner. Walt, she'd told me, was from an old Virginia family. His great-grandfather had been lieutenant governor and, while it was true his main income came from lot rentals at several trailer parks, when his father finally died, he would be a zillionaire. I'd watched him get out of his Volvo in a rumpled seersucker suit, his face long and red and his nose looking like it was constructed entirely out of raspberries. Mostly she just listened, her ear pressed into the receiver, but occasionally she said *Oh stop that* or *You're so bad.* I thought this was odd as Sheila told me her mom had met Walt at First Baptist. If he didn't call, Sheila's mom fretted, saying he was probably chatting up his secretary, who was clearly after him. While she ate she looked through magazines, compiling lists of hors d'oeuvres to make for Walt's surprise birthday party.

✦

On Saturday my mom dropped me off at the mall. Sheila had ridden in early with her mom, as she did every Saturday. She hung around the makeup counter while her mom loaded the cash register and set out the makeup. I had assumed we'd meet in the French Quarter, but unlike me, Sheila preferred the Orange Julius on the ground floor.

"Sorry I'm late," I said, throwing myself into the orange plastic seat.

"It's OK," she said.

When things got quiet, Sheila stared like babies do at a point just over my head. Her silence was the opposite of my dad's. With him, you felt the strong current of his interest and that that interest was not focused on you. But Sheila's silence was empty, like a dog's or a cat's.

The Orange Julius mixer whirred. The boy behind the counter told the girl he was waiting on that he'd signed up to join the Marines. The orange wall behind Sheila's head vibrated. I watched people coming into the dark mall from a rectangle of pure light.

"What's up with the party planning?" I asked.

"My mom is obsessed," she said. "Last night she made three kinds of mushroom caps."

Besides being a key-carrying member of the Playboy Club and a trailer-park mogul, Walt was also a Redskins fanatic. His car was covered with bumper stickers and he and his friends from church some-times caravanned it up to Washington for games. If he stayed home, he took Sheila's mom to the Fiji Island to watch the game on the TV that hung over the bar. Afterward they went to his place. I imagined Frank Sinatra playing on the stereo, Walt sitting in a sat-in smoking jacket, like Hugh Hefner, eating stuffed mushroom caps off a silver plate.

I wasn't sure what girls did at the mall. My only experience had been with Jill and I knew there was no way Sheila would want to smoke bean pods in the French Quarter bathroom. Sheila just sat there, more like a cow than a dog. Her inertness was horrible and fascinating. I had hoped we'd move from Chess King to Spencer's Gifts, trying on tops, buying flip-flops or rhinestone studs set into plastic. Mostly I had hoped that kids from school, who also roamed the mall on Saturdays, would see us together. This was the one public place where people could see us together because at school Sheila didn't speak to me. That hardly mattered, though; my worship of her was too fierce to be called love. It hardly mattered if she never spoke to me at all, as long as I could bind myself to her by a secret vow. I followed her down the hallway at a distance. When she hung around the audiovisual room talking to Mr. Ramin, I waited outside, pretending to search for something in my backpack. Mr. Ramin sat surrounded by overhead projectors and filmstrip canisters, with his feet up on his desk. He wore Earth shoes, a Western shirt with silver snaps, and bell-bottoms with rust-colored stitching on the pockets. Sheila did the Bunny perch on the side of his desk and listened to him talk about his band, Earth Tone, and how they were about to get a record deal.

Time inside Tanglewood was like time in Narnia: it stretched out like Silly Putty and had no relation to time outside. After we browsed the crocheted penis-warmers and the candy underpants and each bought Playboy Bunny shot glasses at Spencer's Gifts, we sat on the fountain's edge and watched the lid of a plastic cup stuck in the bubbling water. I had the feeling

Sheila was waiting for someone. Maybe Mr. Ramin had said he would be shopping for drumsticks at the mall music store. Maybe they'd agreed to meet and I was the cover. I'd stand in front of the bathroom while they had sex inside.

When I asked if she was waiting for anyone, she acted the same way she did when I mentioned her father—completely blank as if I hadn't said anything. Senior citizens sat around us waiting for the A&W to open so they could get their lunches for $1.99. A group of boys walked by us; one pushed another toward us while the rest laughed. It was funny that I was ugly and Sheila angelic.

Finally, Sheila pointed, and I saw the woman she'd been waiting for. When I tried to ask her if she was Walt's ex-wife or some teacher who had tortured her in elementary school, she put her finger to her lips and grasped my hand, and we followed the woman. The lady's hair was clearly synthetic, her ankles thick, and her stride a bit too wide. Even though the woman was middle-aged she seemed much younger, a girl even younger than myself, trying to figure out how to apply makeup and walk like a lady.

She rode the escalator up to the French Quarter and we followed her through the darkened halls, past the wishing well and the thatched-roof shops. She stopped in front of the bridal shop and gazed at the rhinestone tiara and lace veils. The woman moved through the French Quarter and back down the escalator. When she was nearly at the mall's front door, she looked over her shoulder and I saw up close her heavy foundation makeup and her large, angular nose. Fear flashed over her features as she realized we were following her, and she ran through the doors into the bright parking-lot light.

"Who was that?" I asked.

Sheila didn't answer, though I could tell by her flushed face how upset she was. She walked out of the entrance of J.C. Penney where my dad had said he'd pick us up.

When we got back to Bent Tree we went right up to Sheila's room where she paced the floor, saying it was gross and creepy to dress up like a girl if you were really a man. She put Donna Summer's "Love to Love You Baby" on her record player. A weird expression came over her face.

"Make the sex sounds," she commanded.

I laughed.

"I don't want to."

"Do it now or I'll tell everyone how after gym class you smell like vegetable soup."

I weighed my options. On the one hand if I didn't make the sex sounds Sheila would betray me by telling everyone I smelled, but if I did it, she might betray me worse by telling everyone I'd made the sex sounds. I closed my eyes and let the sex sounds come from deep in my belly. I panted and made the vowels last a long, long time.

"OK," she said, "that's enough."

✦

One day, during a commercial break while we were watching *General Hospital*, Sheila told me her father's landlady had called to say that her dad was missing. She said this without looking at me, looking straight ahead at the Magnavox screen, as an ad for Tang played.

"Where do you think he is?" I asked.

"Who knows," Sheila said. "My mom called my aunt, his sister, in West Virginia and she hasn't heard from him. He just stopped showing up at the bank where he worked."

"Maybe he wants to start a new life?"

"All I know is, if he doesn't come back soon, his landlady is going to take his stuff to the dump."

Sheila hadn't seen him since he tried to speak to her after she got off the bus six months ago. When he called on the phone, which he hadn't done for a while, both Sheila and her mom hung up as soon as they heard his voice. He'd finally gone away, like she and her mother were hoping, probably to a gay place like Greenwich Village or Atlanta.

"He can fuck whoever he wants," Sheila said, "and I'll fuck whoever I want."

I had heard that sex put you in a great mood, but whatever Sheila was doing with Mr. Ramin, making out, going to third base, cunnilingus, blow jobs, whatever, only made her more anxious. I knew Sheila went into Mr. Ramin's AV room, and he locked the door and taped black construction paper over the window. Now instead of zoning out during *GH*, she was jittery, chewing her cuticles and spilling her Tab on the white carpet.

Most days after *General Hospital* she wanted to do beauty rituals, mash avocado in a Tupperware bowl and slather it over our faces and lie down with slices of cucumber over our eyes. If our skin was oily we made oatmeal and pressed it over our noses and foreheads. Because I had a few red spots on my chin I had to have a milk of magnesia mask.

Sheila made me scrub my face with salt and lemon juice. She used a tape measure to check the space between my thighs, just below my private parts, and told me it was too wide. The fashion magazines said an inch to an inch and a half was the proper space; less than that meant your legs were too fat. More than that meant your legs were too skinny.

We mixed peanut butter and eggs, put it on our hair, wrapped Saran Wrap around our heads, and heated our gooey scalps with a blow dryer. We made a bucket of tea and stuck our heads into it. We mashed bananas and cornmeal to rub on the bottoms of our feet. We did sit-ups to make our tummies flat, and rotated our ankles to make them thin. Sheila read that beatings with oak leaves improved circulation, so we collected branches up in the woods, bound them with yarn, and she hit my back until the skin was pink and raw. We started the paleolithic diet, eating only hamburger and nuts, and then switched to the lemonade diet, drinking lemonade mixed with cayenne pepper. We spent one whole afternoon trying to catch a snake, as Sheila had heard Asian beauty experts used them for massage.

We made lists, as the magazines instructed, of our most hated body parts. My list read: (1) *head* (2) *torso* (3) *waist* (4) *arms* (5) *heart*. Sheila said I couldn't include heart, as it was inside the body and we had no idea what it looked like, if it was ugly or beautiful.

After that we went on to Bunny practice. We'd graduated from our bathing suits to the black leotards Sheila's mom had bought us. We clipped on the paper cuffs we'd made from poster board, securing them with cuff links borrowed from Walt. We wore black bow ties that we'd found in the J.C. Penney boys' shop. We'd also sewn tails to the backs of our leotards. Once our uniforms were completed with Sheila's mother's high heels, we practiced tailing the nightstand, and then we did the Bunny dip, asking Mr. Hefner (he was our only customer at this point) if he wanted a cocktail. We ran through the stance and the perch, judging each other on a scale of one to ten. If I got less than a five, Sheila morphed into the Bunny mother and gave me demerits and told me I'd never be Bunny of the Week. Then Sheila turned on the radio and we danced on top of her bed, pretending it was the grand piano at the Playboy Club.

After that, Sheila wanted to play orgy. Everybody knew the Bunnies were the key elements in Hugh Hefner's orgies at the Playboy Mansion. So we rolled around on Sheila's bed until we were both flushed. She got a carrot from the fridge and made me watch her give Hugh a blow job and then said I had to get up on all fours so she could *do it* to me. Afterward, sweaty and disheveled, we got trays from the kitchen and high-carried them around the living room to Sheila's favorite 45, "Love Machine."

For Walt's surprise party, Sheila's mom had a stack of albums she was testing by the stereo. Walt and his friends were fifteen years older than Sheila's mom. They'd all gone to Virginia Tech, wore heavy college rings, and loved to play golf, driving around in the cart wearing their Redskins baseball caps. They were obsessed to the point of madness with Redskins football and talked about Billy Kilmer as if he were God. Walt loved to mention that while all the other pussies wore double-bar helmets, Kilmer was the only quarterback who had the balls to wear the one-bar mask.

Sheila's mom wasn't sure what sort of music Walt liked. He'd said he enjoyed the jazz they played in the Playboy Club, but she also knew he liked Bread, and the radio in his car was tuned to the oldies station. She'd bought half a dozen records and listened to each with a worried expression. Would Walt and his friends like Burt Bacharach or Dusty Springfield?

She was worried about the food too. She wanted
the food to seem high-class and so she tested punches,
one with Sprite, lime sherbet, and vodka; another
with pineapple juice, rum, and frozen strawberries.
In the fridge there was always a plate of deviled eggs
sprinkled with curry power or celery sticks spread
with pimento cheese or cucumber finger sandwiches
with the crusts trimmed off. We were encouraged to
sample the food and give her our honest opinion.

+

One day when we got home from school, Walt was
waiting in the living room. He sat on the couch in his
white golf shirt and polyester shorts drinking a can of
beer. His nose was red and his eyes bloodshot.

"Hi girls," he said.

"Where's Mom?"

"At work," he said, sitting up on the edge of the
couch. "I was nearby and I thought I'd stop in and see
if you might want my expert opinion."

"On what?" Sheila said.

"You all want to be Playboy Bunnies, right?"

Sheila nodded.

"Well, go get your outfits on and I'll let you know
how authentic you look."

Sheila looked over Walt's head and into the wall.
She had perfected keeping her brain in another
sphere from her body.

"OK," she said.

I followed her up to her bedroom. I assumed we'd lock the door, or call her mom from the phone upstairs. But Sheila just moved like a robot, pulling open a drawer and grabbing two black leotards.

"Hurry!"

I tried not to stare at Sheila as we changed. Her full breasts, so white compared to her tan, flat stomach, slender hips, and thighs. Her pubic hair was blonde so I could see the pink slit between her legs. It was supposed to be nothing, us changing in front of each other, but it was everything.

We helped each other attach the homemade Bunny tails, the white cuffs we'd cut out of poster board.

Sheila rolled gloss over her lips. Cotton candy flavor, with just a tinge of pink. She threw her head down, fluffed up her hair, and then swung her head up again, looking at her face in the mirror that hung over her dresser.

"Here goes nothing," she said.

I walked down the stairs behind her, watching her tail and the fishnet tights against the skin of her thighs.

"Hot dog!" Walt said as we entered the living room. "You girls look fantastic."

Sheila's face was still as she walked over the carpet. I followed her maybe a little too close behind.

"Your friend is a bit stiff," Walt said, tipping his beer up to his lips. "She should relax."

I nodded.

"What about me?" Sheila asked.

Before he could say anything she threw herself down onto his lap. She sat the way I used to sit on my Dad's lap, with her legs thrown over his knees and her head on his shoulder. He moved his arm around her in a way that was not at all fatherly.

"You, doll," he said, pressing his lips into her forehead, "are perfect."

✦

After Walt left, we went up to Sheila's room. She said she needed a sequined tube top stored in a milk crate at the back of her closet. If I found the tube top I could have anything else I wanted in the crate. Sheila had given me several items of clothing and I treated each like a shred of holy scripture: the black Bunny leotard of course, but also a terry cloth tank top and a pair of white shorts with red piping. I'd always wanted to look through her closet, smell her nightgown, and touch the material of her dresses. I climbed into the closet and squatted down over her shoes.

Then I heard the door shut, and Sheila pushed her desk chair against the knob. I was left in the dark, confused and unsure how to proceed. If I asked to be let out, I knew Sheila would be less likely to let me out. Really it wasn't that bad, there was a comforting smell of musk and talc and I could relax and not worry about what I said or if I smelled bad. I knew, too, that I deserved to be locked in the closet. I needed to change; I was too nerdy and awkward. I hadn't been able to access beauty or light. In the closet I might transform, from sweet Patty to Tania, a glamorous rebel.

Sheila walked to her bed; the springs shifted as she lay down and opened up a magazine. Maybe if I didn't say anything, she'd let me out in half an hour. I was like a load of laundry in the washer; once she felt I was clean, she'd let me out. At least a half hour passed. I smelled my own sweat and I was getting thirsty. I stood up behind the rack of dresses.

I thought of the girl kept in the box under the man's bed, how she lay there in the dark and didn't try to escape. I'd read that after a while he let her go home and visit her mother, but she always came back and got right into the box.

"Let me out," I finally said, pushing at the door. "This isn't funny."

"Why should I let you out?" she said.

I tried to think of a good reason.

"I have to pee."

"Sorry about that," she said.

"Let me out," I said again.

"Say you want to give David Bowie a blow job."

I had to think. If I said it, she could easily tell everybody at school I wanted to give David Bowie a blow job without including the fact I'd been forced to say it while trapped in a closet.

"No," I said.

"I'm going to walk down to the Hop-In," she said. "Want anything?"

"Let me out," I said. "I want to walk with you."

"I'm sending him in now," Sheila said, "and he's going to fuck you really good."

I sat down again on the shoes, my head sandwiched between the hems of her dresses.

"Say you want to be fucked really good."

"I want to be fucked really good."

"I knew it," she said. "You act so sweet and innocent, but I knew you wanted it."

+

When I got home my face was pink in the bathroom mirror and I was sweaty under my clothes. I lay on my bed for a while, trying to calm down and waiting for a good song to come on the radio. No good songs came so I turned on my cassette player. I'd taped my favorite Bowie song, "Starman," every time I heard it come on the radio, so I could listen to it over and over. The first few notes were cut off, but the fact that it sounded scratchy made it seem like Bowie actually was up on the moon.

I liked how he said *boogie*; people used the word all the time in a stupid way, but Bowie said it like a little prayer. The way he said it reminded me of Jill. I jumped up off my bed and decided to call child protection again and see if they'd tell me where I could find her.

The lady told me that Jill was no longer in their system.

I took the phone book on my lap and looked up the number of Woolworth's and asked for the Pet Department. I knew her grandmother had worked there, but the guy who picked up said he'd never heard of a Brendy Minkler.

I walked down to Dwayne's duplex and knocked on the door.

"What do you want?" he said, stepping out on the slab of concrete.

"Do you know where Jill is?"

He looked at me. I could see that his little mind was moving but whether he was building up a lie or telling the truth was impossible to tell.

"Actually I just heard from her."

"Are you bullshitting me?"

"She called in the middle of the night. Said she was living out in Bedford with her grandmother."

"Did she give you a number?"

"No," he said, "but she was shit-faced drunk. She said all kinds of crazy stuff."

I ran all the way up the hill and into my duplex, throwing myself at the wall phone in the kitchen. I called information and asked for the number for Brendy Minkler and then dialed. I listened to a few rings until a message came on saying the phone had been disconnected.

+

One afternoon, after school, while I was in the closet, Sheila said she'd let me out only if we could show my dad our Playboy outfits.

"You mean just the leotards?"

"No," Sheila said, "I want him to judge us like Walt did, to see if we're doing a good job."

I wanted to get out of the closet but I knew that my dad did not want to see me dressed as a Playboy Bunny.

"He'll get mad," I said, "and I won't be able to come here anymore."

Sheila just turned on the radio and sang to a Carpenters song. I could tell by the way the light was fading at the bottom of the door that it was getting late.

"Let me out!"

"Promise."

"OK."

Sheila made me call my dad and arrange for him to come over to her duplex after work. I told him we had a surprise for him. I knew he figured we'd drawn a forest scene on poster board or set up a science experiment.

We got into our outfits and practiced a few Bunny dips. Sheila wanted to grade my performance, but I kept slumping my shoulders. I heard our car pull into the driveway and my dad open the car door. I pulled my sweater over my leotard and put on my painter pants.

"What are you doing?" Sheila said.

"I can't go through with this."

The doorbell rang and Sheila ran down the stairs with me following behind.

"Pastor," she said, "thanks for coming"

She said the word with a sort of giddy respect as she grabbed his arm and pulled him into the living room. My father didn't want to minister to the people of Bent Tree, he didn't feel qualified anymore, but once again he was being forced into it. He stood in the white living room, trying not to stare at Sheila's outfit, staring instead at the conch shell on the glass coffee table.

"What's this about?" he said to me.

"We need your advice," Sheila said.

"For what?" my dad said, taking off his jacket and handing it to Sheila.

"For God's sake, cover yourself up!"

"No thanks," Sheila said, trying to Bunny-dip away from him.

"I insist," he said, throwing the blazer over her shoulders.

Sheila's face got red.

"We want you to judge us on how we walk."

"You walk fine," my dad said. "What's all this about?"

"Nothing," I said, pulling him out the front door and toward his car.

I convinced my dad that Sheila was trying out a Halloween costume. He didn't buy it completely but it settled him down. She called me after dinner desperate to go to the Coffee Pot where Mr. Ramin's band, Earth Tone, was playing. I lied to my mom and we walked down the highway, arriving as it was getting dark. Sheila flitted around the back door trying to get somebody to tell Mr. Ramin she was waiting outside. I hung around the parking lot. The neon beer sign shone red against the asphalt. The Coffee Pot was a log cabin with a giant red coffeepot balanced on the top as if God's hand might reach down, pick it up, and pour a gigantic mug of steaming coffee. Inside Mr. Ramin beat on the drums and the singer wailed as if he were trapped inside a wet mitten. When the door opened a puff of smoke escaped and the music flamed up like a fire encouraged by gasoline.

I leaned against the side of a pickup truck and looked over the parking lot at the strip mall across the street. The moon was full and, because we were down in the valley, mist rose up off the ground. I moved outside the oval of entrance light. Winter had morphed into spring. The bugs were loud. In a truck a few parking spots away, a man handed a joint to a girl in a flannel shirt with the sleeves cut off. At the other end of the parking lot, a group of men passed a flask around and smoked cigarettes.

I walked to the back door and watched Sheila talking to an older man in a leather vest. Near my feet

was a patch of moving jagged-leaf light. Mr. Ramin
came out and he and Sheila walked to the other side
of the building and went behind the Dumpster. I
watched the patch of light so long I convinced myself
it was a soul trying to get my attention. How could
I help the poor soul? I laid gravel in the shape of a
cross and repeated some words my dad had taught
me three times. I thought of going over to Sheila and
Mr. Ramin, pulling her away from him or maybe just
standing near them as if I were part of whatever they
were doing. This would be creepy but undeniably
exciting.

Sheila yelled my name and I popped up from where
I sat. She was running toward the road.

"Let's get out of here," she said, moving between
cars and then onto a block of tiny white houses, all
glowing pale purple in the dark.

"What happened?" I said, running after her.

She wiped her eyes against the back of her hand.

"Did he do something to you?"

"Yeah," she said, stretching the neckline of her shirt
to show a dark spot.

The skin was unbroken and I knew it was a hickey.
Deep purple marks I'd seen all over the necks of what
my mother called the trampy girls who worked at
fast-food restaurants. A girl at Hardee's had linked
mouth marks that ran like a choker around her neck.

We walked toward Bent Tree, into a subdivision
of ranches with lawn jockeys painted white, past

the donkey pulling the cart filled with plastic flowers, the miniature windmill, and the cast-iron teddy bears. Our shadows stretched out in front of us and the moon was large and bright.

When we finally got to Sheila's duplex, where I was supposed to be spending the night, I saw that her mom's car was gone. It was not unusual for her to stay overnight with Walt. Across the street was a Pacer. Mr. Ramin was sitting inside smoking a cigarette. Sheila told me to go on inside.

I walked into the dark duplex and stood for a minute by the front window. I could see that Sheila had gotten into the passenger side of the car, and in the moonlight I saw Mr. Ramin's profile.

While I waited, I perched on the side of the sofa. I had on the T-shirt with the Bunny logo Sheila had lent me. I saw that the light was on in our living room and that my father was reading by the lamp. I knew he would not approve of my Bunny lifestyle.

I didn't care. I was a Bunny in training, like a ninja but with a better outfit. As I waited for Sheila to come back, I practiced my Bunny dip and imagined having a long conversation with Hugh Hefner about which drink was better, an old-fashioned or a martini. After about an hour, I decided to check on Sheila. I pulled the curtain back and looked out the window. The moon had disappeared behind clouds and I couldn't see what was happening in the Pacer. I wanted to sleep in my own bed but if I came home in the middle of the night

I knew my father would be suspicious about why the sleepover hadn't worked out. I thought about going out and interrupting whatever Sheila and Mr. Ramin were doing so that maybe Sheila would come inside. But I knew she'd be furious if I did that. I got the metal tray from the kitchen, filled a glass with water, and practiced the high-carry back and forth across the living room. I did this for so long my arm got sore and I had to rest.

+

The day of Walt's surprise party, I got down to Sheila's duplex hours early, at eleven. We were going to lie out in the sun before we started our beauty ritual. The big news was that Sheila's mom had agreed to do my makeup. She had brought home her kit from the department store.

We stretched out in the sun, turning over every half hour and pushing our straps down so we would not have any pale marks. She told me how she and her friends had once hiked up the hill so they could see the porno movie at the 220 Drive-In. She'd seen on the shining screen a penis the size of a tree trunk hovering over a woman's gigantic mouth. The mouth was open and black and the monster penis had disappeared slowly inside.

Ever since Sheila had started to lock me in the closet, she'd begun acknowledging me at school. Most days after *General Hospital*, she'd open her closet door and without a word I would get in and sit on her shoes. She'd close the door, not even bothering to put the chair under the knob, while she did her homework or painted her nails.

At school she sat with me at lunch and we talked about Laura and Scotty, who was cute but dim. Once she'd even come to my locker and said she liked the picture of Cher I'd taped to the inside.

We went over what our duties would be at the party: make and deliver mixed drinks, empty ashtrays, and carry around plates of stuffed mushroom caps and clams casino.

After we were dark enough, we got the jar of mayonnaise out of the fridge and smeared it over our hair. Then we mixed dirt with lemon juice and spread it over our cheeks and foreheads to make our pores smaller. We lay on the bed and Sheila read from her mother's new paperback, *The Happy Hooker*, by Xaviera Hollander. I was surprised her mom would read a book about a prostitute. But Sheila explained that Walt had given her the book as a joke. Sheila read the parts that might help us understand our clients at the Playboy Club. She read that bankers were the best customers and that stockbrokers were a *horny bunch of brothel creepers. When the stocks go up, the cocks go up* became our favorite line. I wasn't sure yet if I was headed toward being a good girl or a whore. I'd been hoping for a little bit of both, but listening to Xaviera, I began to think there was no middle ground—you were either one or the other.

At five we took showers. I'd brought over my hot curlers and so we both, after blow-drying, wrapped our hair onto the hot white plastic. Sheila put on her makeup, while Sheila's mom, who was also in hot curlers, took me into the bathroom.

"OK, Jesse," she said, "you ready?"

I nodded, gazing over the thirty kinds of sparkly eye shadow and the ten shades of lip gloss and blush that she'd brought home from the store.

She shook a bottle of foundation and spread the paste over my face. She'd already done her own makeup and penciled in her eyebrows, which at some earlier point she must have plucked off completely. She'd used gray shadow, which made her eyes look large and supernatural. She was, I realized, as beautiful as my mother.

"You're young to have such dark circles," she said, pressing the concealer over the bags under my eyes, then blending in the foundation.

"I get anxious," I said, "and it's hard for me to sleep."

"It's the Devil," she said. "He's tormenting you."

I knew she was talking about the local Satanists. According to the newspaper, they drank cats' blood out of crystal goblets and had fires where they burnt Bibles along with red satin underwear. Black masses performed in basements included the sacrifice of both hamsters and mice. Mrs. Smith claimed the Satanists sent away for books of incantations to cast spells on the elderly. My dad said all this was crazy. He said he'd never seen people so obsessed with the Devil as people in Roanoke. It wasn't the nightly news without at least one report of some demonic activity.

+

At my school in the morning, the Christian Athletic Association prayed out by the flagpole and, at lunch, Crusaders for Christ prayed beside the smoking block, asking God to free the stoners from the Devil's snare. I had even seen the principal, his eyes clenched shut, his face flushed, begging for protection.

"Do you ever pray to Jesus?" Sheila's mom asked.

Here we go.

"No," I said.

Actually I did pray. Sometimes I prayed to the memory of the altar at our old church. Not on Sunday mornings but in the evenings, remembering the times after dinner that I'd snuck over to run around on the dark altar, with its linen cloth muddled in gold light. On the altar I'd seen a lady in her coffin, the skin of her face slack and her features completely still, and also a bride so pregnant that the zipper on the back of her dress had to be safety-pinned. I believed that the altar was a soft spot, an opening between our world and the infinite one. Now, though, God was mundane, something old and pretty, but broken, like the bronze door handle, or the

263

odd crystal from a chandelier, things you might see in a box at a junk shop. At times I still felt the open God feeling, not so much in objects but in the space around them, like in the space around the couch or the area between the lamp and my bed: it was in that vacuum that something might happen, though it was impossible to know how to pray to nothingness and if it was crazy to do so.

"Well, you should pray," Sheila's mom said. I could see her lip liner and how she had expertly filled in the color by using both gloss and lipstick. "You need to accept Jesus as your personal savior."

A few girls in school had been talking about getting saved, not just the usual pack of Christer kids but even the regular kids: a few of the cheerleaders, and a handful of girls on the drill team. After the assistant football coach got saved, most of the team followed. It was like the flu, my dad said, everybody was catching it.

"If you let Jesus in he will wash you clean. Close your eyes," she said.

I felt the wand with the soft sponge moving over my eyelids. In the dark, I saw streaks of light moving from one side to the other over my eyeballs. Maybe this was the moment. After I had my face made up, I would finally transform. I'd become shining and whole in an instant.

"If you accept Him all your sins will be washed away and you'll be like a little baby."

I didn't want to be like a baby lying in a crib. I wanted to go out into the world, I wanted to sin, I wanted to sin a lot.

At seven, after we'd painted our nails and spread lotion over our tan arms and legs, we pulled up the black tights and our black leotards, clipped on our cuffs, and hooked our bow ties. Our hair was huge. The bell rang and the first couple arrived: Walt's college roommate from Virginia Tech and his girlfriend. The couples kept coming until finally Walt drove up and we all crouched in the dark living room. He came in, calling out, and we sprang up and Sheila flipped on the lights. Walt put a hand against his chest, took a step back, and his mouth fell open. Sheila's mom threw herself on him, wrapping her arms around his neck. He hugged her back and smiled.

Sheila and I took our Bunny duties very seriously. I carried gin and tonics on my tray and delivered them with a perfect Bunny dip. Sheila passed a tray of mushroom caps from couple to couple. One man stared at her for so long his wife nudged him.

"You all look soooo cute," the wife said.

I picked up empty glasses and dumped ashtrays into the trash. One man grabbed my ears off my head and stuck them onto his own bald one.

After lots of drinks, the couples played musical chairs. I'd played this game at birthday parties when I was little, but this version was different. The men sat on the chairs the whole time, while the women scrambled whenever the music stopped to find a seat on the men's laps. The women had to jump onto the men and the men hugged them and snuggled their faces in the women's hair. The one lady without a lap was out and, while everyone laughed, I could feel she was humiliated. It finally got down to Sheila's mom and another lady in a pink dress and white go-go boots. When the music stopped Sheila's mom was farther away, but she threw herself through the air and landed on the birthday boy's lap.

After musical chairs was over, Walt went into the bathroom with the lady in the pink dress and go-go boots. Sheila's mom stared at the bathroom door from the living room. "Fly Me to the Moon" played on the stereo. Black eyeliner tears ran down either side of her nose. No one said anything to her. A couple of the men who weren't too drunk looked at her as if they might go over and try to say something to comfort her, but they didn't. The women looked away or looked down at their shoes. Sheila didn't say anything either. She just looked at me and walked slowly up the stairs. I followed and we lay down on her bed, silently looking out the window at the streetlight. After a while Sheila got up, walked over to the closet, and opened the door.

✦

Mr. Ramin, it was rumored, had taken off for Canada, where the cops could not arrest you for sleeping with a minor. At least that's what Dwayne told everybody on the bus. After they got caught in the AV room, Sheila got two weeks' suspension. Her mother grounded her, and the only sign that she hadn't killed Sheila was the globe of light shining through the shade of her bedroom window.

Sheila came back to school for the last few days of junior high. She wouldn't speak to anybody. She sat alone on the bus and at the far end of the last table in the cafeteria near the garbage can at lunch. The cheerleaders pretended to bump into her every time they brought their trays back. Eventually, she fled to the smoking block. The kids out there with their hunched shoulders and dark circles under their eyes were vampires, and now Sheila was one of them. I watched her, in an angle of sunlight, doing the Bunny stance all by herself.

+

CHAPTER FIVE

DWAYNE

On the last day of ninth grade, on the bus back to Bent Tree, Dwayne and I fought about the Civil War. He said, as he always insisted, that the Confederate soldiers were just fighting for *what they knew*. I inferred the Confederacy was a lot like Nazi Germany. Dwayne lost his cool completely, yelling about how his great-grandfather had nailed horseshoes to the bottoms of his boots to make them last longer and that he'd had to wear the uniform of a dead man.

He stood behind my seat, even though the driver yelled at him to sit down. He no longer wore his Skynryd T-shirt and faded army jacket. Instead he'd dressed up for the last day of school in a blue oxford and khaki pants, with his hair slicked back with gel; he reeked of his dad's Old Spice.

"You think the world would be perfect if you could just get rid of us rednecks!"

"Wouldn't it?" I said.

At first I thought he was going to spit at me; his face collapsed in on itself and he made a noise in his throat and put his hand up to cover his eyes. He flung himself into the backseat and turned into the corner so no one could see him cry.

✦

After that it was like he'd found a trapdoor at the back of my head. When I saw a layer of dust on the base of a lamp, I wondered would Dwayne feel like I did, that it was the smallest snowfall in the world? When I swung open the refrigerator door my eyes went first to the bologna in white butcher paper, a food I knew he liked. What was Dwayne's favorite color? My guess was ivy green. "My Eyes Adored You" came on the radio. Did Dwayne agree it was a cheesy throwback and should be dynamited off the dial? I spent a lot of time playing back things he'd said to me over the years and trying to figure out if they had some secret message. When he said he liked my shirt with the brown piping was he serious or did he really think I looked like an idiot? When he asked if I wanted to go riding with him, I knew I should say no, but I just nodded my head.

I told my mom I was going to a friend's. She asked a few questions. What did my friend's father do?

Insurance. Would they drive me home? Of course. I made up some stuff about the mom being a nurse and how my friend was first chair on flute in the high school orchestra. While I spoke to her, I sang the Carpenters song "Top of the World" in my head. I had taken to doing this while she told me about the plans for Rose Kennedy's birthday or that Teddy Kennedy was still drinking. My mother knew something was off; even as out of it as she was, she could sense I was lying.

✦

I sat in the backseat beside a twelve-pack of beer. Dwayne's friend Larry drove and Dwayne sat in the passenger seat. I recognized Larry from pictures in the newspaper. He had blond hair with dark eyes and handsome features. He was the son of Louis Hancock, who owned the store in the French Quarter where Dwayne worked. He'd gotten into trouble in Blacksburg, where he'd been at college.

Besides my brother, I had never been alone with boys before. Should I ask about football or horror movies? If you didn't know their lingo, boys made fun of you. As the jeep turned onto 419, I found it hard to believe that I was actually sitting in a boy's car. And I was with Dwayne, the same Dwayne who'd gotten suspended from school for spray-painting curse words on the wall of the boys' bathroom and setting a pile of towels on fire in the locker room, the same Dwayne who was seventeen and going into 10th grade because he'd failed both sixth and seventh grade, the Dwayne who had given me an Indian handshake so violent my wrist was sore for a week.

Luckily, I didn't have to say anything, as he started to talk about Hutch. How all day people came into the store and told him he looked exactly like the TV character. He broke down a fight scene from a recent episode, first pulling his arm back, then tucking his head sideways. He gently punched the dashboard and then sunk back deeper into the seat.

"All you talk about is Hutch," Larry said. "I'm sick of it!"

"It's just not fair," Dwayne said, "that David Soul gets to be Hutch and I just get to look like him."

People loved to look like famous people. Sheila loved that she looked like Laura, and my mom often mentioned how, when she was younger, people said she looked like Grace Kelly. There was a girl in school who looked like Jodie Foster and a boy who looked like David Cassidy. Even our neighbor Mrs. Smith was always pointing out how she looked just like Mrs. Robert E. Lee. But what good did it do to look like a famous person? You were not that famous person, you didn't even know them, and looking like them didn't make you their sister or cousin. It made you smaller, not bigger, to look like somebody else, as if the famous person had swallowed you whole and you were just a tiny worn-out doll stuck inside their stomach.

"You could be an actor," I said.

"You are not getting it," Dwayne said, turning around to glare at me. "I am Hutch!"

Drops of water stabbed the window and it started to rain. Steam rose up off the asphalt. The headlights lit up the monkey grass and milkweed by the side of the road. Splotches of blurry gold-and-red light came through the window.

"Hellhole number one," Larry said as we pulled into the parking lot of the Ground Round. The Ground Round parking lot was the best lot in all of Roanoke. It had spaces in front but also in back. In back the kids hung out along the tree line or near the Dumpster. Back here it wasn't glaring with dusk-to-dawn lights like most of the lots on the highway; there was just a single lantern suspended near the restaurant's back door. The downside was the stench of fryer grease. Also, the manager came out every now and then and chased everybody off.

Tonight the lot was packed with cars and clumps of kids standing under umbrellas. Larry hit the brakes and slowed the jeep to a stop. They checked out all the cars. Not seeing any vehicles they recognized, they pronounced the Ground Round lame. Larry spun the wheels a bit on the wet pavement as we pulled away from the lot.

We moved on to hellhole number two, the Happy Clam. The Happy Clam was a seafood restaurant that featured beach music at night. Beach music was a throwback to fifties swing. For some reason the rich kids loved to dance to it. The dance was called the shag and had lots of turns and twists and was maybe fun to do but really stupid to watch. We parked in a big lot completely devoid of character. I was unclear why we didn't go to the Pizza Inn, with its dark and cozy lot. Even the Hardee's lot had more charm. The band must have stopped because kids streamed out, boys wearing madras pants and Izod shirts and girls in bright pink or yellow wraparound dresses.

"There's Naomi," Larry said, pointing to a girl with long, dark hair wearing a white shirt with a giant scallop shell on it and a blue skirt.

"You went out with her?"

Larry nodded.

"Three years. Then that asshole Willmont Vanhoff is with her two weeks and gets her pregnant. He was a loudmouth about it too. He might as well have put flyers under every windshield wiper at the mall."

"That's sick," Dwayne said.

"Hey Naomi," Larry called to her and her friend. Her friend was short with broad shoulders, while Naomi was tall and skinny, with a gap between her front teeth and bangs cut straight across her forehead.

"Larry," she said, walking over to us. "I heard you were back."

"I want you to know it was bogus," he said. "They dropped the charges."

"You'll go back in the fall?"

"My only plan is to party all summer long."

Naomi laughed.

"Same old Larry."

"No, not same old Larry. Different Larry. New-and-improved Larry."

"Yeah right," she said.

"Seriously," he said. "You all need a ride?"

"No," she said, "I'm spending the night with Josie. Her mom is on her way to get us."

"Sluts," Larry said, as soon as we pulled out of the lot. "That little one fucked Buddy Eclor while his friend watched."

I knew Larry was lying. I glanced at him in the rearview mirror. Even features, his Star of David necklace illuminated in the oncoming headlights. I saw his cheek move as he clicked his jaw. He rolled his window down all the way and leaned out so the wind was full in his face. As we drove on 419 past the mall, the electric sign flashed over a huge and empty lot: GO GET 'EM KNIGHTS. The windowless mall looked like a space station and the asphalt like the domesticated surface of the moon. I wanted to break the tension in the car, worse even than the force field of static at my own house—but how? I could say something about Cher, how long it must take to sew the beads on one of her fantastic outfits. Sometimes to go to sleep at night, instead of counting sheep, I'd imagine a pair of hands sewing one small bead after another; sometimes I even thought of them as tears threaded into a tapestry of water. But that sounded, even to my mind, girly and ridiculous. Maybe they'd be interested in my dad's dream theories. He'd just told me that fluxes in the earth's magnetic fields made dreams more bizarre.

Dwayne turned on the radio and Skynyrd came blaring out of the dashboard speakers. Larry pushed the gas pedal and we zoomed by the mechanic's shop with the giant tire out front, a strip mall with a pet supply and an ABC store, past the beauty parlor in the trailer, and into a stretch of woods. Headlights showed leaves, gray trunks of trees, fern fronds, a stump turned over, red with mud. Sheila told me she'd been to a bonfire at the dump where boys drank moonshine and one girl got so drunk she took her shirt off and danced around the fire.

I knew Dwayne might try to kiss me or even zipless fuck me. Parking, like babysitting, was dangerous. Everyone knew about the couple who heard a strange scraping sound. They raced away only to discover a hook dangling from their door handle, left by a one-handed mental patient escaped from the local loony bin. Those two got off easy, though, compared to the boy who went out in the woods to pee. His girlfriend waited all night for him to come back, but it wasn't until sunrise that she got out of the car and saw her boyfriend's head stuck onto the radio antenna!

We pulled onto a dirt road and drove, cones of headlights on a swath of kudzu vine that smothered the underbrush and reached up into the trees. Light illuminated two boys in army jackets, one holding what I knew was a roach clip; then they fell back into the dark. We drove into an opening where the trees had been cleared and I could see the stars overhead; a few cars were parked and kids sat up on the trunks. Inside the tree line was a bonfire, and I saw kids' faces illuminated in slashes of orange and red.

We pulled into the far end of the opening and parked. The air smelled of wood smoke and sweet rot. I'd heard about the dump as a place where girls lost their virginity and boys puked and passed out. The blanket beside me had taken on scary implications. I was worried Dwayne and Larry were going to make me walk into the woods.

I heard the door click open and Larry got out and walked away from the car. I heard his zipper and the flat sound of urine hitting the ground.

Dwayne turned around.

"Want to get out?"

"What's the alternative?"

"I could come back there."

"Let's get out," I said, pushing the handle down and stepping out onto the ground.

We sat on the trunk. Dwayne passed me a beer. They were warm now and tasted terrible. Larry came back, leaned against the trunk, and bent forward to the flame of his lighter, his profile illuminated and then gone.

"How are the lovebirds?"

"Better than you," Dwayne said.

"Shit, man," Larry said, "I don't know why I'm hanging around you preschoolers."

"Maybe because you don't have any other friends."

"You better shut your mouth," Larry said, "if you want to keep your job."

"Did you know that elephants cry when they're lonely?" It was something Kira had told me and it just came down from my mind and blew out of my mouth like a soap bubble.

"Is that so?" Larry said.

"Leave her," Dwayne said.

"What do elephants do after they fuck?"

"I'll tell you what they don't do," Dwayne said. "They don't hold a gun to a girl's head."

"It was a joke," Larry said. "Can't anyone take a joke?"

Light shimmered back in the woods toward the highway, first dim and then brighter as a car drove into the opening and pulled up near us. The Volvo doors opened and boys in Izod shirts, madras shorts, and docksiders got out. One was holding a bottle of bourbon and the others silver Jefferson cups.

"It's Willmont," Larry said, motioning with his head to a kid wearing a blue button-down and a puka bead necklace.

"Be cool," Dwayne said.

"You know me, I'm Mr. Cool," Larry said, though he stood straight now and glanced with undisguised hostility at the boys.

"I mean it!" Dwayne said.

"Fucking preppies," Larry said.

"Dirtbags," Willmont said, and all the boys laughed.

"You going to stand for that?" Larry said, holding his arms out.

"Be cool," Dwayne said. "Don't let them get to you."

A lit cigarette flew from the group toward us like a tiny shooting star, landed with a spray of red embers on the back window of Larry's car, and rolled down the trunk onto the ground.

"Don't." Dwayne tried to hold Larry back but it was too late; he flew like a fly out of an open car window, swung his arm back, and punched Willmont in the head. There was a sound like a bag of flour falling off a table and hitting the floor and then voices rose one over another, like birds squalling. Larry pulled his shirt over his head; his stomach was pale, muscular, and shiny with sweat.

"Come on," he said. "Hit me, pussy."

"Get in and lock the doors," Dwayne ordered.

I got inside, rolled up all the windows, and locked the doors. Out the back I watched kids from the other side of the dump run toward us. At first I thought they were going to try to help, but then I saw their faces and how several screamed out "Fight!"

Dwayne tried to pull Larry back, but he kept slipping out of Dwayne's embrace.

Willmont stood, one hand on his hip and the other touching his bloody lip.

"You fucker," Willmont said. "You're crazy."

"Come on," Larry said. "I'll show you how crazy I am."

Larry reached out and grabbed Willmont's necklace, and the string snapped and beads flew up and then down, landing on the ground like hail.

Willmont threw himself at Larry, and when Dwayne tried to pull Larry back two preppy guys started to hit him. He tried to twist out of their reach, but one boy punched him in the stomach and he doubled over, and the other hit him in the side of the head. He fell forward, but maintained his balance until a third guy kicked him from behind and he fell, his head in a rut of rainwater.

When I got home that night everyone was already sleeping. Upstairs I saw something in the mirror at the end of the hallway. I moved my head sideways and the head of the intruder also shifted. I raised my right. Ditto. I walked forward and looked into my own dark face. I turned and went to the bottom of the stairs and then walked toward the figure. I did this too many times to count, sometimes walking very fast, sometimes in slow motion, pressing my body into the wall, other times with my head pressed into the top of the other's head, as if we were conjoined twins. Finally I heard mattress springs shift inside my parents' bedroom.

"Stop whatever it is you're doing," my father said, "and get to bed."

✦

I had to lie to my mom again to get her to drive me to Tanglewood. I said I had a job interview at the Orange Julius. Once up the escalator, I walked under the archway into the French Quarter. The French Quarter was looking shabby. Some of the stores, I read in the paper, were complaining about being stuck away in the corner of the gigantic mall. And there was a terrible rumor that the dark streets would be torn down, replaced by a giant sporting-goods center. I still loved the arches painted to look like brick and the lanterns suspended on the stucco walls. It was always a clear and starry night in the Quarter.

The Hancock's window featured loafers on pedestals. The place was wood-paneled with racks of sports coats and windbreakers. Dwayne stood next to a table covered with cashmere sweaters. His right eye was purple and there was a scab on his bottom lip.

"You came!" he said.

"I said I would."

He introduced me to the other salesman, a chubby guy who was folding shirts by the cash register, and then to the floor mannequin, Mr. Potato Head, with his bow tie and seersucker suit. He led me through a back door and up a few stairs into the attic stockroom. The night before, after Larry had dropped us off, I'd cleaned up Dwayne's face with a washcloth and listened to him fret about getting scars that would make him look less like Hutch. His father was at the bar and so he'd played me his Allman Brothers record and told me how he was planning to quit high school, get his GED, and move to Los Angeles.

The attic stockroom with its sloped ceiling and rough wood floors was the place Jill and I had envisioned renting in the French Quarter, a cozy apartment with a view out the tiny beveled window of a dark European street. Dwayne led me to a little table where he had set out sandwiches and cans of soda.

"Thanks about last night," he said.

"No problem," I said.

I took small bites of my sandwich so I wouldn't get mayo on my chin.

In bed the night before, I had fought with myself. Larry was at worst an agent of evil and at best a lunatic. Dwayne was trying to do better, but he was clueless and pathetic. Also I was lonely; my brother had no interest in me, my mom was giving me yet another silent treatment, and my dad was preoccupied as usual. And then there was summer itself; my job babysitting Phillip and Eddie was so dull and repetitive, I thought I might kill myself. Dwayne was just my momentary escape hatch. But I knew I was lying to myself. Because if Dwayne loved me, I'd be a girl loved by a boy. Once this happened, everyone else would realize I was adorable and loveable too. My eyes would shine, I'd look delicate—even delectable— and whether there was a place for me on earth or not would no longer be in dispute. I wanted my own story to get going. Not my mother's story or my father's story, not Sandy's story, or Jill's, or Sheila's, but *mine*.

"Did you know a snail can sleep for three years?"

Dwayne smiled, moved my hair off my face, used his hand to cup my cheek, and pulled my mouth closer to his. I could smell the cold cuts on his breath and then his mouth was on mine, his hurt lip rough; his tongue darted between my teeth and moved fervently against my gums.

✦

The next day, after feeding Eddie and Phillip a late lunch, I was just settling down to watch the soaps when I heard a shot explode from in front of the house. I ran outside. Eddie had a shiny piece of coat lining tied around his neck and Phillip was wearing his new glasses. Both wore black felt minutemen hats. Their bikes lay on the gravel beside them as they squatted down, marveling at the hole in the ground and the ants streaming over the red dirt.

"That's cruel!" I said.

"They're ants," Eddie said, as if I didn't know. "They'd bite you as soon as look at you."

"Where'd you get the firecracker?"

"What firecracker?"

"Come off it," I said.

"Dwayne gave it to us."

"Really?" I said.

"It was weird," Phillip said. "He just walked up the hill and handed it to me."

I walked down the mountain toward Dwayne's duplex. Mrs. Smith had unrolled a Confederate flag from her second-story window and several people were setting up grills in the front yard to celebrate. Most of Bent Tree was at the stadium downtown for the parade. Mr. Ananais had gone to see the antique car show and the wrestlers Bobo John and Billy the Red.

At Dwayne's the blinds were closed, but I could see the TV was on and I heard muffled voices. I'd come down to tell him how disappointed I was that he'd give something so dangerous to kids. But I had a deeper reason. I had decided to let Dwayne do whatever he wanted to me. He could even kidnap me or rape me if he wanted. He could handcuff me and tickle me with a feather, or give me an Indian handshake. I tapped a triangular pattern six times with each foot; my toes in my flip-flops looked long and odd as if they were giving me away as a space alien. I heard a sharp laugh and the door sucked open. Dwayne stood in his khakis, his oxford open to show his bare chest, his eyelids sunk down halfway.

A sweet smell wafted out on a wave of cold air conditioning.

"Come on in," he said. "It's the fucking Bi-cen-tenn-ial."

I stepped inside and looked around the dark room. Larry and Sheila sat on the couch and Dwayne's dad sat in a lawn chair up close to the television, which was balanced on a box. Sheila glared at me. I knew she thought I'd ratted out Mr. Ramin.

"Close the fucking door," she said. "You're letting all the cold air out."

"Watch your language, missy," Dwayne's dad said, though he did not turn around, just sat in his bathrobe with a glass of scotch in his hand, watching the television screen.

"Come on, Dwayne Senior," Larry said. "Loosen up."

"Yeah," Sheila said, "loosen up!"

Dwayne tossed me a can of Bud and I sat down on the shag with my back against the wall. I realized I had played right into his hands. He knew I'd come down if he gave my brother the firecracker.

"Tell her what you did to Willmont," Sheila said.

"I caught him coming out of the 7-Eleven," Larry said, "and beat the shit out of him."

"Can you keep it down," Dwayne Senior said. "I can't hear the president."

One part of me was saying: *Get out. Get out now while you can.* I was also worried about my little brother and Eddie, whom I was supposed to be watching. But another part of me was fascinated with the white-blond hair on Dwayne's forearm, by his sad crooked smile and his drunken dad.

I'd read how boys asked you out, bought you dinner, and kissed you at the door when they drove you home. I'd read about dances, where you drank punch from crystal bowls and danced with a different boy every song. But this particular social situation—sitting around drinking beers while your date's dad sat in a stupor watching television—I didn't have any information on.

"Did you see the nigger moving into 21A?" Dwayne's dad asked.

I had seen the van pull up and a white man and his black wife carry boxes into the house. There was a little girl who ran around the yard trying to catch butterflies. My father had walked over to welcome them.

"Come on, Dad," Dwayne said.

"I got fired because of a nigger."

"You got fired," Dwayne said, "because you were out a whole week and didn't call in once."

"I was sick," Dwayne's dad said. "You know I was sick. They would have let me off but that nigger salesman told them he'd seen me down at the bar."

"But you were at the bar," Dwayne said.

"All I'd done was gone down to get a hot toddy for my throat."

Everyone was quiet. When you were with boys you let the boys talk and you just laughed a lot. If you did say something, it had to be adorable. You could say something funny, but dumb-funny was better than smart-funny. I thought of cutting the silence by making a joke about the movie *Jaws* or saying something about the *Apollo* spaceship that had just splashed down, the pale astronauts coming out only to go into isolation to make sure they didn't have some crazy space virus.

Dwayne's dad stomped upstairs, changed his clothes, and went out, he said, for cigarettes. We all knew it was 6:00 PM, his time to go to the bar in the strip mall next to the card shop.

"We could go downtown," I said, "and see the fireworks."

"Fuck that," Larry said. "It's showtime!"

He closed the blinds and got the movie projector from the closet and took a reel from a paper bag. Idiotically, as it turned out, I first thought he'd show us a documentary about the Revolutionary War. The light flicked on against the stucco wall: an Asian girl in bell-bottoms and a red halter top pushed a cart through a grocery store. The film quality was grainy and I could hear the film moving inside the machine. The girl stopped in front of the bananas and made eye contact with a bald guy in a white T-shirt. The man and woman left the grocery store. Then they were in an apartment and the man unzipped his pants. The girl licked her lips slowly and dramatically and then they fell on each other in a frenzy of body parts and extended tongues.

The man sunk his finger between the woman's legs and sucked her nipples, an expression on his face as if he were going to have a seizure. The camera floated down to his penis, hard and bobbing like a sea creature. The woman grabbed the penis with her tiny hand and started to pump it, as if trying to get water out of a well.

When the film was over, Dwayne jumped up to turn off the projector. Sheila and Larry had dissolved into one another on the couch. Dwayne put his finger over his lips and walked over to the stairs. I hesitated. I certainly couldn't stay down here where Larry had his hands up the back of Sheila's shirt, his face pink and desperate. But I wasn't sure I wanted to go up the stairs with Dwayne. He shrugged his shoulders and went on up alone.

A part of me knew I was in over my head. I wanted not to go home so much as to be little again, sitting on my dad's lap while he read to me from my book of children's Bible stories. But here I was terrified and thrilled at the exact same time. Dwayne paused at the top of the stairs, glanced behind him, and walked down the hallway toward his room. I watched Larry, still entwined with Sheila, move his hand up to the lamp and turn out the light. The duplex was dark as I moved up the stairs.

Halfway down the hall, Dwayne jumped out of the closet where he'd been hiding.

"Get in the car!" he shouted at me.

I was confused.

"You mean go outside and get in the car?"

His features had rearranged and his pupils were dilated. I knew he'd been drinking, but now I was worried he'd taken acid. I had heard stories of kids jumping out of windows or walking into traffic. One girl, thinking she was a seagull, had jumped off the top of a Ferris wheel. And a boy, the next town over, had stabbed himself with a steak knife.

He stood with his hands on his hips. Should I try to kiss him or hug him, try to snap him out of his bad trip? He balled up his fist, swung. I flinched as he punched the air, then fell back against the wall, moving his head back and forth as if being slapped this way and that.

He was Hutch. I wasn't sure, though, which particular episode we were in—the one where Huggy Bear gets kidnapped by the psychotic drug lord? Or maybe the one where the delicate country music star is stalked by an obsessive fan? As he shook off the slaps and stood back up, he brought his fists up in front of his face. I realized we were back at the dump with the preppy boys. But this time Dwayne was Hutch, taking out one after the other, punching the air, flying sideways into karate kicks.

I took a baby step toward the stairs, but Dwayne pulled my arm, he wanted an audience, as his bangs stuck to his sweaty forehead and he threw up his elbows, knocking some poor kid in the chin.

"Stop," I said. "You're hurting them."

He looked at me, blinking. At first I thought he was angry, that he felt stupid for pretending, but then he smiled. We heard an explosion and then another. We ran outside. The few people who hadn't gone downtown sat out in lawn chairs. The girls from 4B waved sparklers and we could see, up in the sky, the blooming light.

✦

The summer crept forward with nothing much happening until one hot day in August. Eddie, Phillip, and I were sitting down to eat peanut butter sandwiches when an unfamiliar convertible drove up the hill and parked in front of 17A, across the street and down the mountain a little from our duplex. A dark-haired guy in a denim leisure suit and a woman in a long floral dress with a pointy white collar got out and walked up to the front door. They didn't knock. They just stood under the hot sun in their big sunglasses, smiling. Other cars parked and by the time I finished my lunch, the line of people stretched down the sloping street almost to the Bent Tree sign. They were all dressed for a party, women in makeup and false eyelashes and men in ties, although it was nearly a hundred degrees. Among the group was a man in a Hawaiian shirt and white pants, his bald head shining in the sun. Beside him was a tall, skinny woman with twin boys, both in blue blazers and red bow ties.

A few days earlier, a man had driven up to 17A, a heavyset guy with just a folding chair, a card table, and a few boxes in his trunk. The young woman who lived in the duplex, a dog groomer named Dolores, was visiting her mother in Richmond. I figured she must be letting a friend use her place while she was gone. Through the front window I'd seen the new guy watching the black-and-white television with tinfoil on the antenna, and drinking from a martini glass. Maybe the man had come back to Roanoke and was throwing a huge party and the people lining up now were all old friends. Maybe he was a well-known doctor and the people all suffered from undiagnosed illnesses? Or could he be giving away, to the first one hundred folks, coupons for free television sets?

Eddie and Phillip weren't interested in speculating about what the man did. Instead, they wanted to take advantage of the crowd. Their entrepreneurial streak had been awakened that spring. They'd sold the dessert off their school lunches and used the profits to buy candy bars, which they then peddled at recess for twice what they'd paid.

Now, with a gathering crowd of people, they brainstormed about what to sell. It was a hot day, so Eddie suggested setting up the sprinkler and charging people to jump through the cool spray. Phillip suggested linking extension cords out the front door and charging for a few minutes of cool fan air. I vetoed these ideas.

"I got it!" Phillip said. "We'll sell Kool-Aid."

As we were setting up the card table, Dwayne walked up the hill. He wore white jeans, a white belt, and his Dingo boots. He'd blown out his blond hair and looked like the angelic version of his usual self. I asked if he knew what was going on and he smiled widely and said, "Casting call," reaching in his pocket and pulling out an ad he'd torn from the morning newspaper. He handed it to me.

Do you have talent? Universal International Studios is looking for extras, dancers, singers, and horseback riders for a Civil War film to be made in the area. Those interested apply at 1:00 PM to Glen McCabe in Bent Tree, 17A. August 10, 1976.

"See," he said. "I told you the South would rise again."

A van pulled up with an airbrushed eagle on the side. The door flew open and people dressed for square dancing jumped out, the men in Western shirts and Texas ties and the women in calico skirts and crinolines.

"Gotta go," Dwayne said. "I'm going to cut the line."

At one o'clock sharp as promised, Glen McCabe, his hair slicked back, wearing a shirt open to show a slew of gold chains, came out onto the stoop. Everybody cheered.

"Welcome," he said, "and thank you for your interest in our little production. The director told me it was a long shot that I'd find extras here, but you all have proven him wonderfully wrong. I look forward to meeting each and every one of you."

Dwayne, who'd been standing on the grass, walked up to the man.

"I have riding experience."

This was the first I'd heard that Dwayne was a horseman, but in the days that followed he'd claim that, thanks to his Confederate ancestor, he knew how to handle a saber and light a cannon fuse.

✦

Glen McCabe was the most exciting thing that had ever happened to Bent Tree. His arrival derailed the idea that Bent Tree was purgatory. All day folks went into 17A with hopeful, subservient expressions and came out beaming. Every hour Glen walked down the line, tousling the hair of the twin boys in red bow ties, pulling a coin from the ear of a lady in a halter top, admiring the Civil War artifacts people brought to show him: letters, Confederate jackets, swords. Some even brought photos of relatives, somber-looking young men with beards holding guns. Because the United Daughters of the Confederacy had held a Civil War Ball a few years ago, a few women wore hoop skirts and carried silk parasols. Even my own family stood in line. McCabe promised my mom the part of an antebellum lady and Phillip was going to be a drummer boy.

Mrs. Smith called an emergency meeting of the UDC and asked me to help pass the punch and finger sandwiches. Most of the ladies had gray hair and wore shirtwaist dresses and practical shoes. One exception was a woman who claimed to be the descendent of a captain who had fallen at Shiloh. She had dyed black hair and wore a long white dress.

They ate pimento cheese sandwiches and drank sweet iced tea.

Before the meeting started I passed around a plate of deviled eggs.

"Are you the new junior member?" the lady in the long dress asked. Mrs. Smith had told me about the children's wing of the United Daughters of the Confederacy.

I shook my head and felt my cheeks warm up.

Mrs. Smith called the meeting to order. She told the Daughters about Glen McCabe and the Civil War movie; how Cary Grant was to play John Bell Hood and Mickey Rooney would play Stand Watie. On set the Daughters would make sure period details were accurate. The precious historical items they had gathered for so long—gloves, Bibles, letters—would finally be seen by millions. Glen had also offered a thousand dollars to the Daughters for on-set catering.

Mrs. Smith nodded at me to bring out the lemon cake and the pink dessert dishes. I asked who wanted coffee. After they were done eating Mrs. Smith went to her piano and started to play. The women sang loud, particularly the last verse.

And here's to brave Virginia!
The Old Dominion State
With the young Confederacy
At last has linked her fate.
Impelled by her example, now other states prepare

To hoist on high the bonnie blue flag
That bears a single star.

I slipped out and into the kitchen to do the dishes and lay them out on the linen dishcloths. I rinsed grounds out of the percolator and wiped down the countertops.

It was dark by the time the Daughters finished singing the song about Shiloh. Mrs. Smith called me back into the living room to help her pass around candles like the ones my father used for Christmas Eve service, white wax with paper drip skirts. She turned out the lamps and the orange flames lit each woman's face. Mrs. Smith read names off an index card. *Adam Ickis, private*; *William Marr, private*; *Chester Adams, private*; *Tilman Valentine, private*. After each name and rank was read, his great-great-granddaughter extinguished the flame, until all was dark and the women sang "Dixie," without accompaniment, into the dark living room.

✦

When I got home my mom had the stereo headphones on and was singing to her favorite musical, *Fiddler on the Roof*. Phillip had his head wrapped in paper-towel bandages and was making a saber out of tinfoil. My father was on the couch reading. Mrs. Smith had come over to see if my dad was willing to be a Civil War chaplain but he'd refused, saying everyone had lost their minds.

I ran up the stairs and locked myself in the bathroom and placed my hands on my invisible hoop skirt and said, "Oh you do run on, teasing a country girl like me." And I practiced slapping Rhett and then kissing him using the pillow I'd brought in from my bed. "Atlanta's burning," I said into the mirror dozens of times. I tried to mist my eyes up by thinking of how Mr. Ananais's cat, Hector, had gotten his paw run over and now had only three legs, and how the kids still teased Pam on the bus, calling her butt-ugly and Kool-Aid face. No matter how hard I tried, I could not make myself cry.

In the mirror I was stiff and unnatural. I could not be like the girls at school and cry whenever I wanted. I'd never be an actress and live in a castle high up in the Hollywood Hills, eating lobster tails and chocolate éclairs. I'd thought it was adorable the way Dwayne went on about Hollywood. Even before Glen McCabe, he'd talked of wanting to move there, getting a house with a pool, learning to surf, and going to parties where he'd meet David Soul and Keith Carradine. I knew he was dreamy, but I liked to put my head on his chest and listen to him go off into La La Land. There was something soothing and familiar about the tenor of his voice.

I could hear people on the street. Most of them had disappeared for the day once auditions were over, but some camped out, sleeping in their cars. I could see Mr. Ananais picking up the garbage with a stick and looking sadly at the trampled grass.

+

The next day people started getting in line at 6:00 AM. I heard them talking below my window about how Glen said he'd pay ten dollars an hour, fifteen if you had a beard. One guy said if he could get hired, he'd be able to make his car payment. Another said he was going to pay for his mother's hernia operation.

By nine o'clock over a hundred people had lined up. Eddie and Phillip carried Lulubell over and Glen gave the cat a part as a lazy Confederate kitty lying out on a porch. Her job, Eddie told me, was *to act uninterested*. Yesterday the people in line had all looked vaguely theatrical. Today the people looked more ordinary: guys in gray work shirts, housewives, teenagers. Everybody thought they had hidden talents. Even those who had no talent thought that having no talent must be a sort of talent.

Dwayne appeared just after nine, saying he'd quit Hancock's for a job helping McCabe. His duties included collecting the ten-dollar application fee, distributing forms, and asking people if they had experience singing, dancing, riding, or sword fighting. Dwayne told each applicant that, once registered, he or she would be a full member of the Screen Actors Guild. I heard him tell several people that, after Glen's film wrapped, he was going to move to Los Angeles. To think of him living the good life while I was stuck in Bent Tree made me sick to my stomach.

Dwayne ran out of the duplex to tell me that Glen knew David Soul and that Soul was interested in the part of Jeb Stuart! I tried to ask him to take me with him to LA, but he was so excited that Liza Minnelli was going to lead the Southern belles in the big ballroom dance scene, I didn't have a chance. Just before lunch he told me George C. Scott had agreed to play Grant, and Al Pacino wanted to be Ambrose Burnside. Glen was in negotiations with Sylvester Stallone to play Longstreet. Late in the afternoon Glen got the OK from the studio to burn down a barn. He and Mrs. Smith were going to scout locations in Vinton in the morning. Mrs. Smith was going to do the paperwork with the fire department this afternoon. She'd invested in the film, and so she would have some creative control. Dwayne roamed up and down the line, mostly dealing with girls. One nervous girl in a tube top and feather earrings burst into tears, and Dwayne rubbed her back till she got ahold of herself. He fed ice cubes to a girl who fainted and waited with her until her mom arrived.

Near dinnertime Dwayne came to get me for my audition. I'd been in the bathroom practicing, going over my facial expressions and trying to make my smile look genuine. I'd rehearsed for so long in the bathroom mirror I had no idea when my expression looked natural and when it didn't. We walked in silence, side by side, to the door of 17A. Inside, the duplex was cool, dark, and smoky. The rooms were the same as ours, the gold shag and plaster swirl ceiling, but with pictures of puppies and stacks of magazines about dogs. Glen sat on his folding chair, a shoe box full of money at his feet. He stirred his drink with his pointer finger, then put it inside his cavernous mouth and sucked.

Time wobbled off its usual track and seemed to elongate.

"This is the girl I told you about," Dwayne said.

"Can you act, my dear?" Glen asked me, leaning his massive form back into the chair.

"I thought you wanted extras?"

"We have a few speaking parts," he said. "For the right people."

He tipped his glass to his mouth, holding his pinkie out, the ice clinking against his teeth. Even though it was freezing in the duplex, his upper lip sweat like Nixon's. He closed his eyes.

"I see you as a girl dressed as a boy," Glen said, "so you can fight for the motherland you love."

A girl inside a boy. I liked that.

"She has a certain look, don't you think?" Dwayne said.

"I see a scene where you show the soldier boy you love your womanhood."

I was not exactly sure what he meant; the term *womanhood* had always confused me.

He opened his eyes and looked at me.

"Would you be willing to do that?"

"No," I said, "I don't think so."

McCabe frowned and turned to Dwayne.

"I thought you said she wanted to be in our film?"

"She does!"

"Apparently not," McCabe said, standing and walking into the kitchen. He swung open the refrigerator door and got out a bottle of vodka.

I waited for him to say something more.

"You're free to go," he finally said. "Good luck with your life."

+

I retreated to my room and lay there, staring up at the ceiling. I stared into the eyes of the Egyptian on the poster above my dresser. Was this really my only chance? Was I actually blowing everything? Like everybody else, I wanted to be saved.

I walked over the shag, down the hallway, and locked myself in the bathroom. I stared into the mirror. I was skinny and pathetic. I pulled off my dress and reached around to unhitch my bra, letting the white cotton cups fall. I looked in the mirror. I didn't want to see myself the way I did every day when I pulled my clothes on in the morning, or pulled them off and put my T-shirt on at night. I wanted to see myself the way Glen McCabe wanted to see me. My nipples were small like pearl buttons, a washed-out pink flooding up around each.

I heard a knock on the front door and Dwayne asked my mom if he could see me. Normally my mom would have never let a boy come to my room but something about McCabe's movie had pushed aside her anxieties and suspicions. I heard her say, "Go on up!"

I pulled my shirt back on and ran to my room. Quickly, I tore down the kitten poster, throwing it under the bed. After that I arranged myself against the pillows and moved my face into a smile.

"Hey," Dwayne said, coming through the doorway.

I knew what was coming.

"Are you sure you don't want to be in the movie?"

"Not if I have to show my womanhood."

"You could think of it like a stepping stone."

The overhead light made his blond hair glitter and his eyes, while vacant, were the prettiest shade of blue.

"OK," I said.

"Really?"

I nodded.

He jumped on the bed and kissed me.

"You won't be sorry, I promise!"

He kissed me again full on the mouth and turned and walked out of my room and down the stairs. I heard the front door close and I watched him moving into a cone of light and then out again into the dark. Each time he moved into the streetlight in his white pants and shirt, his hair shone like a movie star's.

After an hour of trying to get to sleep, of turning my pillow over and over, I decided to pray. But this time I wasn't going to pray to Cher, with her black hair as powerful as crude oil, or to Bowie, with his red hair and different-color eyes, or even to a giant mushroom, imagining myself lying prostrate under it. I wanted to contact God directly, but the ways I'd been taught to connect didn't really work anymore, it was like trying to talk on a phone with terrible reception. Maybe it was because God was gone. On TV I'd hear hippies say that God was dead, but what was left after someone died? A hole, a space that was just as affecting as when they were alive. Just because the body was gone did not mean someone was not real. I was going to pray into the hole, yell down: *Do I really have to bare my womanhood?*

I'm not sure exactly what I expected. Only in the Bible did God speak to people directly; these days He occasionally showed His image on frosted windows or dirty dish towels. I'd never heard an actual voice, though sometimes my attention had been focused in a way that felt outside my control; I'd noticed a drop of water falling from the bathroom faucet, or the weave of the material of my jeans. I waited, I knelt until my legs got numb and I heard Phillip in the shower. My knuckles were white, my teeth clenched, but bits of my brain were falling asleep. I opened my eyes and the first thing I saw was the business card lying on the night table. McCabe had given it to me on my way out in case I changed my mind. I grabbed it and walked across the hall into my parents' bedroom. I sat on the side of the bed and picked up the receiver. Under Glen's name was printed UNIVERSAL

INTERNATIONAL STUDIOS. I dialed the number. I was afraid my mother would come in and catch me calling long-distance. We never called long-distance. We never called anybody until the rates went down after eleven.

"Stay Bright Laundromat," a woman said with enthusiasm.

"What?" I said.

"We close at midnight."

I hung up. My palms sweat. I dialed the number again.

"Stay Bright Laundromat."

I slammed down the phone. The number must be printed on the card wrong. I unfolded the sheets McCabe had given everybody who auditioned. The words were purple and I could tell the sheets had not been printed but run off on a mimeograph machine, like my father's church bulletin. A few words had been misspelled, blocked out with XXXs, and then retyped.

Maybe the number had changed since McCabe had had the cards made up. I dialed information and waited for the California operator. I asked for the number of the studio.

"Are you sure you have the name right?"

"I think so."

"Checking again."

I listened to the rushing silence over the line.

"There is no listing under that name."

I hung up, walked into the living room, and sat down on the couch. The radio dial on the stereo glowed and

I watched the lighted windows of the duplexes down the main road. My dad came in, closing his umbrella; he looked exhausted from his shift at the psych center. I turned on the lamp.

"I have to talk to you."

"Now?" he said.

"Glen McCabe asked me to show him my womanhood."

"That movie guy? You didn't do it, did you?"

"No," I said.

"Well, thank God for that," he said, walking over to the phone. He picked up the receiver. "I'm going to call the police."

✦

The next morning Glen's car was gone, but people started to show up as usual and Dwayne, who assumed he was out scouting locations with Mrs. Smith, got everybody in orderly lines. After a while Mrs. Smith came out and said she hadn't heard from Glen since yesterday but that the police had called and asked a few questions. She looked small and worried, telling everybody that he must have had an emergency meeting out of town. People moaned when Dwayne announced auditions for the day were canceled.

It took a few days for it to sink in that no movie was going to be made. No grand battle scene with thousands of extras, no ballroom scene with a full orchestra. James Taylor would not be playing Jubal Early.

✦

Dwayne got his Hancock's job back. I'd see him through the window lying on his couch after work with his oxford unbuttoned, doing bong hits. He claimed he'd known all along that Glen was a fake, that he'd promised him a cut of whatever money they made off of dopes who wanted to be movie stars. It didn't make sense. Had he really wanted me to show McCabe my womanhood for the ten-dollar application fee?

On Saturday night I could have hung around outside the pizza place down in the strip mall by the highway or lain on my bed and stared up at the ceiling. If I were a boy I'd have shot hoops or worked on my karate moves, but for a girl there was only one kind of adventure. I walked down the hill to Dwayne's duplex. As he opened the door, I threw my skeleton against his skeleton. It was like we'd lived our whole lives, died, lain down in the dirt, and were now meeting as elements. He put his arms around me. Over his shoulder I saw the little altar on top of the television, one of his mother's dangly earrings, a postcard of Little Sorrel, Jackson's horse, and a star-base bullet that Dwayne claimed had killed his great-great-grandfather in the Civil War.

+

CHAPTER SIX

JESSE

The morning I got up for my first day of tenth grade, my parents were sitting on the couch. My mother's face was white, but she was smiling. Dad, on the other hand, was gray, exhausted. My mother said after school we were going to have an important family meeting.

What would the meeting be about? I asked diplomatically. The night before they'd had a terrible fight, yelling, slamming doors. My mother screamed *you want us to eat air* and my dad said that actually there was a sect of monks who trained themselves to survive only on oxygen. My mother went from a 3 to a 1, and my dad fled, left the house, and drove off in the car. I couldn't tell if they'd made up or if they'd decided to end everything. My parents responded together that we'd have to wait and see.

I was feeling queasy by the time I climbed on the bus fifteen minutes later and caught a whiff of vomit and cleaning fluid. One of the little kids from the earlier elementary-school run must have thrown up. The wheels rolled into a pothole and I was tossed in the air and had to hold on to my seat. Dwayne had dropped out of school to work and Sheila was going to the Christian High School in Salem. The only person I recognized was Pam, who sat in her usual place a few seats behind the driver, her long bangs over her birthmark, her nose, as usual, inside a fat book. Halfway to school, she turned and looked at me.

"What's wrong?" she said.

"Why?"

"You look sick."

"I think my parents are going to split up."

"Join the club," she said.

"Your parents are divorced?"

"Mine never even got married!" she said.

I waited for her to explain further but her eyes drifted back to the pages of her book. She was famous for sneaking a library book onto her lap and being so mesmerized by it that she wouldn't even hear the teacher call her name. The door clunked open and a kid got on carrying his black tuba case. The driver yelled at the boys in the back who were chewing tobacco and spitting brown juice out the window. As we turned off 419, into the high school lot, Pam told me how Eleanor Roosevelt often read straight through bath time and, sometimes, while sitting up in a tree. Eleanor was terrible at making conversation and so she'd go through the alphabet to come up with things to say. *A–apples. Do you like apples, Mr. Smith?*

I glanced around to see if anybody was laughing, but nobody seemed to care what we were doing one way or the other.

✦

At Cave Spring High, which went from tenth to twelfth grade, the halls were not as noisy as they were at Low Valley. Boys didn't jump on each other's backs pretending to ride each other like horses. Girls didn't scream when they heard a surprising bit of gossip. I'd expected to be threatened with a knife while watching kids copulate. I'd expected to be offered Thai stick and to watch girls snort coke in the bathroom off their geometry textbooks. But while there was a strong undercurrent of sex and misery, the students moved subdued through the hallways.

My homeroom teacher, a middle-aged woman with a small, shriveled face, looked over us female sophomores with contempt poorly disguised as cheerfulness. In health class, the eager young student teacher told us our first unit was to be on grooming. We'd each have to do an oral report on some aspect of our morning routine. Hands shot up to volunteer to talk about hot rollers and curling irons.

The only teacher who appeared nervous was Mr. Higgins, who taught sophomore english. He paced the front of the classroom in black dress pants and a blue button-down, his face pink. He spoke in an unhinged way about infinity. On the board he'd written out a quote by Emerson:

> A sentence in a book, or a word dropped in conversation, sets free our fancy, and instantly our heads are bathed with galaxies.

He had a lunatic's enthusiasm for the Transcendentalists. He told a mesmerizing, if tangential, story about taking a bee out of his little sister's white ankle sock. How tiny her foot was and how hard she'd tried not to cry. Pam, who sat beside me, was clearly as thrilled as I was by Mr. Higgins's energy. He was like the preachers on television, but instead of God's law, he was talking about the possibility of becoming *pure love*. My classmates rolled their eyes at each other while he spoke, but I felt that, like Cher and Bowie, he had a message intended especially for me.

In the hallway, Pam made the boys uneasy; when she passed they looked down at their tennis shoes. In the locker room a girl whispered something to Pam. She put her hands over her face but she wouldn't tell me what the girl had said, and she didn't want me to tell the teacher. High school, she'd hoped, might be different than junior high, but clearly that wasn't true.

I felt bad for her, with her slumped shoulders and marked face. I reached a hand out to her, but she just shrugged me off and quoted Muhammad: *When people throw garbage on you, remember that it's their garbage.*

+

When I got home my parents were sitting on the couch again. My dad had on his suit and my mom wore her good dress. My brother was called down from his room and we all walked outside and got into the car. I sat next to my brother just as I had on the drive down to Roanoke from Philadelphia. He started to cry. My mom turned and told him softly that there was no need. I knew we were headed to Sans Souci to see where my dad was going to live. I figured he was the one who had decided he was not rooted in our life together. We'd visit him on weekends, he'd make us eat his terrible cooking. I'd used to long to hang out with my dad in his bachelor pad, where we could sit reading, him with his Alan Watts book and me with my *Big Book of Burial Rights*, no one moving from a 3 to a 2. But now that it was happening all I felt was carsick.

My dad did not drive the car toward the airport and Sans Souci; he turned into a subdivision not far down 419. The place was called Nottingham Hill, and we passed a split-level with a speedboat parked in the driveway and one with a deer figurine beside a boxwood bush.

"Are you getting divorced?" I finally shouted.

My mother turned around as we pulled into the driveway of a red-brick ranch with yellow shutters.

"No, silly," she said. "Your father and I bought a house!"

✦

As I got off the bus the next day I saw Jill holding hands with a dozen kids out by the flagpole. She wore a long prairie dress with a white collar. A boy with a receding hairline asked God for protection from the Devil. He asked Jesus to walk alongside each of them through the hallways and into every classroom. Jill's eyes were clenched shut, but when she opened them and saw me, she ran over and threw her arms around me.

I'd been hoping to see her, but now that she was in front of me I felt angry. After she hugged me she started to talk fast, telling me that after the Swensons' she'd been placed in another foster home. It wasn't a bad place, just weird, with odd smells and hot-pink towels. Her grandmother had finally gotten custody of them last Christmas and they'd moved into her trailer in Bedford. Now they lived in Sans Souci.

"The big news is my mom came back," she said.

"Where was she?"

"She won't say," Jill said. "The only clue we have is a tattoo on her ankle of a rattlesnake."

"Weird!"

"She just came in the front door, got a beer out of the fridge, and threw herself down on the couch."

"Why didn't you ever call me?"

"I kept meaning to, but the more time went by, the more I got afraid to dial your number."

Her accent was thicker than I remembered. She was still skinny and hunched, and her face was pale and beautiful like a girl in an old painting. She asked if I wanted to ride the bus home with her one day after school.

+

Jill was in standard while Pam and I were in accelerated, so we had different lunch periods. I ate my tuna fish sandwich. There was something really sad about the tuna fish sandwich, especially because the bread was soggy and mayo was smeared onto the plastic bag. We were finally buying a house and moving. I knew this was supposed to make me feel good. But instead of making me feel more substantial, somehow I felt less so, like a ghost girl roaming the hallways with my feet floating above the floor. Between me and everything there was a space, like an enormous canyon I could never hope to bridge or cross. It was like I was dead. A ghost girl didn't need to worry about being popular, and it didn't matter if she was sitting beside the freakiest girl in the whole school. Pam tried to cheer *me* up, which was pretty ironic. She reminded me that

Mr. Higgins had told us the Transcendentalists felt unseen things were eternal and that the life inside us was like a river. She told me that when Eleanor Roosevelt wanted to swear, she said *Oh Spinach!*

After lunch I gave my report in health on how shampoo buildup dulled hair and how important it was to rinse your hair now and then with cider vinegar to cut soap scum. I had a picture of soap scum on a bathroom tile to illustrate my point. The girl after me explained how by using an ice cube you could numb your eyebrows before plucking, and the girl after that showed us how to clean our pierced ears with a peroxide-soaked cotton swab.

Pam walked up to the front of the room swinging a tote bag. She was supposed to talk about highlighting your hair with lemon juice. She picked up a piece of chalk and wrote *nevus flammeus* on the board. After she set the chalk down, she looked out over us, gazing into each of our eyes before taking a damp washcloth from her bag and running it over her face. The makeup came off beige and greasy and her birthmark revealed itself as purple-red with a lattice of tiny black capillaries just under the skin. It was as if she were showing us that while she could pass for human, she was actually a space alien and that, on her planet, people's hearts were located not in their chests but inside their cheeks.

I wanted to shout *Stop! Go back! Have you lost your mind?* But it was too late; a space had opened, one rawer and realer than the classroom we'd originally entered. All eyes fixed on Pam. She didn't seem shy or embarrassed. All her movements were matter-of-fact. I was reminded of how, on the rare occasions she spoke up in class, she always said something so wise that the teacher had a hard time believing she was not reciting a quote from a book.

She told us her birthmark was often called a port-wine stain or other nicknames, such as salmon patch, stork's bite, or angel kiss. The medical term was the word on the board. *Nevus flammeus.* For a long time, she explained, people had thought birthmarks were caused by things your mom had done while she was pregnant. You'd get a red patch if a jealous person touched your mother's stomach; you'd get a red patch if someone slapped her face, or if she'd been frightened by an animal. Saints sometimes had red marks that were reported to give them divine power. A woman with a mark on her forehead might say she could cure babies of colic. All of these were false. *Nevus flammeus* was just a bunch of blood vessels all in one place, too close to the skin's surface.

"I've been called Kool-Aid face, throw-up face, fire face, monster," Pam said. "Also sambo, retard, cootie queen. I've been called ugly in so many ways—ugly monkey, Ugly Mcfugly—I've lost count. You'd think by now we'd be too old for name-calling but the first day of school someone called me cutworm. It was worse in the fifth grade. A boy said I was possessed by the

Devil. On the playground he'd sneak up on me and make devil horns over my head. Pretty soon all the kids were doing it."

Pam held up a jar of white cream.

"It was after that that I started to use this. And I'm going to show you how I do it." She stuck her fingers into the stuff, spreading it over the mark that stretched from her forehead almost down to her chin. When it was covered she looked like she had sunscreen over half her face. Then she squeezed the thick beige foundation onto her fingers and spread it out in a circular motion. As she did this her real face disappeared and the one we all recognized came back into focus.

✦

Sans Souci consisted of two rows of three-story apartment buildings surrounded by gravel parking lots. Jill and I walked from the bus stop with a fat girl named Bitsy, past the reeking Dumpster full of diapers, pizza boxes, and a busted lamp shade. The Bamburgs' apartment was on the second floor. The living room had a low ceiling and walls painted industrial gray. An electric cord hung down from the overhead light and connected to the back of the television.

In the kitchen I could hear the upstairs neighbors laughing and, through the wall, "Free Bird." There was an uncovered pot of beef stew on the stove and, in the fridge, a twelve-pack of beer and a jar of mayonnaise.

Jill started to tell me how she went to both Sunday and Wednesday church services. At her church sometimes people looked up at the ceiling as if they were seeing right through the roof and spoke in tongues. Others were slain in the spirit and fainted. Now she felt closer to Jesus than her own family. He was always nearby, sitting on her bed or walking beside her through the halls at school.

She read her Bible every morning, during lunch, and at night.

"So you found God?"

I tried to sound bored.

"He found me," Jill said. "I was too lost to find anybody."

"Lost how?"

"First I started drinking. Then huffing. When I was huffing I would go with anybody."

Jill looked down at her hands. She'd bitten her nails down to nubs but her fingers were still long and elegant.

"What does Jesus tell you?"

"It's personal," she said. "He doesn't want me to say."

I remembered when we'd smoked the bean pod in the bathroom at the mall and Jill had seen the black catfish that looked like her dad.

"Jesus will talk to you, too, if you ask him," she said.

There was a mildew smell coming from the wall adjacent to the bathroom. I did not want to do a Bible study. Jill was talking about Jesus like he was her boyfriend. I just wanted to leave. But the clock said my father wasn't supposed to pick me up for another half hour, so I'd have to sit in her room and listen to her testimonial.

Jill's bed was made up with the same afghan she'd had at Bent Tree, though now it was in tatters. She didn't have a dresser. Her clothes were carefully folded and stacked against the wall. I watched her move around the room. The skin on her face was grayish with lavender pouches under each eye. She had on that long prairie dress, the white one with the lace collar. Everything she did irritated me. I had loved her once but now I didn't even want to look at her.

She put "Stairway to Heaven" on the portable record player she'd found in the Dumpster. According to the newspaper this was a song the satanic kids loved, but Jill claimed it was about Jesus.

"Buying a stairway to heaven means the lady is tithing," she said. "And with a *word* she can get what she came for. The word is the Word of God!"

"If you say so," I said.

She could tell I was unmoved, unyielding to her lover boy Jesus.

Jill reached up to the top of her closet and got down her Ouija board.

"Did you know there were unicorns in the Bible?"

"Unicorns?"

"Numbers 23:22. God brings them out of Egypt and is for them like the horn of the unicorn."

The Ouija board's box was cracked at the sides from heavy use. In Philadelphia, I'd been to a birthday party where girls got out the Ouija board and asked if the boys they liked liked them back and how many kids they'd have. But I'd heard darker stories too, about the girl who'd started talking in the voice of Jack the Ripper and how during one session a toaster had flown off the counter and smashed on the floor. I watched Jill unfold the board on her bed. On each side was a different occult symbol: a sickle, a moon, a crown, a raven. The wooden planchette was shaped like a triangle.

"Are you sure your minister would approve?"

"I'm careful," she said, turning down the music, squeezing her eyes shut, and interlocking her fingers.

"Saint Michael, archangel, our protector against the wickedness and snares of the devil, thrust into Hell all evil spirits who wander through the world for the ruin of our souls. Amen."

She opened her eyes and asked: "Do you want to ask the first questions or should I?"

"You go first," I said, as we put our fingers on the planchette.

"I'll start with the basics," Jill said. "Lord Jesus, are you here?"

The planchette moved to the *Y*. Then the *E*. Then the *S*. *Y-E-S*.

"You go now," she said to me.

"I don't know what to say."

"Just ask anything."

I had a lot of questions for the Son of God but none I really felt like asking through a Ouija board.

"What is your favorite color?"

The planchette moved. *R-E-D*.

"I could have guessed that one," I said.

Jill knew I wasn't taking this seriously, just like the bean pods in the mall bathroom. But now she was less angry than determined to convince me that Christ was real.

"I have one," she said.

She closed her eyes.

"Is my dad in heaven?"

The planchette hesitated then jerked hard to the right and spelled out *M-I-S-T*.

"That's weird," Jill said. "My dad is a part of the weather? I don't know if I like that."

"It's a nice word, though," I said. "Maybe he's lost inside the letters."

I heard a car horn outside and I looked out the window to see my dad looking skeptically up through the windshield at the apartment building.

I jumped up and said I had to go.

Jill grabbed my hands.

"You think I'm pathetic, don't you?" she said.

"I don't," I said, pulling away.

"I can see it on your face. You think I've gone crazy."

Dad beeped again, longer this time. I picked up my book bag and Jill followed me to the front door.

She hugged me so hard I felt her breasts pressing against me. She turned her head, her breath warm in my ear.

"How was it?" my dad asked when I got into the car.

"Weird," I said, looking out my window. "Jill got saved."

My dad nodded.

"She thinks Jesus is talking to her."

"Maybe he is."

I went from a 5 to a 3. My heart valves thumped, silver threads shimmered at the edge of my vision.

"Man suffers," my dad quoted, "only because he takes seriously what the gods made for fun."

"Pull over," I said. "I want to get out."

"What's wrong?" my dad said, his voice shaken.

He was surprised I was angry, that this question, to me, was a real one. I was sick of his bullshit. Either God existed or He didn't. If He did, my friend Jill was not crazy; we were.

✦

That night, I lay on my bed. "Bridge Over Troubled Water" came on the radio. It wasn't as sad as "Cat's in the Cradle," but I still found my eyes getting warm and water leaking out of them. It was almost better when Jill had disappeared.

On Monday she ran up to me while I was getting books out of my locker. She pushed a mound of tinfoil at me.

"They're brownies," she said.

"Thanks."

I knew she wanted me to invite her over to Bent Tree. I knew, too, that seeing her should have made me feel better, but I had an empty place in my chest. Though I had found Jill, it was like I had lost her. And every time I saw her, praying in her long dress out by the flagpole, reading her Bible in the cafeteria, that spot got bigger and started to hurt, until I had to run into the bathroom and lock myself into a stall to get ahold of myself.

✦

On the day before we moved into our new house, my dad and Sandy's fiancé, Steve, loaded all our furniture except the beds and the dining room table into the U-Haul. I heard Mr. Ananais's brush moving back and forth against the hallway wall. Already he'd painted over the doorway where Dad had marked our heights, and filled in the holes where Phillip had shot the wall with his BB gun. The kitchen smelled of ammonia instead of hamburger, and the windows, without curtains, flooded the duplex with light.

I'd packed my clothes, wrapped my perfume bottles in newspaper, my busts of Shakespeare and Emily Dickinson, taken down my Egyptians—even my Venus flytrap was going over to the new house. Last were books. The one Pam had lent me, on Eleanor Roosevelt, went on top. Pam talked to me about Eleanor's ideas, how she'd done very specific things to help people poorer than herself. Pam knew a lot about the congressional bills the first lady had gotten passed and she could talk about them for a long time, in a passionate way. She kept a notebook filled with quotes by famous women. Her favorite: *As a woman I have no country. As a woman the whole world is my country.* She and her mom were Quakers. A Quaker, she told me, sat in silence. Every summer she spent two weeks in New York City with her dad and his friend Henry. They ate dumplings in Chinatown and went to see French films at the revival movie theater in the West Village. Besides her dad, Pam had correspondences going with three pen pals, one in Ohio, one in California, and one in Brazil! She told me sometimes a good idea got stuck in her head behind a mediocre one. And she thought cute things—babies, kittens, puppies—were actually dense patches of God.

My dad was going to drop me off at Pam's house so I could spend the night, and then pick me up in the morning and take me directly to the new house. I set my horse notebook, my nightclothes, and my toothbrush inside my little black suitcase. We planned on finishing the story we were writing about Mr. Higgins's college days, how he'd read philosophy while lying on his bed and taken long walks in gardens. We were both completely obsessed with our English teacher. On Friday, he'd told us how Thoreau's friends had spread wildflowers over his dead body at his funeral and on the black board, he'd written a dream from Emerson's journal.

> I floated at will in the great Ether, and I saw
> this world floating also not far off, but diminished to
> the size of an apple. Then an angel took it in his hand
> and brought it to me and said, "This must thou eat."
> And I ate the world.

Pam and I had looked at each other. *We wanted to eat the world too!* Pam had read some of my unicorn girl story and she liked it so much she wanted to make a Super 8 movie. Already she had gathered props: a stuffed squirrel, an old saddle, and a bunch of dried lavender. I was going to write the screenplay and Pam was going to direct.

Downstairs my mother sat at the table. Instead of old photographs she looked through paint-color samples, putting them against squares of carpet. "What do you think?" she asked me, holding up a patch of orange against a brown carpet.

"I like it," I said.

I knew now never to say what I really thought. It was better just to tell her what she wanted to hear. With this strategy I was even able to feel for her; it was more pity than love, but that was better than being jerked around by her mood swings.

My dad sat beside my mom, paging through a seed catalog Mr. Ananais had lent him. On a yellow pad he drew rows of tomatoes and corn and made a square patch for strawberries. In our new backyard, he'd already pulled up weeds and turned over the dirt with a shovel.

Our neighbors had all come to say good-bye. Julie, who had quit drinking, took my mom out to lunch in the French Quarter. While they were gone I went over to Kira's room and she let me hold Snowball on my lap. I fed him a carrot and let him lick the tip of my pinkie. When Eddie first heard we were moving, he and Phillip fought and he threw a lump of modeling clay at my head. But when Sandy brought over a tuna casserole, Eddie had come along and given me one of his Sargent Rock comic books as a going-away present. Now he and Phillip were downstairs watching television.

Mrs. Smith, like Eddie, was mad when she first heard we were going. She told my dad he was the only person she could talk to and she grabbed his hands in both of her wrinkly ones.

✦

In the day I lived at my new house, unpacking my stuff, setting up my room, but once I was asleep I was back in Bent Tree. People carried out boxes, loaded their cars, and then drove off. New people parked, climbed out of their cars and carried boxes through the front doors. This all went on very fast, all night long, like a sped-up movie, so Bent Tree resembled a frenetic colony of ants. Sometimes I'd dream that there was a fire in 34K. I'd see the pink flames shooting out the windows and I'd wake up terrified until I realized that 34K was not a real duplex, but one, as Jill said, that was in the next world.

✦

Jill kept calling, asking me to come see her get baptized. The last person I'd seen baptized was a premature baby. My dad called all the children to come out of the pews and gather around the basin of holy water. The baby was tiny and hairless, more like a woodland creature than a child. She slept in her godmother's arms until my father cupped water and poured it over her forehead. She didn't scream like most babies, she just opened her eyes and looked up at my dad as if he were God.

It was one thing for a baby who didn't know anything to be baptized, but Jill was desperate. At first I said I had something else to do that day. She persisted, stopping me whenever we passed in the hallway and asking if I'd come see her get baptized. Even at night when I closed my eyes I'd see her in her long white dress, begging me.

My dad thought I should go.

"Why?" I said. "You don't even like church."

"I'll drive you," he said.

"I have not been inside a church since we left the rectory; why should I go now?"

"Do you love your friend?"

"No," I said, "not anymore."

✦

On the Friday before her baptism, Jill cut class and tracked me down in the cafeteria where I was sitting with Pam.

"You have to come!"

"I can't," I said.

"You could," she said, clutching the large Bible she carried with her everywhere. "You just won't."

Because Jill was yelling, kids turned around and stared.

"Look," I said. "I just don't want to see you get baptized."

"Why not?"

"You used to make fun of those people."

"I know," Jill said. "I feel bad about that."

I moaned and rolled my eyes at Pam.

"Just come," Jill said.

"I don't want to watch you make a fool of yourself."

Jill flinched like I'd hit her, put her hands over her eyes, and ran out the cafeteria doors. I felt bad, but at least that was the end of it. She'd be insane, I thought, to ask me again.

After the final bell rang, Jill was waiting for me in front of my bus. She'd made a sign on a piece of notebook paper that read PLEASE PLEASE PLEASE

COME! All she had on was her dress, so her arms goose-pimpled and her teeth chattered. She had lost her mind. She stood there, hair hanging around her face, begging me. Cold smoke moved out of her mouth as she asked me again to come.

She called me several more times over the weekend. Once my dad answered the phone and Jill pleaded with him. My dad told her he would drive me over to the church in the morning. He used his Buddhist mumbo jumbo on me, saying everything was connected to everything else, that every fragment fit somehow into the whole. When he saw me rolling my eyes he said, "A real action is one only you can perform."

The next morning I felt a hand on my head and opened my eyes to see my father sitting on the edge of the bed. It was ironic. There was a time, not long ago, when I'd have been thrilled just to get his attention.

"It's time to get up, Jesse," he said.

"I don't want to go!"

"We're leaving in twenty minutes."

I dressed in a sweatshirt, my worst pair of jeans, and ratty sneakers. I figured he'd see how inappropriate I looked and let me stay in the car.

On the way I told him again I had no intention of going into the church and I quoted Emerson to prove it: "God enters by a private door into every individual."

He quoted a line back at me, one of Mr. Higgins's favorites: "Always do what you are most afraid of."

"Doesn't that go for you too?"

"Me?" he said, shaking his head. "I'm beyond all that."

"In what way?"

"I'm post-crucifixion."

"What?"

"I wouldn't recognize Jesus even if I saw him."

He never talked about the services he'd been part of in the sixties anymore, where he'd worn a black turtleneck and read from Neruda and T. S. Eliot. All he said lately was that God, if he even existed, was too big a concept to fit into his head.

"I am not going to go, unless you go with me."

My father was silent. As the car ran down the asphalt the winter trees, naked without their leaves, were a blur of gray. Mist hung over the road and floated like bits of cotton candy around the mountain. I tried to do silence, to sit in a space like an open doorway or a flower.

"OK," he finally said.

We parked in the lot, got out of the car, and walked up the stairs. Snowflakes swirled around in the air and clung to my hair. Some perched on the shoulders of my sweatshirt.

Bibleway Church was a one-story rectangular building covered with white aluminum siding. Inside, an usher showed us to a back pew. We'd come in late; the band—drums, electric guitar, and bass—were midsong. Our church in Philadelphia was all dark wood pews, organ music, musty hymnals, and heavy bronze light fixtures. Our stained glass showed Bible scenes in deep syrupy colors and the altar was dark, lit only by candles. Jill's church had painted cement-block walls and the altar, lit by a fluorescent panel, held only the baptismal font, a big plastic rectangle filled with water and a table covered with a wax cloth. One small, round stained glass window, a crown of thorns surrounding three bloody nails, was suspended over the back door. It felt unfinished, even ratty, or what my mother called *tacky*; I prayed nobody would start speaking in tongues.

At the altar stood the minister, a short man with a full face. Instead of a robe he wore a white suit. He motioned for the baptismal candidates to come forward. There were three: a pear-shaped boy, his bangs clinging to his forehead; a middle-aged lady who wore her long hair parted down the middle like Cher; and Jill. She was smiling. Her dark roots showed above orangey strips of Sun-In. Even from the back of the church, I could see the constellation of pimples over her forehead. I thought of all the rituals Jill and I had made up, the bean pods, the Halloween turnip, setting fire to the *Vogue*. We'd chanted over our math textbook and recited poems as we sacrificed flowers to the garbage disposal. Now, she danced awkwardly to the music, elbows in the air, the melody catchy, like a song you'd hear on the radio.

The band stopped and the minister stepped forward and talked about the boundless love of God and how Jesus was the ragged figure who moved from tree to tree in the back of our minds. Dad had kept his coat on and sat with his shoulders straight as if he feared if he got too comfortable, he'd be trapped in the pew forever. He reminded me of another Emerson quote. Mr. Higgins had recited it on Friday, just before the bell rang: *Thou art to me a delicious torment.*

The minister took Jill's hand and pulled her forward. Her body under her robe seemed constructed out of bird bones and confectionery sugar. Seeing her so fragile reminded me of one of my dad's children's sermons. He'd held up a small cross made out of sticks, then snapped it so the yellow wood inside showed. Laying the broken cross on the red carpet, he'd held up a second stick cross, saying that our weakness needed God's strength. He pressed nails into the back of the cross, knotted string around the two, and passed me the new one, asking if I could break it. As hard as I tried, it was impossible.

The minister told how Jill had been coming to church for a year, how she'd not only gotten her mama and little sister to come, but had also helped out in the kindergarten Sunday-school class and started an animal adoption program, finding homes for kittens and dogs nobody wanted. Throughout the summer and fall she'd tended the church's flower beds. She'd collected cans and bottles by the side of the road to raise money for bulbs. It was cold now, he said, freezing, but in the spring, right around Easter, her tulips and daffodils would bloom.

"There is no doubt in my mind that the spirit is at work in our little sister," he said.

"Jill," he said, looking into her eyes. "Are you ready to take the Lord Jesus Christ as your personal savior?"

"I am!" Jill said, going up on her toes.

"Is there anyone here today you'd like to have up here with you at the altar?"

I assumed she'd pick her mother or Beth. Instead, I heard Jill say my name.

Everybody in the pews in front shifted to see who was going to come forward to help Jill. I blushed and glanced at my dad. We'd been living in a world without prayers or church for so long, the whole idea of God seemed embarrassing. I was afraid he'd grimace and whisper to me that we should leave, but he smiled, a raw and uncalculated expression that opened up his face, and he reached around and grabbed me by the shoulders, gently lifted me out of the pew, and pushed me in the direction of the altar. I walked up the center aisle, my legs wobbly and my eyes darting down self-consciously to my faded jeans. I climbed the steps to Jill, her eyes glittery, her smile wide and kooky. When she grabbed my hand, I saw she wore a POW bracelet and that her fingernails were covered with chipped polish.

"Ready?" the minister said.

Jill shook off her plastic high heels, the kind of shoes my mom said were worn exclusively by tramps. Jill took the minister's hand and stepped over the edge and into the water. The minister showed me where to place my hands, one on her shoulder and one against her heart.

"Do you give yourself completely to the Lord?" the minister asked.

Say no! I thought. Say you want yourself all for your own self. Say that you have no specific country, say that you are important without any story from above, say that your home is with me and the other girls up in the sky.

"I do," Jill said. She took in a breath, then reached up and squeezed her nose shut. She was on the trolley now, moving along the tracks that would feed her body into the retort. Whether she was moving into truth or bullshit, I did not know. Either way, I couldn't stop her. I could only help her along. I tipped her so the back of her head eased into the water.

Under the surface, her robe floated around her like seaweed, showing her bare feet and legs. I thought of the swan-obsessed Layona, how they tied feathers to the wrists of their dead before sinking them down into the recesses of the riverbed. Jill's robe soaked transparent and her body showed itself in outline, white, writhing. A chain of silver bubbles escaped her lips and her hair was loose, each strand free and swaying. She was every girl caught in a dream, her face alive with anguish and joy.

Keith Solit. A special thanks goes to Jin Auh and Sarah Chalfant at the Wylie Agency for believing in me and standing by me. Thanks to Matt Chittum, Beth Macy, and the Virginia Room at the Roanoke Library for help with research. Thanks to Alex Ruiz for being a fierce girl. A huge and bottomless thanks goes to Tin House, to Rob Spillman and Elissa Schappell for giving my book a home, and to Nanci McCloskey, my publicist, for getting it out there into the world. To my editor Tony Perez whose careful and brilliant attention made this book better by far; I am indebted to you. Finally to my husband Michael Hudson, first reader and stupendous mate, and my daughter, Abbie, who amazes, inspires, and delights me every single day.

✦

ACKNOWLEDGMENTS

This book you hold in your hands was supported and nourished by many wonderful people and I want to thank them all. To my early readers Rob Sheffield, Elizabeth Mitchell, Michael Parker, Rogelio Martinez, Natalie Standiford, Will Blythe, Stephanie Papa, Sister Leslie, Michael Parker, Elizabeth Gilbert, and Michael Plekon: thank you for your enthusiasm, encouragement, and careful reading. Thank you to my student assistants Noah Blake, Luke Wiget, and Nora O'Connor, all of whom have become wonderful writers in their own right. Thanks to Douglas Martin, Idra Novey, Susan Wheeler, Jeffery Greene, Judy Hottensen, Marnie Weber, and Rene Steinke for keeping me afloat. Also to my family—David, Lauren, Jonathan, and Nicole—and to my Dad; I know it's not always easy having a writer in the family. Thanks to